JACKIE FRENCH i[...] children's books, w[...] gardening for the [...] and [...] *Garden* amongst others, and presents segments on various radio stations around Australia. For several years she was a presenter on the television show *Burke's Backyard*. She has written many books on plants, their ecology and history.

Jackie's writing has earned her awards both in Australia and overseas (her books have been translated into a number of languages), including the ACT Book of the Year and the Australian Booksellers Association/Nielsen BookData Book of the Year Award.

Jackie lives in the New South Wales bush with her husband Bryan in a house made of stone from the creek. She has one son, two stepdaughters and three step-grandkids.

www.jackiefrench.com

A War for Gentlemen

A War for Gentlemen

~ a novel ~

JACKIE FRENCH

HARPER PERENNIAL

HarperPerennial
An imprint of HarperCollins*Publishers*

First published in Australia in 2003
This edition published in 2004
by HarperCollins*Publishers* Pty Limited
ABN 36 009 913 517
A member of the HarperCollins*Publishers* (Australia) Pty Limited Group
www.harpercollins.com.au

HarperCollins*Publishers*
25 Ryde Road, Pymble, Sydney NSW 2073, Australia
31 View Road, Glenfield, Auckland 10, New Zealand
77–85 Fulham Palace Road, London W6 8JB, United Kingdom
2 Bloor Street East, 20th floor, Toronto, Ontario M4W 1A8, Canada
10 East 53rd Street, New York, NY 10022, USA

National Library of Australia Cataloguing-in-Publication data:

French, Jackie.
   A war for gentlemen: a novel.
   2nd ed.
   ISBN 0 7322 7776 0 (pbk.).
   1. Veterans – New South Wales – Fiction.
   2. United States – History – Civil War, 1861–1865 – Fiction.
   I. Title.
A823.3

Cover: photograph of soldier from American Memory Historical Collections;
         image of formal room from Getty Images
Cover and internal design adapted from the original by Gayna Murphy,
HarperCollins Design Studio
Typeset in 11 on 15 Sabon by HarperCollins Design Studio
Printed and bound in Australia by Griffin Press on 50gsm Bulky News

5 4 3 2 1   04 05 06 07

TO
Edward

Acknowledgments

The lyrics on page 18 are from 'Molly Pitcher' by Kate Brownlee Sherwood.

The extract from the poem 'Jock of Hazeldean' on pages 17 and 69 is by Sir Walter Scott (1771–1832)

The extract from the poem 'The Field of Waterloo' on pages 94–5 is by Sir Walter Scott (1771–1832)

Contents

AUTHOR'S NOTE

This book was inspired by an Australian who fought for the Confederacy in the American Civil War; who deserted and escaped north with a woman who was a slave; who married her and was disowned by his family.

This is not the history of that man, nor that woman; most of their story is unknown, and unknowable. In places, I have deliberately changed what happened. But sometimes fiction can capture the essence of a story in the way that history cannot.

I spent many years trying to trace the original Charles and Caroline. I have come to care for them deeply. I hope that if either of them read this book they would feel I had done them justice.

Jackie French
2003

CHAPTER 1

1863

CHARLES FITZHENRY KNOWS
THAT HE IS GOING TO DIE

Lying in a crowded cart, in a foreign country, there came a moment when Charles Fitzhenry knew he was going to die; knew it with such certainty that the heat of his body and of the others pressed against him faded, and he shivered, as though a breeze from his grave washed over him.

Through it all, he burnt. Burnt with fever; burnt with the sunlight that scalded down onto the cart; burnt with thirst, with pain, with hunger for home and the smell of gum trees after rain.

There were other bodies in the cart. Charles didn't know how many. He had tried to count the arms in the dusty light when they'd carried him to the cart, but the light swam and he did not know if he'd counted them all. At first the bodies had been piled three deep, with Charles in the middle. He had been cocooned in their heat, felt their moisture dry on them and in moments of clarity wondered if it was sweat or blood.

The body on one side of him was warm. The other had been cold all day. It was a boy's body; fifteen, perhaps. The boy must have lied about his age when he enlisted. His face was blown off at the jaw. A rag held the remnant loosely, stiff and black with blood. The boy's face was black too, but with gunpowder, not because he was a nigger. No man would put a nigger in a cart with white men. The boy's eyes were very white. It was only after many hours, when the eyes failed to close, and the body grew ever colder, that Charles realised he was dead.

Earlier, the boy had muttered foreign names through the blood and rag: Susannah, Annabelle Lee and Ma, names from this land, not the land where Charles was born.

This was the land of death.

Years later Charles remembered the most frightening thing about that land: the knowledge that every rule of life — safety, comfort, predictability — could be broken.

The cart lurched into a rut. The bullock droppings fell like cannonballs. Charles could smell them as the cart rolled over them. His bad arm knocked against the body next to him. The world was black; for a moment the pain vanished, and then it came again. Someone sobbed; in the cart, perhaps, or on the road.

The wounded were everywhere. This was a war where men were more expendable than guns or cannon. (If ten of his men died for every rebel killed, said the Northern General Grant, he'd be content; he didn't mention the diseased or wounded.) You learn to close your eyes, your ears, your soul. The mind had room for only so much cargo, so much pain.

The cart rocked again. Water splashed under the wheels. There had been so much water in the last two years; an extravagance of water for a boy brought up in a dry land. The swirling Potomac, treacherous underneath shaking bridges, so unlike the thin brown streams of New South Wales; the rain that drizzled through gun-smoke and the smoke so thick the rain turned grey; the frozen dew that dripped into your collar; the brackish swamps; the streams that ran so sour the troops claimed they were filled with Union piss, but you drank from them to fill your belly, to still the pain that came from having nothing more than four ounces of old bacon a day with a cup of rice and weevils, till even those were gone and your belly cramped and tore at you.

The air was calm above the cart; the bullock moved too slowly to make a breeze. The cart smelt of blood and sickness and the sullen taste of death. Charles wondered if your senses grew more acute before you died, as though you wanted to hold on to what was left of life.

The cart stopped. There was less pain when it stopped but he now had time to think about the pain.

The rocking cart kept him occupied in tensing his body against the jolting.

Moses held water to his lips. Moses was his body servant, his personal slave. Cousin Ralph had lent Charles Moses, just as he'd lent him the horses that he rode. All the bodies in the cart had been placed there by their slaves. If Charles hadn't had a servant he would have been left on the battlefield, one of thousands waiting for an army surgeon who would never come.

It was Moses' hands that cleaned him every night, wiped away the filth of cholera. Not the smell; the smell couldn't be wiped away. Later he realised it was Moses driving the oxen.

Moses lifted the dead boy from the cart and placed him by the side of the road. There was more room now. The cart began to move again. The sun came out. Charles' arm screamed in the heat. His tongue swelled till it filled his throat. He wondered vaguely if the army was in retreat, or were they just moving the wounded beyond the Union lines. He couldn't ask. Finally, he couldn't care.

They stopped. There was water. Perhaps they'd found some forage for the bullocks too. The grass had all been eaten round the battlefields. They moved on again.

Men moved along beside the cart, wounded men who could walk. Even after all these days they were still walking. They rarely spoke. When they did their voices jarred. Charles had thought he was used to the Southern accent. He thought: a man should die with his own voices round him.

4

Men with bandages, or eyes blackened with the cholera, who leant on sticks or on each other. At one time there were others on the road as well. Old women, huddling away from death, and pregnant women, their arms instinctively around their bellies, as though hands could fend off rape or cannonballs. He saw their profiles against the sky, heard the thin cry of a child. Refugees. The hot air shimmered and melted them together. He closed his eyes. Time shifted around him. The days were crushed together like bodies in the cart.

Memories sucked at him, fiercer than the flies: memories of corpses bloated like cattle after too much green grass; the whistle when a long dead body was pricked by a bayonet; a massive Percheron carthorse, bred to pull a plough and not a gun carriage, with its legs blown off at the knees. It screamed and the bones were white. No one had told him about the death of horses.

He remembered walking away from camp after the second battle. (The second battle was the worst. You knew what was coming in your second battle. You were numb from shock during the first.)

There had been trees — away from the ploughed fields they had camped and fought on — and under one tree was a horse's leg, the blood still bright and the tendons white. There was no sign of the rest of the horse. An animal must have dragged it there, he had thought, though there was no sign of gnawing. He wondered what animal would dare to penetrate this world of men.

Sometimes, in the first months of war, he had put his face down against Elijah to feel the scent of horse sweat, the roughness of its coat, to close his eyes and think of home. Now he'd learnt that horses sweat fear too. Their scent changes after battle, just like men's.

It was night in the cart now. Mosquitoes sipped, replacing the flies, though the flies still crawled in the warmth at the bottom of the cart. The cart kept moving. They must have found more bullocks or perhaps a horse. Surely the starving bullocks could not have pulled the cart for long. Or had they? How many days had they been travelling? He didn't know.

The cart stopped. It was a horse that pulled it now. He heard him wheezing. When had the bullocks gone?

Moses spoke: 'Come now Mas' Charles, up an' easy now.'

The blackness grew as Moses lifted him. The cart rolled off again, into the night. Or did the darkness belong to him alone?

'Resten you easy Mas' Charles,' said Moses. 'Now we's home.'

Moses' voice faded. He never heard it again.

CHAPTER 2

1863

RESPITE

Sunlight. The scent of jasmine swam through the window. The sheets smelt of lavender and linen.

The world was quiet. Only his ears sang. He wondered if they would always sing, the song of cannon and muskets and the dying, noise so loud you couldn't hear it, only feel it, so loud you couldn't hear the sobbing of the boy behind . . .

He opened his eyes. The dust motes danced in a stream above the window seat, the curtains hung smooth and straight and heavy. Their silk tassels drooped like horses' tails.

Was he home? It smelt like home. Home and peace.

He shut his eyes again.

She was there when he woke, sitting by the bed. Her white headscarf was bright against the green curtains. Her hands were pale cream against the sheets. They were delicate hands, long and tapering, though roughened by work. Even ladies' hands had toughened in these times. The sheets were linen, not cotton. Linen sheets from Ireland, just like home.

The girl nodded, seeing him awake, and stood up. She made a movement to go out.

'Cousin Elizabeth?'

The girl shook her head. 'She gone back to Mont Alba wit' the chillun, Mas'Charles.' She pronounced it all in one word. 'She was worrit 'bout the typhus. Miss Lillian, she still here.'

At the sound of her voice he shut his eyes. It was a black voice, despite the pale hands against the sheets.

No, he was not home. And there was no peace either.

CHAPTER 3

1845-61

EDUCATION OF A HERO

Charles' first memory was of hands splashing water about his body in his bath. They were white hands, with red knuckles. None of the hands that tended Charles Fitzhenry as a child were black, although other properties employed black stockmen and black house servants. Blacks were cheap. You paid them food and some tobacco.

But Charles' father liked white faces about him. James Fitzhenry had grown tired of coloured faces in the Indian Army, before he was retired because of fever and came to New South Wales to see if the dry climate would restore his health.

James Fitzhenry liked the colony. Though the great land grants were past James Fitzhenry had money to buy a good property, and there were still the free teams of convict labour to help him build his estate. So he stayed, and slowly his health improved, away from the heat and flies of India, in the house he built on a hill by the sea and the farmland he carved from the bush. (They spoke of farms being carved out in those days, as though the surrounding bush was granite that needed a strong man to grind it down.)

The hands Charles remembered belonged to Jane. Square hands, with swollen knuckles, that washed his secret places; he must have been no older than three, but already he knew that they were secret. The towel had been warmed on the towel rail by the fire. It felt rough against his skin as she rubbed and dried him.

The clothes had been warming, too: stockings and trousers and linen shirt. Dressed at last he held up his arms to be carried.

Jane laughed. 'You're a big boy now, Master Charles!' But she lifted him anyway, pressed him against dark cloth and soft bosom, jigged him on her hip over to the window.

'What can you see?' the child demanded. It was a game they played.

'I can see ... cows. See, there they are down there. And Ezra building a rock wall. I can see fences and the waves. I can see the road ...'

Jane turned at a noise behind them — Lily, the upstairs maid, bringing in the nursery lunch tray of prunes and custard and buttered bread. Lily came to the window. She patted the boy's hair smooth. 'Funny to think all that out there will belong to a scrap like you,' she teased.

Charles frowned. He knew what ownership was. He owned his furry monkey, his special pillow, his lead soldiers. The rest of the world, all he had ever seen of it, belonged to Papa, and bits to Mama too. But this was a complexity of ownership he hadn't thought of.

His. All his. It made sense. He was prince of his small world and of course it would be his: four thousand acres with endless acres of sea beyond it; sand, whiter than a dinner shirt at midday, yellow as clotted cream in the afternoon; paddocks bordered with hawthorn hedges; the gum trees like a tribe of blacks clustering at the paddock edges, to be gradually pushed back by the ringbarking — five minutes per tree with a good axe, once you got your hand in.

Even after fifteen years in the colony his parents found the gum trees strange; ungainly, shabby things that shed their bark and never lost their leaves. But Charles' short life had been spent with both the bush and the sea. He'd flung his small body into both. He wondered if they belonged to him as well. Yes, he decided, still gazing out at his world from Jane's hip, the sea and trees must certainly be his too.

A rest, after lunch, then down the stairs, along the hall and out the front door. Jane used the front door only when she accompanied Charles. Servants never used the front door on their own. When Lily polished the front doorknob and the lion's-head knocker she would go out the back door and round the side.

Charles looked at the rosebushes, the laurel trees, everything, with new eyes. He owned the garden then, as well as Mama and Ezra too.

Mama had designed the garden. She'd ordered the shy flowers from England that lost their subtlety in the harsher sun and grew rampant, the straggly pansies and roses with lax stems, and the tulips — a great rarity these — for the frosty hollow below the orchard. But Ezra felt the soil and rocks with his grimy hands. Ezra touched the garden, while Mama only touched the flowers.

Ezra had been a convict. He refused to speak of that part of his past, as though the days of his servitude had been chopped out of his life, and only what had been before or after was real. 'That be my business, Master Charles, and you've got yours, I reckon, and the two of them will mix when horses cover cattle.'

Today Ezra was building a stone wall around the vegetable gardens with the sharp stones that seemed to grow overnight among the leeks and lettuces. Charles let go of Jane's hand and ran to him.

'May I help? Ezra, may I?'

Ezra grinned, showing his two remaining teeth, long and yellow at each side of his mouth. One day, thought Charles admiringly, I'll grow teeth like Ezra's.

'I'll look after the lad,' Ezra said to Jane, and she shrugged, not wasting a smile on Ezra who was too old to be interesting to a girl in a colony where men still outnumbered women, and went back to put her feet up by the nursery fire.

Charles squatted on the ground by Ezra. It was too cold to sit, although the frost had melted. Ezra looked at the rock pile consideringly. 'That one there, Master Charles,' he instructed, and Charles handed him the stone. He had to use both hands to lift it, but in Ezra's callused hands it hardly looked big at all.

Another stone, and another, placed lengthways or crossways, each somehow tying the wall together so it grew slowly higher and stronger. Charles waited for Ezra to speak. Ezra had good stories, but you couldn't hurry Ezra.

'See that water race, Master Charles?' asked Ezra at last.

Charles nodded.

'I cut that race, eight year ago now, to bring the water from the spring round to here. Said I were mad, they did. Said water that close to the sea'd be brackish. Laughed at me all the time I were digging it.'

'Was it brackish?' Charles asked, handing him another rock.

Ezra placed it carefully. 'You taste that water Master Charles. You tell me now if that stream's brackish. Wouldn't have no vegetables this high up the hill if it weren't for old Ezra and his water race.'

Last winter Ezra had piled the dray high with horse dung. Charles had wanted to help with that, too, but

13

Jane had said no, it was too dirty. She had let Charles watch while Ezra sifted the horse manure and scattered it over the vegetable garden. In summer, the dung turned into cabbages so firm you could sit on them, radishes so fiery they bit your tongue.

It was the fault of the sun, said Ezra, radishes never grew as hot as this at home. The Australian sun sent the asparagus bolting and soured the lettuces at midsummer.

Other memories.

He was eight, sitting on a cushion at the long polished table in the dining room, still in his going-to-Church clothes. Now he was older he ate Sunday dinner with his parents every week. He had a bedroom, not a nursery shared with Jane. George was in the nursery. George was his brother, but George was to be pitied, just a little bit. The farm and the house would never be George's and, besides, George was too young to play with and whined to be carried if he was expected to walk for too long.

Sunday dinner after Church dragged to a close, the brocade curtains and the smell of mutton and potatoes and ginger cream stifling, his dangling legs longing to be moving away. Outside, Charles could hear the yells of Marjory-in-the-kitchen's children by Sam Southwell, the boundary rider.

Marjory's children were different from him and George. Marjory's children played all day, or so it seemed to Charles. Charles had to learn his alphabet with Jane while Marjory's children looked for eggs or firewood or learnt to fence the paddocks and yards — outdoor jobs that seemed like play. Charles had to lift his hat; to sit attentively in Church; to listen and not speak at table. Charles was a gentleman. Gentlemen had duties.

But today there were visitors, English cousins touring the colonies. Charles was excused the drawing room after dinner, ducked out of the side door and went to find the laughter.

Marjory-in-the-kitchen's Sam and Mary, Ned and Anne were playing knucklebones by the barn. Charles led them to the garden — Marjory's children were forbidden to go into the garden. It was another world to them, like the gentlemen's world beyond the kitchen door, the world with carpet and wallpaper, and beeswax candles instead of tallow candles or smoky lamps.

Charles showed them the daffodils, the last of the pomegranate fruit split on the trees, and how to roll down the grassy hill to land in the mud and clover of the water race; hours of dirt and laughter and glimpses of Anne and Mary's knees under their skirts and once a flash of white and pink higher up. For the first time he realised how girls were different, and manoeuvred himself into a better position in case the pink flashed again.

'Master Charles!' It was Jane. She'd seen him from the nursery window as she roused George from his nap.

Charles was stripped to his breeches by Jane and washed in the back courtyard while the others were sent home.

'How could you, Master Charles? You should know better.' Jane was cranky as she bundled his damp clothes.

'The others played too.'

'The responsibility's yours. You should show them how to behave.'

'Why?'

'Hoity toity! What a question! You'd be whipped, my lad, if I told your father. Because you're your father's son, that's why. You should know better.'

~⁂~

At nine he had a tutor. He had to study with Mr Lucas, who had pimples on his neck where his stiff collar rubbed, and whose black suit was rusty under the armpits from sweat. They studied Latin and Greek, two cultures that had men of noble mind and action at the top of society, whose job it was to rule and set a good example, and slaves at the bottom, the way it had always been, and always would, it seemed. No more rolling in the clover.

At ten he was to be sent to Sydney, to school. But his mother had been ill for a long time after George's birth. She cried, and so Charles stayed at home until she recovered. The tutors came and went. Finally, he was never sent at all.

Mornings in the sunlit room, where his mother sewed after the lessons finished; afternoons galloping after cattle. They never walked through the bush in those days. They always rode, on the fast stocky Waler horses, that were a reminder of his father's time in the Indian Army.

Quiet evenings. The snicker of the fire and the smell of the saved apple wood prunings, to keep it sweet, or of the lavender that Mama threw on the coals before she went to bed, to scent the room in the mornings. Sometimes there were visitors: Aunt Euphemia from Sydney, playing the piano while his mother sang the songs her mother had sung before her, songs as sweet and colourful as her embroidery cottons.

Why weep ye by the tide, lady?
Why weep ye by the tide?
I'll wed ye to my youngest son,
And ye shall be his bride.
And ye shall be his bride, lady,
So comely to be seen.
But aye, she let the tears downfall,
For Jock of Hazeldean.

Sometimes she would sing 'A Maiden's Prayer' and visitors with the right accent would sing and stay a night, a month. (Visitors with the wrong accent were sent round the back to eat with the men, or to the kitchen with the servants.)

Other times his mother read aloud — Dickens or Sir Walter Scott or the stirring story of Molly Pitcher, heroine of the American War of Independence, who fetched water to her husband during the battle of Monsmouth and when he fell, took the ramrod of his cannon and kept the cannon firing all the day.

Molly Pitcher sprang to his side,
Fired as she saw her husband do,
Telling the king in his stubborn pride
Women like men to their homes are true.

One day I'll have a wife like that, thought Charles. And I'll be a hero too — while George fidgeted until told to sit still or leave the room; tales of brave heroes and braver deeds that she adored. Books with yellowed leaves and brown age spots or mildew or sea water stains from the voyage out, with woodcuts and gold edges and the smell of mustiness and cleanliness combined with the smell of paper, the smell of ideas.

Sometimes his father read out loud: news items from the *Sydney Morning Herald* or the *Illustrated London News*, months old and marked with salt water; letters from Sir Roland's wife at Montfleur, the family seat in England, from Cousins Roland and John fighting in the Crimea, or Great-uncle Duane on his estate in the United States.

Slowly, as Charles grew older, the world outside seeped into the orderly life of the house on the hill.

CHAPTER 4

1861

THE WORLD OUTSIDE

There are few times we can look back and say, 'That was the moment. That was when I changed.' But, years later, Charles remembered two moments, of such clarity that afterwards nothing was the same.

It was summer. The eucalyptus oil shimmered above the trees. Charles had been supervising the shepherds as they cut the tails and testicles from the lambs. The tails were thrown into bloody heaps — in a meat rich land there was no need to keep them for lamb tail pie — though some of the testicles in the bucket, like tiny sodden eggs, would be sizzled in dripping by any shepherd who felt his manhood waning or wanted to show off.

Charles took the long way home through the bush, feeling the power as his horse jumped logs, the vaguely exciting warmth between his thighs, the exhilaration that was partly animal and partly the human controlling the horse, the smell of salt from sea and sweat ...

... and suddenly he was flooded with the knowledge that he could ride all day and it would still be only this: the sky, the trees, the endless acres, that tomorrow or in ten years' time his life would be the same, with the addition of a wife, perhaps, and children, but otherwise unchanged. The sudden, piercing grief was shocking: life should be more than this. Life was happening somewhere else, if only he could find it.

The horse was tiring as they cantered up the hill to home. The hooves clattered on the cobbles in the back courtyard. He tossed the reins to one of the men, who would groom the horse and feed it. The mail sat on the hall table as he came in; Burroughs must have been to town. Fortnight-old *Sydney Morning Herald*s; the months old *Illustrated London News*; letters in still crisp cream envelopes; and on the top a letter from Duane.

Great-uncle Duane had an estate in Carolina, where he had settled after his resignation from the army. Duane had been on Wellington's staff at Waterloo. The Fitzhenrys were a family where younger sons entered the army, while the eldest cared for the family estates.

Sometimes, as James Fitzhenry read Duane's letters aloud to the family, Charles regretted that his father hadn't chosen Carolina instead of New South Wales. The South of the U.S.A. was a land of gentlemen in a way that brash, colonial Australia would never be. Its architecture was more gracious, its schools finer. It had a rich and cultured life that this young colony lacked, and more literary magazines per head of population than any nation on earth.

'It is no accident,' said one of Duane's earliest letters, 'that the other great cultures of Greece and Rome have been built on slavery too. How else can men find the leisure for ideas and music?'

But as the years went by the tenor of Duane's letters had changed. The gracious, cultured Southern way of life was under threat.

There were even calls for slavery to be abolished. 'To any man of sense,' said Duane's letters, 'the very concept is a cruel one. The black mind is different from the white. Blacks are a childish race, the sons of Ham. What black man can succeed without protection in this modern world?'

War was coming. A war that would determine if the Southern glory would survive. Now Charles gazed at Duane's letter. He would have liked to open it. But it was addressed to his father and must wait till after dinner.

Charles glanced at the headlines of the *Sydney Morning Herald* instead, then snatched the paper up: 'Shots Fired at Fort Sumpter'; 'The South Secedes'.

The war, it seemed, had finally come to Duane's gracious acres and, like most of its gentlemen readers, the *Sydney Morning Herald* had no doubt who was in the right and who would win, declaring:

The South will not, we may imagine, lose the immense advantage of a vast region where they can retreat upon their resources ... it is difficult to see how an invasion can be successful in a country, often fatal, under the utmost precaution, to European life.

Our readers will observe that the quotations from the American papers call the Southern forces 'rebels'. It was so with their own fathers, for they were so called by the English Government when they were arrayed under Washington ...

The North has marble and iron, the South is an unfading Eden. All the best genius and all the best eloquence spring up without cultivation in the slave states, under their fiercer climate and more careless life.

Later. The men of the family gathered in the study before the dinner gong had sounded. This was not a matter for the ladies. James sat at the desk, Duane's letter in front of him. George sat on the sofa, and tried to keep his hands from scratching at his pimples. Charles stood by the fire, not so much to warm his legs but because it galled him to sit still.

His father slit the envelope, perused it slowly.

'What does it say?' demanded George.

My dearest family,
War has come. It is a war for all men who believe in the right of a people to choose their own destiny. The South cannot and should not face this alone.

James stopped reading and put the letter down. 'It's only a matter of time before England declares war on the North,' he said slowly. 'They need to protect their cotton supplies.'

England's mills were dependent on the cotton from the South. Without raw cotton the mills would close, the workers starve, the fortunes of the mill owners wither.

Charles shook his head. 'Surely England will enter because the cause is right.'

His father didn't answer. He was calculating, perhaps, how the loss of raw cotton might affect the price of wool.

Charles picked up the letter. He was shocked at how much the news had affected him. He tried to tell himself it was because the war the South faced mirrored the political battles in Australia, from the hordes that had flooded the country looking for its gold and who clamoured for democracy. 'One man, one vote,' the rabble cried. A ludicrous idea to any man of sense; almost as unthinkable as votes for dogs or women. How could an ignorant Irishman straight off the boat play any sensible part in government either here or in the United States? How had that Irishman in the Northern states of America any right to order Southerners what to do?

But deep within himself something else uncurled: a young man's need to have a cause that he believed in, the need to passionately commit. Years later, looking back, he would long for this innocence. The world would never be as clear or simple for him again.

CHAPTER 5

1861

DECISION

And the second moment?

It was a week later. There had been no more letters from Duane, nor any further news in the *Sydney Morning Herald*. But Charles had not forgotten.

They had been playing tennis, on the new court paved with crushed ants' nests: George, of course, but no one ever really noticed George, and Sally Begman from the property next door; Augustus and Evelyn Brennan from Laranwood, and Edgar Riles, who was down from Sydney on a visit. Charles had partnered Sally, whom he had kissed in the moonlight last month after the ball at Wangarilla.

Afterwards the girls sat in chairs under the apple trees, except for Evelyn, who lounged in the hammock and showed her ankles. Charles watched Sally instead:

the pucker of her top lip with its faint beads of unmentionable sweat. Where did you start to touch a girl? he wondered. Lips would meet lips, of course, but what about your hands? On her waist? Then up or down?

If he had been to school would someone have passed on the necessary lore? He could ask Augustus . . .

The sky stretched clear and blue above them. The bees droned in the fruit. No, thought Charles contentedly, there was no need to ask. As far back as he could remember his life had fallen into place, and so this would. For the moment he would enjoy the wondering. Soon Morton would bring down lime juice and thin, hard biscuits made by Marjory the cook. Charles was half asleep.

Evelyn talked of Sydney; the words washed over him. It was pleasant to listen to girls talk, even if what they said was nonsense. Evelyn had seen a play, and told them all about it. She had been to Church and listened to a sermon.

'He was so passionate,' said Evelyn, looking at the males under her eyelashes, as though talking of passion, even religious passion, might inspire a different, albeit gentlemanly, passion in her companions. 'Every Christian man — and woman too, he said — must abhor the curse of slavery. It is our Christian duty to . . .'

Charles looked up. 'Nonsense! You know nothing of the matter!'

The others woke up at that. It was strong language to use to a woman, unless she was your wife or daughter, and even then only in the privacy of your home.

'And you do?' Edgar's voice was lazy, amused. He was twenty-five, seven years older than Charles, and had been educated 'back home' in England.

'As a matter of fact, I do.' Charles took a breath. He wanted Sally to admire him — his knowledge and his convictions. He wanted to prove himself more of a man of the world than Edgar, that Sydney fop! 'A Southern slave lives in more comfort and security than any so-called free black in the North's factories!'

'But freedom ...' began Evelyn earnestly, no longer the coquette. 'How can any Christian man condemn another to be a slave?'

'What is freedom? Freedom to starve? Freedom to die uncared for in old age? Who has the better life — a child in an English mine or a slave in the South?'

'You mean slavery is good for them?' Augustus was mildly incredulous.

'Is that so strange? Do you give your own black stockmen money?'

'No, of course not. They'd spend it on drink, or give it away.'

'Exactly. The primitive races need our care and our protection. Has the North even thought what war might mean? A famine of cotton in the north of England would be infinitely worse than a famine of bread; idleness breeds sloth as well as hunger.' A quotation from Duane, or was it a *Sydney Morning Herald* editorial he remembered now?

'But the brutal slave owners, the whippings ...' Evelyn refused to concede.

'Of course they're wrong. But this is not about slavery! Slavery is a topic for the yellow press and demagogues. What is at stake is the struggle of a brave and high-spirited people to free themselves from a nation of pedlars and storekeepers.' Another quote. He had never realised how deep the words had burnt.

'But surely slavery is more important ...' began Evelyn.

Charles took the words and arguments from Great-uncle Duane's letters; he took the passion and the dream of heroism from the songs his mother sang him as a child, from the stories of Sir Walter Scott and the regimental histories in their library. 'These people are fighting for freedom, the right of a people to secede from a government they abhor. That is a right that free people everywhere should fight with them.'

Edgar Riles grinned. 'It sounds like you're planning to join them.'

There was a pause. Had Charles already half considered it? He loved the farm, the bush, his parents, even George, at a pinch. But they were familiar. This home was a backwater. Charles had been born with the instincts of a hero. Now he needed to commit to a cause.

The pause grew longer. And then he said, 'Yes. I plan to join them.'

George blinked. Edgar lost his grin. Sally gasped. 'When?'

Charles Fitzhenry's words came out as grave and adult as he intended. 'When I have put my affairs in order.'

He said it to impress Sally. It did impress her. She and Evelyn (her anti-slavery sermon forgotten) clustered about him. Charles gave a short lecture on military tactics to George, Edgar and Augustus.

He told his father of his decision that evening.

Three days later, after reflection, his father agreed to let him go.

His mother cried, but you could see that she was proud. (Or, at least, Charles thought he saw.) George looked envious, but also pleased that he would at last have a chance to shine without the brighter presence of his brother.

Charles rode over to Sally the next morning. Sally cried as well. Charles promised to write. He left her as heroes ought, with a pink rose pressed in his Bible.

This is how he decided to go to war then — casually, in flannels, damp with tennis sweat, with a glass of lime juice in his hand.

～⚯～

The reality was slightly less heroic. Charles and James — and Duane in Carolina — believed this war would be a war of adventure, not of armies and fixed battles.

It would be a war of gentlemen, a replay of the American War of Independence, where gallant raiders and fine riders outwitted and out-waited the invader.

They believed the war would last a year at most. If the South didn't win immediately (and an immediate Southern victory was a strong possibility, even without the expected help from France or England) the North would soon capitulate and accept terms that granted at least partial Southern independence.

Charles was not a younger son. He had an estate waiting for him. But James was well aware that his son needed to see more of the world before he settled on the family acres. If he had been a different boy he might have gone to Oxford. But that would not have suited Charles.

Charles did not want a soldier's career, decades of training and promotion in another backwater like India. He would taste a few months of war and the command of men, have a little of his colonial brashness worn away in the well-mannered homes of his American relatives then, when the war was over, tour the Continent and look at the German cattle breeds, or come home via South Africa to buy sheep.

But Charles was still a hero. This war was an adventure; it was also an ideal. If you do not understand this about him, you do not understand him at all. Charles Fitzhenry went to fight because the cause was right.

As for Sally: he promised to write. He didn't ask her to wait for him. He had never, in fact, thought he would marry her. She probably hoped he would. The Fitzhenrys were wealthy, and Charles was unquestionably attractive.

Charles dreamt instead of silken English cheeks, or a Southern belle with flounced skirts and wasp-tight waist, who, as in all the best novels, waited for him to rescue her from the Northern invader.

CHAPTER 6

1 8 6 1

SAILING TO WAR

Charles Roland Fitzhenry (now aged nineteen) sailed on the *Lady Allison* to Dover ('superior accommodation for cabin and intermediate passengers, surgeon on board') with a banker's draft and corded chests and all the accoutrements of a gentleman soldier, except his horses and his uniforms.

Neither Duane's letters (which had stopped now that war was formally declared; the Unionist blockade was preventing most ships from leaving or arriving at Confederate ports), nor the reports in the *Sydney Morning Herald* had told Charles what the uniform of a Southern officer was. It appeared the matter was still in dispute.

Arriving in Dover he put up at the Ship Inn, intending to stay for one night before undertaking the day's journey on the mail coach to London, thence to the family estate in Surrey, while Sir Roland's secretary arranged a passage for him to America. Events, however, proved different.

Dear Mother and Father and George,

I write this in haste aboard the Esther Deane *in Port at Dover, and will give it to the steward to post tonight. As I mentioned in my letter yesterday, which You should receive in the same mail as this, I arrived in Dover the day before yesterday, viz the 23rd, and hoped to travel to Montfleur before embarking again. A most cordial letter from my Uncle Roland greeted me at the hotel, pressing me to accept their hospitality and assuring me of his good graces and determination to assist me in any way possible. I was informed by the waiter at the hotel this morning, however, that the* Esther Deane *was to sail for Wilmington via Nassau tomorrow morning. He urged me to take ship at once, as passage to the Confederacy has become increasingly scarce and unreliable.*

I therefore wrote to my Uncle, giving my apologies and hoping I might make his and his Family's acquaintance on my return from the South, discharged my bill at the hotel and took coach to Liverpool, where the Esther Deane, *a merchant ship, lies at anchor. I have not yet enquired as to her present cargo, but gather she will attempt to return with the cotton that the English mills so badly need. According to my informant the waiter Captain Travers has run the blockade twice before, and is a good and capable captain.*

There is one other passenger aboard ship, an Englishman John Williams, who like myself is joining the Confederate cause. We have spoken only briefly as yet at dinner, to which Captain Travers had invited about twenty persons, all mill owners or connected with that trade, and indeed John Williams' Father owns a mill in Yorkshire. He seems however a Gentleman, and I look forward to companionship upon the voyage.

The Esther Deane is as unlike the Lady Allison as is possible, scarcely catering for passengers in normal times, but my cabin if not commodious is sufficient. Captain Travers says we should weigh anchor at 9 tomorrow. I cannot express my feelings at being able to take ship so soon; I had resigned myself for several months wait in England. I will write from Nassau, and remain, Your Loving and Obd. Son, Charles Fitzhenry

CHAPTER 7

1862

ARRIVAL

Captain Travers succeeded in running the blockade for the third time. (And the last: his ship would be confiscated by the Northern forces on her next voyage out.)

The *Esther Deane* docked at Wilmington, not having seen a Union ship, much less been fired upon or boarded. As well as her two passengers, the Englishman John Williams and the Australian Charles Fitzhenry, the *Esther Deane* unloaded gunpowder, medical supplies, silk, and wheat flour, and uploaded some of the vast store of cotton already rotting in warehouses.

Charles had expected all ports to smell the same. But Sydney had smelt of the gum trees that crowded the hot harbour; Liverpool had smelt of oil and shit. Wilmington smelt of spices and cotton oil. The sky was different here;

a clear, soft blue where Liverpool's had been smoky grey, and Sydney's brightness almost painful in its clarity.

John Williams went directly to his father's contacts in Wilmington. Charles stayed one night in a Wilmington hotel while transport to his uncle's farm, Mont Alba, was arranged, and looked at the new land with the wonder of a colonial.

Dear Mother and Father and George,

Tomorrow I travel to Mont Alba. It has taken me three days to bespeak a carriage and driver, so many horses and men are gone now to the army. I had expected indeed more signs of war, but of course the armies are many leagues from here. My driver is a Negro, the first I have spoken to, and to my surprise is a free man, employed by the owner of the coach. I enquired why he had not joined the army, and he replied in an accent almost unintelligible that the army did not want such as he.

The port is less prosperous than I expected from my Uncle's letters. John Williams told me however that the richness of this land is in the country, and those who can afford to, avoid the city and live there. The houses as I drove through the port today were drab, their front doors open to the street, the walls unpapered, the interiors bare of even carpet. Green shutters are attached to doors and windows to keep out the heat, which is oppressive. The roads are mud, and flocks of hens and geese scatter among the traffic, but again I am told that this was the poorer part of town and if I had more time I would see handsome houses enough.

You see the Negro faces everywhere. The drivers swear at each other, at their horses, at the mud, in a musical cacophony. The piccaninnies have thin legs and stiff black braids and short coloured skirts. They grin up at the traveller from the gutters and hold out their hands for coins. House niggers as they are called stand at the front doors in their long drooping skirts and bright white turbans.

This land is as different as possible from Sydney and even London. Even the food at the hotel seems strange. Last night's dinner encompassed a stewed chicken with spices, which was very good, and fine ham glazed with marmalade, buckwheat cakes and dishes of what were termed preserves, jams and fruit, plenty of strong coffee as well as a large jug of milk upon the table to drink, as though the diners were still in the nursery. Last evening I saw two ladies, in dress respectable, spit tobacco juice onto the street.

I will entrust this letter to Capt. Travers tomorrow, and remain, Your Loving and Obd. son, Charles Fitzhenry

Mont Alba was blue-green grass bordered by white fences and the house the most elegant Charles had ever seen, but Duane was no longer the vigorous man in command that Charles had expected. War had aged his great-uncle; the opinionated man in the letters kept to his bed most of the day, his heirloom firearms of Waterloo already added to the motley weapons of the army — swords, duelling pistols, squirrel guns and English rifles.

The house seemed to be run by the black butler, who was almost as old as Duane and a female slave with pale skin and watchful eyes, who seemed neither housekeeper nor housemaid, but who the other slave deferred to. Two days later Charles rode one of Duane's horses — not his best; the best were already with the army — to his Cousin Elizabeth's. Her husband Ralph, a Colonel, would organise his commission.

If Wilmington had been a disappointment, the grandeur of Mont Alba and Cousin Elizabeth's were startling to a boy from the bush, where the grandest of homes were no more than overgrown farmhouses, with a piano to show their gentility.

Cousin Elizabeth's house was no larger than his childhood home on the hill, but it was beautiful, graceful, from its wide staircase to its chandeliers.

Cousin Elizabeth, too, was almost dreamlike in her perfection, precise with her children and her Negroes, kind to Ralph's elderly aunt who lived with them, her black taffeta swaying on its wide stiff hoop, her soft slurring voice, her liquid vowels and gentle consonants.

It was easy to dream of glory here, in the ordered beauty of Cousin Elizabeth's. Charles was unquestionably in a land of gentlemen, a world of grace and ordered living that made their colonial life at home seem blunt.

Buckwheat cakes for breakfast with ham and syrups; the parlour with its French furniture and gilded ornaments, loops and loops of curtains, its net and lace to keep out light and dust; the deference of Negro servants; the women's waists so small and tight you could circle them with your hand; the breasts that bounced so slightly above the hard cups of their stays.

Charles Fitzhenry was a romantic stranger come to help them. Cousin Elizabeth's friends and the daughters of her friends smiled at him, danced with him, their eyelashes fluttered at him above their fans.

Cousin Ralph equipped him with two horses, his uniforms and a black body servant, Moses.

Charles protested at the body servant. Cousin Ralph looked at him: 'Son, this is the South. If you want to be an officer for our country you'll follow her ways. You understand me? In the South we go to war with honour.'

Going to war with honour meant not behaving like the Yankees in Missouri, Tennessee, Virginia and Kentucky: raping and pillaging, and torturing small children, people gutted or bayoneted as they pleaded for a cherished animal commandeered, their darkies roped in chains and taken for the army. General Lee had issued orders that no private property was to be touched — no matter what the army's need — that looting was punishable by death. The Southern Army would pay for everything requisitioned.

A war of honour.

So far this was what Charles had dreamt of. (Almost, at any rate. He did feel a certain shock when he discovered that half of Cousin Ralph's income came not from horses, but from the slaves he bred and sold to Southern cotton and rice fields. Babies were as much the product of his acres as his foals.)

The glory Charles imagined was also slightly strained. The valour and determination were genuine. General Lee was an extraordinary strategist and was almost worshipped by his troops. But Lee's Army was already ragged, the men smelt of shit and disease, and according to Ralph there were few tents or boots, too few horses, an incredible shortage of food.

Yet even these privations were a source of pride. The South would win — and in early 1862 *was* winning — by sheer courage alone. Charles too was proud that he would be part of it.

The Northern forces were, in fact, stronger than Charles had imagined when he left home. The North had money to hire mercenaries from Europe, as well as to equip them. They also had the naval power to blockade the South's ports, so Southern cotton rotted in the warehouses and neither guns nor ammunition, nor medical supplies, could be replaced. There was not yet the expected help from France or Britain; no European power had formally acknowledged the government of the South.

Dear Mother,

... Our company is made up of planters, sons of planters, farmers, these being most adept at arms and horsemanship, as well as merchants, clerks, saw millers and carpenters. We even have a lawyer and a marble cutter in our ranks, two gasfitters and an iron moulder. Colonel Timber is from the regular army and a veteran of the Mexican war, where he distinguished himself with some honour. He greeted me warmly, and indeed I have had much kindness from all my fellow Officers.

The Men here march to their meals. The food is plentiful but not what our Men receive at home; there is much pork, fresh or salt and

generally stewed with dried vegetables especially beans, and thickened
with cornmeal and milk at every meal and gingerbread that the Men
seem partial to. I mess with the Major and Captain. The Wife of
one of the Men cooks for us, and the Major's man sets our table,
white tablecloth, whiteware and fork and spoon, no bread or damper
but what the Men here call biscuits, much like a scone at every meal.
Ours are made from wheat flour but those of the Men of cornmeal,
insect infested and often hard. Last night some of the Boys carved
holes in their 'biscuits' and filled them with powder and blew them
open, saying it was the only way to break them into pieces to eat . . .

Charles rode northward with Lee's Army and crossed the shallow Potomac. Even though many in the army were already starving, and despite the thin horses and the men with blistered feet wrapped in rags, they were still sure the North would be forced to negotiate a peace conceding independence.

The axles on the gun carriages shrieked for want of oil; men in the lines dropped on the spot from hunger and disease; but, to an officer who was well fed (Moses was an excellent scavenger, and Charles' fat was a bank account he would draw on over the next year), all this was bearable. It was still, mostly, an adventure.

Nothing had prepared him for his first battle. Not the regimental histories in his father's study. Not the stories his mother read aloud in the quiet evenings in the house on the hill.

They waited for first light. It was impossible to sleep. Finally, towards dawn, someone scraped on his tent flap.

'Come in.'

Charles expected Moses. But it was a young man, a year or so older than Charles, already promoted to Captain.

Charles sat up. 'Captain Cavendish.'

'Walter. Jus' call me Walter.' Charles was growing used to the soft Southern voices. 'Thought you mayn't be able to sleep, this being your first battle 'n all.'

'No, I ... no.'

Walter sat down on Charles' saddle. 'Still gets to me, even after a year. The thing to remember is jus' to keep goin'. If the line breaks, then we're lost. Jus' keep on goin' forward and you'll be right.'

Charles tried to grin. 'It sounds simple.'

Walter considered that. 'No. It's the most difficult thing in all your life. The noise ... man, you've never dreamt in all your life of noise you'll hear today. But you jus' keep thinkin', I got to kill me ten Northerners for us to win this thing today, and when we beat them finally, why then we can go home.' He smiled, a surprisingly shy smile for a young man who had lived a year in the army. 'That's what keeps us all goin' sometimes, dreamin' on home. Your home's a ways away, ain't it?'

'Australia.'

'What's it like?'

Charles pulled the blanket round his shoulders. 'Browner than this. The trees are often more blue than green.'

'Your family have a farm?'

'A property. Sheep. Cattle.'

'That so? We've horses at home, but I've always kinda hankered after cattle …'

They talked cattle breeds for half an hour while the night sky turned to grey. Then Walter stood to go. He hesitated. 'Jus' remember,' he said. 'The line has got to hold.' He left the tent.

No, no one can prepare you for your first battle.

How can anyone explain how a horse can smell the hatred, how they stamp in terror or in challenge? (Years later Charles would try to explain it to his daughter, then realised that if you have never been there you could never understand even a shadow of what it was like.)

No one can prepare you for the noise, so loud your bones shiver and your ears forget to hear; the stench of black powder; the sulphur smell as strong as hell; the air so thick with smoke you can see no further than your hand. The shock as the cavalry charge around you, and you realise you are charging too, the horse beneath you racing as horses have raced since man first rode them, your sword arm high, and the first thrust is always a defensive one, to stop the arm that tries to kill you as the armies meet; the second thrust is when you realise you have to kill, but luckily the noise around you is too dense to hear any cry except your own.

Hold the lines … but it is impossible in all that noise and death, when you can scarcely see the man beside you, hardly know if he is friend or enemy. How can you even think to hold the line?

But the Southern lines held at Sharpsburg. Men with no boots repelled an army of more than twice their number. Charles caught glimpses of the enemy through the smoke as his troops built a wall of their dead, to lie behind it and keep firing. When they charged — Charles with his comrades — the ground was thick with corpses, so they had to ride on top of them — blue corpses and grey — and pride in his men bit sharper than the terror and the hunger.

By the end of the day he had survived.

Triumph was almost as good as food, or fresh ammunition. (Almost.) The army marched back across the Potomac once again. Their next battle was at Fredericksburg, another stunning victory of strategy over strength, General Lee losing only a handful of his men as opposed to the Northern loss of 12,500.

Dear Mother,
Rain today has kept us in our tents and You will forgive I know the rough pencil with which I write, the paper being too damp to take the ink. Last night I dreamt of rain on the roof at home and the smell of the sea in the storm. It seems so very long since I smelt the sea. I lay thinking of your faces, Papa and George's but Yours was the clearest of all and for one moment I dreamt that Ellen would call me and there would be breakfast on the table and all clean and sweet. Even in the rain the heat here is oppressive, the mosquitoes worse and even the ants seem to have a taste for human flesh. The

worse perhaps is the 'chigger', a small red thing that burrows into the skin and causes the most irritating itching.

You must not imagine me in worse case than I am however. My health continues good. In truth it is news from Home that I most crave, and envy others when the mail carriers arrive, but my new Friend Walter Cavendish with whom I now share a tent — a large equipage with high walls that allow us to stand in comfort — also shares his letters with me, and in his news of Home and hay making I see our fields and Your faces too. Walter also shares his packages, that are a welcome addition to our soldier's lot, his Mother sending fruit cakes, pickles, butter and cheese and since his last letter to her She now mostly kindly includes a letter for me too. Cousin Elizabeth and her Friends are most diligent too, sending me only last week a new shirt, writing paper, condensed milk, peach preserves and even a turkey roast, and tobacco. So You must not believe me friendless in this land.

Cousin Elizabeth assures me that She will do her best to get this letter and others through the blockade to You. I have received but one of Yours since I arrived here alas, of which I have mentioned before, but We move about so much that mail often times can't catch us even if it escapes the blockade . . .

Charles was back at Cousin Elizabeth's for Christmas.

He had been six months away. He had the watchfulness that every soldier gets as you listen for the step behind that might be an enemy's. His teeth were loose from scurvy, his bowels an embarrassment,

44

though both would be cured by the time his furlough ended. (He regarded neither ailment as serious enough to tell his parents.)

His world had changed. So had Cousin Elizabeth's.

Cousin Elizabeth dressed in silk for Christmas Day. On other days she wore homespun. Like many of the other ladies of the city, her silks had been used to make Confederate flags, her linen and cotton dresses torn up for bandages. Once the bloody strips were used they were taken back to be washed and ironed and rolled again by ladies all through the sweating afternoons.

There was no beef or mutton for Christmas dinner — except for the very rich, who could buy at profiteers' prices — but there was ham and chicken, and corn bread, even if there were no wheat rolls, and there was still gravy to sop the corn bread in.

The cut glass punchbowl was filled with punch of cumquat juice and brandy, even if there were no tea and coffee, or whalebone stays or perfume, magazines or books, and almost no medicines either, not even the householder's iodine and calomel, or the hospital necessities of quinine, opium and chloroform.

There was sweet potato pie for dessert and good wine from the cellar, though most had been offered up for convalescents.

There was even glory again, for a little while, in the admiration of clean women. The women clustered round him, for his double glamour as a soldier of the Confederacy and as a foreigner come to their aid. Girls with white round shoulders and plump white arms and soft powdered bosoms edged with lace, with peacock feathers in their fans and hair, and flowers behind their ears and in their sashes, because their jewels had been sold for the Confederate cause.

They sang 'Your Letter Came But Came Too Late' around the piano in the parlour, sang 'Jacket of Grey' and 'My Old Kentucky Home', sipping at the bitter parched corn and sweet potato roast that passed for coffee out of thin china cups that felt like eggshells after the tin mugs of camp. Charles felt his hands might break them.

It was a short, bright time of comfort, tended by the darkies moving smooth and patient behind the laughter, and seeing their well fed faces, their warm clothes and safe lives, it was hard not to compare the life of a house slave with the starved and weary faces of the Confederate Army.

Charles had grown used to the soft guttural lilt of nigger voices, the relationships that were often closer than a master and a servant's: Moses, loyal and capable, Seneca who opened the door, who ushered in the port and chicken, the small figure in a wide calico apron who brought the supper tray: 'Carrie! Where are you now?'

And the soft obedient 'Yes'm' as Carrie answered.

'She's as slow as molasses in January. Carrie! You come here now and fill the punch bowl, you hear?'

A voice from the crowd at the piano said scornfully: 'And the Yankees want to free the Negroes! Well, the Yankees are welcome to them.'

CHAPTER 8

1863

WAR

Dear Mother,

We are quite settled now in our winter quarters. To think I was excited by my first fall of snow! Somehow the descriptions never included the mud that follows, or the wind that seeps into your bones. But do not think me comfortless. Walter and I now have a hut of wood and mud, with wonder of wonders, a stone chimney, fireplace and even a mantelpiece and real door with hinges. The Men are mostly in Yankee tents captured in the summer campaign; in summer they made do with a woollen blanket and an oilcloth one; two men each slept together, first in the woollen blanket then with the oilcloth one around them, and slept quite comfortable that way. Our camp however increases in luxury each day; the Men have cut trees to let the sunlight in, whenever the clouds consent to part, and have dug trenches to drain off the wet, though as only a few inches depth finds still more water it is often a thankless task. Each day the Men keep the fires burning; at night they are moved a short distance that the Men may move their tents to the warmed earth, and that way achieve some comfort.

Our greatest problem indeed is boredom. Once the day's drilling and camp chores are done there is little for the men to do. Colonel Mountjoy has suggested that our division engage his in a snowball battle, and we hope that this will not only entertain the Men but keep their battle skills sharp.

Again I must assure You that I am well, and hope in my prayers each night that You and father are well too. I remain, your loving son, Charles Fitzhenry

By now there was little hope that the letter would find its way through the blockade, but Charles folded the paper anyway, and left it between the pages of his Bible. The last duty you did for your friend was to check their Bible for any letters they had left for their family.

How much of what he had written was the truth? Yes, he was bored. But boredom implied you looked forward to your release, and any release from boredom here meant battle. By the standards of the camp he was well, too, although his bowels ran water, his skin festered and his breath stank like a dog's. But how could you explain the insanity that was war to the quiet household on the hill at home?

Men, horses, food, ammunition and clothes were scarce. Charles had experienced victory again at Chancellorville, his first defeat at Gettysburg and the retreat. Then had come Chickamunga and another victory, defeat at Chattanooga, and victory of a sort in the mountain passes of Georgia.

There were quarrels among the Generals and among the State Governors. The children on the streets wrapped rags around themselves to keep out the wind. Butter cost thirty-five dollars a pound, cardboard shoes cost two hundred dollars a pair. Cotton sweltered in the storage sheds as the South slowly starved and speculators and government contractors grew richer ...

The war had changed.

So had Charles Fitzhenry.

He lived on a diet of rancid bacon fat, and rice and peas where weevils crawled, the best that Moses could forage for him. Smallpox breathed over his shoulder; measles, typhoid and pneumonia; the stench of dysentery. His gums and those of his men bled with scurvy; their bowels rotted with the disease and maggots wriggled from their anus. No man in the whole camp had steady bowels. The place smelt of shit, impossible to get rid of, and indeed the Colonel called it a patriotic odour, inseparable from an army.

The days of boredom ended. The army moved again.

His boots splintered beyond redemption. Charles walked with feet wrapped in frozen sacking across blue snow and saw red blood turn purple in the cold in front of him, oozing from a stump of leg bandaged in rough homespun. One of his horses died — of starvation, not from a musket shell. He led the other to save its strength for battles, a shell-shocked horse with its stomach cleaving to its back.

He pulled the boots and uniform from a dead Unionist he found behind a tree. A deserter? Scout? He neither knew nor cared. Moses dyed the uniform and the brown walnut stain washed into Charles' skin and blistered it and the creases round his anus festered as the dye seeped through. The boots were too small, but Moses stretched them somehow, or maybe he swapped them for a larger pair.

Charles grew used to the sickly sweet smell of gangrene, the crawl of lice around his body, the torment of mosquitoes, gnats and flies that clustered round the wounds and sucked, that sucked on the sweat from fever. The stench of vomit, the itch of maggots as they swelled in festered flesh. (Skin festered at the smallest cut, even a blister gone sour; flesh seemed to melt with poor diet and non-existent hygiene.)

He had been prepared for privations. He had not been prepared for noise. The clamour of many thousands of men, the bark of their voices, and the bark of muskets, rifles, pistols, so loud in battle there was no noise at all, just a ringing in the head that left you deafened for days after (and did in fact leave him partially deafened for the rest of his life).

Charles heard the voices of Germans, Irish, Poles in the battle around him, mercenaries bought with Northern money, shouting in their own languages in their blue uniforms, and he knew that the dreams of England or France joining the South were gone.

The South was alone. Charles knew that defeat was inevitable, although this was not something he could mention to his companions. Nor did you desert a cause because it was lost. On the contrary, a doomed cause should string your conviction even tighter. Besides, there was loyalty to friends. Charles had entered the war for a dream of justice. Now it was Walter's war he fought, and Captain Johnstone's, and Ward Sutherland's. How could he leave them?

Dear Father

. . . discontent amongst the Men increases daily since the Conscript Act. Many believe that having enlisted for twelve months their obligations are now over, and wish to return to farms and Family. Desertions are common, and are treated with growing severity; indeed many officers believe that if the public firing squads had been instigated earlier this growing disaffection might have been halted and many lives might have been saved. I am not so sanguine; however despite the friendships of my fellow Officers — indeed at times they treat me as a talisman for victory and believe my joining their cause is yet another sign that civilised men everywhere must support the Confederate cause — I am aware at all times that I am a stranger, and keep my opinions to myself.

Yestereve a strapping farmhand was punished for cowardice; he was forced to kneel while his head was shaved smooth as an onion. He was then stripped naked and whipped until the blood flew, then branded with the deserter's 'd' with a hot iron on both hips, then sent howling through the Camp while the Rogues March played.

This however seemed of little effect, and today the entire Camp were forced to witness yet another execution for desertion. Twelve armed guards escorted the prisoner, who marched with his coffin on one side and the Chaplain on the other, with the 12 members of the firing squad behind.

At the grave he was made to sit upon his coffin. His eyes were bound while the Chaplain read a prayer. The order to fire was given; the twelve men lifted their muskets; ten were loaded with powder only, and only two with balls, none among them knowing how their firearms were loaded. Thus no man might know who killed the prisoner, lest the knowledge weigh too heavy on their feelings.

I have written to Mother separately. I would not wish her to be burdened by these things. Indeed we are in bad case here; disease is rampant; our supplies of all necessities are low and at times fail altogether and were it not for supplies we are able to capture our condition would be impossible. Though I have no doubt our Cause is right I wonder if all soldiers have seen the things that we must daily bear and at times long for the counsel You might give me. May God Bless and protect You all. Your Loving and Odb. (Sic) Son, Charles Fitzhenry

Charles was still an idealist. You need a pause, a space to think, before you change your standards. But he was beginning to doubt his ability to live up to them.

As the horses shivered in the cold night, after the sweat of battle, Charles visited Walter Cavendish in the Surgeon's tent.

Walter lay on the black-crusted table. Flies drank the blood from the Surgeon's apron. A pile of severed feet and hands congealed on the ground, waiting to be disposed of. Musket balls destroyed limbs, they didn't simply pierce them.

Charles held Walter down while the Surgeon cut off his shattered leg. It was all he could do for his friend, though Walter screamed at him to let him go, to let him die.

Later, he sat by the fire and dreamt. The fire smelt wrong; it hadn't the acridity of eucalyptus wood that burnt at home. And the smoke behaved differently. This was a better behaved smoke. But it kept away the mosquitoes, like the smoke of home.

Charles no longer dreamt Sir Walter Scott dreams of a girl with warm cheeks and a small waist, to whom he could say: I have come through war and madness to find you, my love.

He dreamt instead of the curl of the water in the creek at home, the sting of the waves as the whiting slipped towards the sand, the flash of silver as the gum tips shivered in the wind.

He dreamt of billy tea at mustering and Johnny cakes at shearing.

Later, he went back to Walter. Walter was muttering, semi-conscious. Charles knew what Walter dreamt of. Not glory; not love either. Walter dreamt of cows. He wanted to breed them, when the war was over.

Later, as the dawn turned cold, he sat with Walter's hand in his. The hand was cold. Walter was crying. Charles wondered if he cried for the cows he'd never breed, as the life seeped out of him and the sky grew pink.

Soldiers dream of simple things in the lulls between battles. A little is enough to keep you going. Charles left Walter's body to the orderly, and wrapped himself in his blanket, and dreamt of roasting mutton.

Soldiers dream of after the war, not because they expect it to happen, but as a magic talisman, to keep them safe. Dreams are other shapes for hope.

Soldiers don't feel fear in battle. They feel fear before the battle, and the mind howls like a sick animal: *perhaps I am going to die.* The hair rises on their neck as it did on our animal ancestors, and they know they have to run, but they still have the remnants of heroism, and they can't.

~∰◎

The army marched again that morning. Charles rode, because although his horse was weak, he was weaker.

His bowels gripped. He dismounted. His horse stood, waiting. It hadn't energy for anything else. Others had already defecated at the edge of the road, the brown streaked red with the blood of dysentery. Charles moved into the trees. He squatted. The sweat ran down his collar till it was over.

There was nothing to wipe with except his hand or the grass beside him. He used the grass. His anus was raw from wiping.

Something flashed pink three trees away. When his breath came back he investigated.

It was a body. It had swollen since death. The pink was its stomach, distended by death, pushing back the ragged shirt and pants. Flies crawled in a glittering sheet over one foot.

Once, his horse had stepped on a swollen corpse. He'd heard it pop. He'd seen the guts shiver in sunlight. Charles backed off from this corpse, and remounted.

No, if there was to be a girl with a wasp waist and silken cheeks he couldn't tell her this. Perhaps he could never tell anyone at all. Wars are fought by the young and remembered, sometimes, when they are old. In between they are silent.

Marching, marching, marching — but this was no longer marching. Men staggered, and dropped along the way, to lie in the muck with flies around them. No one sang these days. Charles' horse stumbled, then stumbled again. Charles dismounted, and waited for Moses to catch up from behind where he walked with the wagons.

'What do you think?'

Moses stared at the horse. He'd grown used to this strange Australian man's questions, asking his opinion like he was white maybe. For a moment he automatically tried to think what answer Charles wanted him to give, then mentally shrugged and gave him the truth.

'He done for, Mas' Charles.'

Charles nodded. Blue eyes met brown eyes, then Charles gestured towards the trees.

Moses led the horse now. He had been a groom before Cousin Ralph decided he should go to war. Charles had grown up with horses, but he had never seen anyone touch them with so much love as Moses.

The horse staggered into the trees, then stood there, head down, gasping. Charles had never seen horses gasp like this before the war. Now he knew what it meant as well as Moses. This horse was dying.

Black powder was precious. Charles shrugged his arms out of his jacket, and Moses threw it over the horse's head, pulling back on the reins as Charles slashed the horse's throat with his sword.

The horse screamed once, then fell to its knees, then sideways. The hot blood flowed onto the ground. Moses knelt to catch it in his mug, pouring it into a water flask. Later he'd boil it with broken biscuit to make blood pudding.

There was little enough meat, but still too much to carry. Charles didn't even consider handing it in to the commissariat. He hesitated. For moment he felt a sudden foolish pain that he couldn't share the meat with Walter.

'Moses — have you any friends back there?'

'Friends, Mas' Charles?'

'Someone you'd like to share the meat with.'

Moses had been a big man before the war. He was still large, but his flesh had shrunk, so his big bones stuck out like spoon handles. He didn't answer, and in the silence Charles realised that, for a slave, admitting friendship might also mean admitting you were conspiring, or owed loyalty to someone other than your master.

'Go get someone — anyone. Quick.'

Moses slid off into the trees, while Charles sat with the meat and the red bones of the horse, and the horse's head grinning behind him. It wasn't only that he suddenly, desperately, wanted a feeling of fellowship about him. Other men would help keep the feast safe. With Walter's death — and Captain Johnstone's, who had died in the same battle — and the half a dozen other friends in the last two months who had died or been captured, he had no one other than Moses whom he knew or trusted.

Five minutes later Moses returned with two men only slightly smaller than he was, and just as black, their eyes wide and brown in their thin faces. The men stood back, uncertain.

Charles gestured at the trees. 'Go get some wood — anything that'll burn.'

They nodded, and walked into the trees.

Moses had also brought a pot he must have borrowed, and an axe. He chopped at the horse's head, for which Charles was grateful, because it looked like meat, not the animal he'd known.

They boiled the head in the pot, and grilled the bones, and roasted as much of the meat as they could on sticks over the fire — a hot fire, with dry wood and little smoke. Charles tore at the meat as soon as it was charred, then stopped to find the others staring at him. It took him a few seconds to work out what was wrong.

'You eat too,' he said awkwardly. 'Please.'

They reached forward, but not towards the chunks of meat. Instead they used rough tongs of wood sticks to hold the hot, charred bones and suck the marrow, and scoop the brains and liver from the pot; all the scraps of the carcass the master would reject and leave for slaves.

Charles had lived in this country for nearly a year. But he had been insulated from the world of slavery around him. Moses had tended his horse, his uniform, had brought him food, had slept with his equipment to guard it, but Moses had never eaten with him before. Watching the man suck marrow from the bones while the rich horse meat dripped juice into the fire, Charles had his first revelation of what it was to be a slave.

Later, the bones discarded, Charles insisted each man take a lump of meat, while Moses wrapped the rest in greasy cloths that might keep out some flies and maggots.

'Moses . . .'

'Yassir?'

Charles wondered exactly what Moses had been eating this past year, as he fed his master with precious chickens and bartered rice and beans. 'The meat is for you to eat. Not just me. It won't last long anyway. May as well eat as much as we can.'

Moses gave a half grin. 'Yassir.'

For a moment, Charles desperately wanted to say more; to ask the man why he was here. Surely Moses could have escaped in the chaos of war, if that had been what he wanted? But what would Moses have run towards? An army chain gang that would capture him and put him to digging latrines; the Union Army that might shoot him as a spy? Did Moses dream of peace and horses back at Mont Alba?

If Moses had been his slave, instead of Cousin Ralph's, Charles might at that moment have given him his freedom. But it wasn't Charles' to give.

So he just said, 'Thank you, Moses. For everything.' He lifted his saddlebags, then realised he was too weak to carry them.

Moses took them from him wordlessly.

'They're too heavy for you.'

Moses shook his head. 'Zachariah — he the one with one bad eye — he go with the wagons. He look after your saddle too.'

Charles bit his lip. Then, carrying nothing but his pistols, musket, powder and sword, he walked back into the straggle of the army.

~·⊙

Night: a sea of campfires spread through the darkness. In the past two years Charles had learnt that light differs from country to country, and darkness is also

59

different; not just the stars, but smells and sounds, the very texture of the air. This air was thin, as though it held not quite enough life for him to breathe it.

Charles slept fitfully. Each time he woke, the night was filled with the sound of coughing, of axes wielded by men desperate for even the slippery warmth of green wood.

They marched, camped, then fought again.

Dear Father,

Is this truly what war is? Is it the glory You knew, and my ancestors? Is there, was there, ever any more than this?

Sometimes in the moment between sleep and waking I am sure that I am home. I smell the polish Jane uses on the bedstead, the honeysuckle out the window. I know I have only to open my eyes and all will be safe and sweet once more.

Other times I wonder if another world exists at all, if all the earth is made of the mud, of lice, the stench of dying flesh, the bitter smell of those who may be dead tomorrow.

Did he write this on the paper, or simply dream he wrote it? At any rate, the letter was never sent.

Charles rose for the last battle he would ever know in the cool dawn, before the heat and dust and flies settled on the world once more. For once the air felt soft on his warm skin.

He ate — something. He drank, and it was hot and black and pretending to be coffee. He talked, but without the depth of friendship. His friends were dead.

He hadn't had the strength for new ones. Even the Englishman, John Williams, had died the previous year of measles, not in battle.

Noise, the impenetrable noise of battle, so loud your body shuddered with it and your ears could no longer hear and even the screams of men and horse seemed silent. The air was black with powder, sulphurous as hell.

Charles knew he was going to die long before he felt the shell that hit him. Then there was only pain and blackness, broken by Moses' hands that brought more pain, and consciousness, as Moses carried him off the field of battle and placed him in the cart.

When he woke again the sheets were cool and smooth, and the girl was there.

CHAPTER 9

1863

REPRIEVE

His head felt heavy against the starched white pillow. He watched the girl go. He remembered her from his period of leave. What was her name?

She was paler than the other niggers, and silent when spoken to. An uppity nigger, said Cousin Ralph. She'd been sent here from Mont Alba to mind her manners. Charles didn't ask what she'd done at Mont Alba to be sent away. He had learnt there were sins here that were strange to someone from another country.

Carrie. Her name was Carrie.

She brought soup that smelt of chicken and roses. It was sweet. It had been a year since he had tasted chicken. That was when Moses had filched a hen from a farm. Charles had closed his eyes to this breach of discipline and ate the meat.

Now he was too weak to drink. She sat without expression, holding the spoon to his lips. The liquid trickled down his chin. She mopped it, tipped it more gently onto his tongue.

He slept again.

She washed his arm when he woke. He could feel it now; an arm, not just pain. He could feel a splint around it, feel the softness of the warm water, feel her fingers as she smoothed on unguent, and wrapped the arm in bandages hot from the iron, and he smelt the stale sweat underneath her arms.

He'd shat himself. He lay rigid with embarrassment. She washed him, his legs and genitals too. She had had towels beneath him and he could see the fouled cloths piled on the floor. She took the towels and went away.

She didn't speak.

Later there was more soup, thickened with rice or meal. And sleep.

This was a time beyond the world.

Everything had gone: the horror of the past year, the strategies, the troop movements, the intricacies of food and shelter. Now there was just his body in a clean bed, waiting for a meal or the chamberpot. He was back in his childhood where life revolved around him. No decisions had to be made. Hands arrived to soothe and comfort him. Towels rubbed at his skin and brought comfort.

Somehow Charles knew that life would never be as simple again.

~◎

The doctor came on the third day. Charles heard him puffing up the stairs. He wheezed into the room, still as portly as he'd been last Christmas, still with a colour like red beef.

'Sorry I couldn't get to you before. I don't know, sometimes, why sometimes I feel there should be six of me these days.'

His breath stank of rotten teeth. (Surely a doctor could pull his own teeth, Charles thought vaguely, but maybe it was harder if they were your own.) The doctor's hands were hot. He muttered, mostly to himself.

'That arm should have come off. No one to see to it, I suppose. Expect me to do miracles here. I don' know.'

He stood up. 'Well, I could take you down to the hospital, but you wouldn't thank me. We've got men lined up side by side in the corridors and you'll get better nursing here. Well, we'll see. It may come to that. I'll call in tomorrow and we'll see.'

He paused at the door. He looked back at the figure on the bed. He seemed to feel that something more was needed.

'It's been a weary fight, son. But we're going to lick them Yankees. We'll lick them yet, you'll see.'

The doctor didn't come again. Later, he asked Carrie where he was. She shrugged.

'Ah doan know, sir. Calliope, she say they're fighting up the north. Maybe doctor gone and went up there.'

The evening was cool. The fever grew again. Colours flashed before his eyes, like rainbows over the sea. He thought the girl sat by him, fanning him with turkey feathers, feeding him rice gruel with a spoon. But it couldn't have been her, because at times she held a child, little more than a baby. She spoke to it in a voice that wasn't a nigger voice at all. Almost like a voice of home.

Morning came. The girl was still there and so was the baby. She was singing to the child. He knew the song; it was Scottish. His mother sang it. Carrie's voice was different as she sang. It was almost like his mother's voice, not like a Southern voice at all.

The child sucked on a small breast, a bubble of milk on one brown cheek. The cheek was much browner than the breast. He shut his eyes for a moment. When he opened them the light had changed and she was gone.

The smell of dust and gardenia floated in from outside. He felt different. She must have shaved his beard, picked the lice from his hair and cut it. He lay revelling in consciousness again, the polish on the door, the fold of the curtains, the shimmering shadow of the shutters on the wall. Pain gripped him — his bowels not his arm. He realised with horror he had fouled the bed again.

She was back. Her eyes were brown below the white scarf. He wondered in embarrassment how to tell her about the bed, but she guessed, either by the smell or because it had happened before.

She worked without speaking. Her hands were matter of fact. She rolled him to one side, gently, easing him on the pillows, pulled the towels from under him, added new ones, wiped him with a warm cloth and then with cream like he was a baby, the faint scent of chicken fat and lavender.

'What happened to Moses? He should be doing this. Why can't he help you?'

'Moses done gone, Mas' Charles.'

'Gone where?'

'Moses done gone with the army.'

He felt the rage rise in him.

'Moses was my servant. They had no right to take him back to the army. Moses risked his life for me back there.'

The girl shrugged. 'Moses goes where he is told, Mas' Charles. Like us all do.'

'Did he want to go?'

Another tired shrug. 'Moses be a good nigger, Captain. He done what he were told.'

Her accent was broader now. Many years later he'd call it playing nigger. Now he leant back and watched the sky. The small exchange had exhausted him.

She came back with rice water. She sat by the bed and fed it to him in small spoonfuls.

He could examine her clearly for the first time. She was younger than he thought, perhaps seventeen. Her features were fine for a Negro. Her skin was pale, much paler than Moses' skin, and he was lighter than the average nigger.

Charles had learnt in the past year that colour was no guide to who was a slave and who wasn't. Some slaves were paler than the farm workers back at home, would pass for white if it wasn't for their voices and their clothes. Household slaves mostly had light skin. Their fathers and grandfathers were the white men of the house. A dark house slave might set people whispering that the master had nigger blood as well. You made sure your house slaves looked good and pale. But Carrie's baby had been dark ...

'Where's the baby?'

Her face was blank. He wondered if she was stupid, but she had seemed competent a while ago.

'I thought I saw you with a baby.'

A shrug. He realised suddenly that she shouldn't have brought her baby upstairs. She'd taken advantage of Cousin Elizabeth's absence to break the house rules. He tried to smile.

'You know, I reckon that's the first baby I've seen in over a year. It made me realise where I was.'

She smiled then, for the first time.

'That was Zanthopee. She's mine.'

'Zanthopee?'

'Mr Ralph, he named her.' The smile was gone.

'Xanthippe then. Socrates' wife was called Xanthippe. The Greek philosopher of ancient times.'

The same blank look.

'She's a pretty baby.' He said it to make her smile again, something he could give her in return for her kindness. It worked. Her smile was wider, though still cautious.

'Will you bring her up here again?'

She shook her head. 'Miss Elizabeth, she doan like babies up the stairs.'

'Miss Elizabeth is at Mont Alba. Is there anyone else here besides you and Miss Lillian?'

'Calliope. She tend Miss Lillian. Calliope say she won't come in dis room case she gets the fever 'n gives it to Miss Lillian.'

'You were singing.'

Her face stayed impassive, neither assenting or denying till she saw his frame of mind.

'I liked it. You sounded different though. You spoke differently when you spoke to the baby too.'

She looked cautious. 'Master Duane, he liked me to speak like he did, like an Englishman.' The accent was less broad now. 'He taught me things.'

'You used to live at Master Duane's? At Mont Alba?'

She nodded.

'Why did you leave?'

No answer.

He closed his eyes. He heard her skirts rustle. He spoke again before she left, hurriedly, in case he lost the courage to ask.

'That song ... would you sing it for me?'

She stood expressionless. Then she nodded. She sat on the chair by the bedside, her hands folded in her lap. Her voice was low and warm, not like the high, tight voices of the girls around the piano on his last leave. She sang with the accent she had used to the baby, Duane's accent, his mother's accent, not the one she'd used to talk to him.

Why weep ye by the tide, lady?
Why weep ye by the tide?
I'll wed ye to my youngest son,
And ye shall be his bride.
And ye shall be his bride, lady,
So comely to be seen.
But aye, she let the tears downfall,
For Jock of Hazeldean.

The words were from a world he'd lost, the world of childhood and of home. They were infinitely reassuring. Her hands reached over and pulled up the coverlet. He closed his eyes and slept.

CHAPTER 10

1863

CHARLES FITZHENRY GRASPS
A FUTURE

Dear Father

*As You will see by the address I am at Cousin Elizabeth's. I have
been wounded, but reassure Mother I am recovering, with every
expectation I shall soon rejoin my Comrades. I . . .*

He let the pen fall. It was no use. The words were
lies, evasions. Nor was there any hope that this letter
could get through the Northern blockade; little chance
that it might even find its way to a port.

Defeat was inevitable. Even if it were not, his spirit
had been killed though his body recovered.

Today was hot. The sun hung white in the still air,
the trees quivered in their shadows. The weather clung

to him like a fever he couldn't shake off. It wasn't like the heat at home.

Carrie had drawn the shutters when she came up with his breakfast: more cornmeal mush. She had left the tray, and removed his chamberpot.

He heard her feet steady down the stairs, then pushed the sheet aside and went to the window. He drew the shutters back, hoping for a breeze despite the heat that would come with it, then climbed into bed again.

He was stronger now, and the thought terrified him.

The angel of death whirled in the burning air outside. What should he do? Go back and fight? Neither his body nor his mind could face it.

He could stay here, and roll bandages with the women, and be called a coward. He couldn't face that either.

There was only one way out. He had to leave.

It was not a sudden decision, as the choice to go to war had been. Years later he would say he left believing the war was endless. To any rational man it would have been obvious that the South couldn't hold on much longer. But Charles was a long way from rationality.

Mostly he just wanted to go home. To reach home he had to desert the army, leave this country of insanity and death and somehow travel north, where he could get a ship to England then Australia.

How? He'd be alone. The thought of loneliness bit into him. Alone in a strange country.

He hadn't been alone before. You are never alone in an army, you are part of it. He'd had the cousinship of Elizabeth and Ralph, the comradeship with Walter, the security of Moses' loyalty, and Carrie's hands tending him. Hands that did everything, so he could lie passive after the agony of the world outside.

And suddenly the solution was clear.

He would take Carrie with him. Rescue her from slavery; take her north where she would be free. That way he could rescue himself as well. He would be a hero in his own eyes, instead of a deserter.

He waited, hot beneath his sheets, till she came back.

She brought rice water, flavoured with cumquat juice, cold from the well outside. She'd stopped the bitter blackberry root now his bowels were steadier. She handed the juice to him without speaking, silent as ever. (She hadn't sung again. He hadn't asked her to. The child had stayed downstairs.)

He took the juice. He sipped. He asked, casually, 'Carrie, have you ever thought of escaping north?'

Her face flushed. 'Why, Mas' Charles, I is a good nigger.' Her hands gripped her apron.

'Carrie, I'm going north. I have to go north to get a ship home. If you want to, if you want to go north, I could take you with me ...'

Her face was blank again, a slave's blankness. He spoke hurriedly before she could protest.

'I've got bank drafts in the North. I can help you once you get there. You could be free.'

Blankness. She watched him. A bird cheeped in the hot air outside. A dog barked far off.

'How you goin' to get up there? The North, it's far away.'

'We'd have to walk. I've got maps. We would have to stick to the bridle trails, the back roads. Up the hills a way. Go across country.'

There was still no expression on her face; not even calculation.

'I could take my baby too?'

He hadn't thought about the child. She was only just walking, and would have to be carried. He didn't have the strength, but Carrie might have. He guessed she wouldn't go without the child.

Suddenly it seemed easier. If they took the child they would seem like refugees. No one would suspect that he was a deserter. A man and a woman and a child — a family. He glanced at Carrie. She could pass for white. No one would look closely, not in days like these. And if the child was darker — well, who looks closely at a child? They could keep her covered.

'Of course we'd take the child.'

She sat down. (That in itself was new. After the first days when she'd had to feed him she never sat in his presence.) Her face was still blank. Then, slowly, she nodded. Her eyes never left him. He breathed relief and let his head rest back on the pillow.

'When do we leave, Mas' Charles?'

'I don't know. Not yet. As soon as I'm strong enough. You understand?'

Another nod. She stood up, went towards the door.

'Carrie ... you won't say anything, will you?'

She looked at him fully. She smiled. She shook her head. Then she was gone.

He lay back. The decision had been made. He thought that he could trust her. That was enough. It never occurred to him, in those early days, to wonder what she was thinking.

CHAPTER 11

1850–55

CARRIE (1)

Tuesdays, Drusilla made the bread. Not Mondays, because the yeast had to grow the day before, and that would make it Sunday, and Drusilla wasn't sure about growing yeast on the Lord's day.

To make the yeast grow you added sugar to it, and a bit of flour and some grated raw potato, and you put it on the windowsill where it sat all night and caught the first sun in the morning, as well as the scent of the roses at the edge of the courtyard, big fat roses. When Carrie was young she thought the rose scent grew the yeast.

By the time the fires were lit and the ashes raked and Drusilla had finished cussing at Big Jim as a good-for-nothing yella sow who never cut the wood right or split it fine enough, the top of the yeast would have been poured into the flour and Drusilla would be pushing it and pulling at it, with white flour on her brown arms as she kept up her cussing, so that years later Carrie was to think bread never would rise right unless you swore at it.

Carrie could never bring herself to swear, though, not even for light bread.

Wheat bread was for the white folks, corn bread for the blacks. 'You there, chile, it's a sin and a shame,' yelled Drusilla catching Carrie tearing at the hot white crusts. 'Lemme tell you sum'ting right now, my lady, you ain't white. Always tryin' to wear the big hat.'

If Drusilla were in a good mood, if Big Jim hadn't sassed her, or the sauce had poured out smooth, she might cut Carrie a crust of the white bread and wipe on guava jelly from the cool stone room beside the kitchen where the bottles crowded on the shelves: rows of jellies, melon pickles, salted butter, lines of hams, the walls smelling of salt and honey that dripped into brown stone crocks on the cold paved floor.

It took time to learn to be a good nigger, especially when your skin was pale like Carrie's, when you had a hankering for white bread and chicken, when white folks like Mas' Duane spoiled you and gave you ideas above your station.

'Girl, you is so bold and brazen,' yelled Drusilla, finding Carrie licking the butter pats under the wide wood table, but then Lina came in and smiled (a smile like a cat sitting up on a shelf and watching you) and said Mas' Duane wanted to see Carrie, and took her up the steps with carpet on them, tugging at Carrie's plaits and checking that her neck was clean.

Master Duane was old. He had fought in a war they called Waterloo. He had built Mont Alba when he'd come here afterwards. Master Duane's wife had died years before Carrie was born, bearing Miz Elizabeth, and now Miz Elizabeth was married herself, but Master Duane liked to have a childer about. That was one reason Lina had been allowed to keep Carrie, instead of having her daughter sold as soon as she was old enough to survive without the tit ... that and the fact that Lina got what she wanted, mostly, from Master Duane.

Lina's father must have been white, and probably her grandfathers were white as well. Lina was a high yella girl, with skin like sweet milk coffee; much paler than Drusilla, who had skin like the blush on a roast chicken, like a bit of crisp crackling heading out for Sunday dinner, but darker than Carrie's. Carrie's skin was as pale as Mas' Duane's, almost.

Years later, in Miz Elizabeth's house, Carrie would hear about the 'octaroon dances' in New Orleans. The octaroon dances were given once a month by the mirror-elegant brothels of New Orleans to display their merchandise to planters searching for a mistress.

Many more years later Carrie would recognise Lina's accent as being more French than Negro, would realise that her mother had been purchased in New Orleans by Master Duane on a holiday after his daughter had married.

Lina had been a high-class slave prostitute in one of the most expensive brothels. She was probably the daughter of another prostitute; possibly the granddaughter or great-granddaughter of a prostitute. Every male ancestor for the last three generations had been white. The high-class establishments sold their slaves, if the price was right, as well as hired them to the white men by the night or month.

The girls were beautiful, well spoken and pale. The whiter a girl was, the higher the cost to buy or hire her. Bought outright, the girl would be taken home to be a mistress while her beauty lasted, a house slave after that. Sometimes a girl might be freed; perhaps (so it was rumoured in the bordellos) even married in a woman-starved part of the country where her past would be unknown. How much of that was hope and how much a real possibility Carrie never knew.

Drusilla's eyes were as brown as the galloping horses Carrie could see in the fields beyond the kitchen window. Lina's eyes were brown like honey, but Carrie's eyes were greenish grey, the same as Mas' Duane's and Miz Elizabeth's.

Lina called her daughter 'Carrie'. So did Drusilla and Big Jim.

Master Duane called Carrie, 'Caroline'. He didn't like the way Carrie spoke. He'd tell her to do it different, speak more like him, not like Lina or Drusilla or Big Jim, not even like Miz Elizabeth.

Carrie supposed the way Master Duane spoke was

the way they made them speak at the war they called the Waterloo.

'Where is this Waterloo, Master Duane? Where you find it?' she asked, and Master Duane shook his head: 'Say, Where is Waterloo? Where do you find it? There is no need to add more words.'

Master Duane took Carrie's hand in his old papery one, and led her down the stairs, across the carpet that smelt of the lavender water Drusilla made in summer and Lucretia sprinkled over the carpet every month to keep out the beetle, and into the library that smelt like shoes, but which wasn't shoes but books, all covered in the same material, as many books as ants on an ant hill, and on the desk, shiny in its beeswax, was a brown and golden globe. Master Duane spun the globe and pointed.

'See that? That's Waterloo.'

'That where you is from, Master Duane?'

'Is that where I came from? In a way. I was born here.' He moved his finger a few inches and pointed at a pink island. 'That's England. And I went to school here.' He pointed further down the pink. 'That's where they taught me to be a soldier so I could serve on general staff.'

'You were a servant?' Shocked.

A smile. His skin fell into folds like an old apple, or like a yam shrivelled at the bottom of the pile in the yam hole in the back kitchen.

'More like an errand boy. I carried the messages to Wellington and I rode and kept on riding, even when

79

they shot my horse from under me. I caught another mount on the field and rode till it went from under me too. They gave me money for that after the war. I'd had enough of soldiering. I wanted to see horses born, not die. So I sold my commission and I came here.'

'Why here, Master Duane?'

'Because I was young. Because it was still an adventure in those days. My nephew James went to New Holland. He thought he'd get good land there. Well, he did, but it didn't call me. New Holland is a convict land, all the riffraff of England, every half-pay Captain who never made it. They call it Australia now, trying to clean it up with a new name so people don't remember. It never seemed to me to be the place for a gentleman. He does well enough there, I suppose.'

'Was he at Waterloo too?'

'His father was. My brother. He died there. They gave his son a scholarship to Sandhurst after that. Sandhurst's like West Point. My nephew was in the Indian Army before he went to Australia.'

'Where are those places, Master Duane?'

Master Duane pointed at the map again. India, Sandhurst, and New Holland, the place they called Australia to make it clean.

Best was when Master Duane gave Carrie books to look at, with colours on the pages and gold round the borders. Carrie's hands had to be clean when she looked at books. She held them in a white handkerchief, whiter than Lina's headdress. She wasn't to move, just sit there.

The books had stories, some of them, but they were hard to read. She didn't know if she was supposed to read them or just look at the pictures. (Had no idea, either, that it was against the law for a slave to learn to read.)

The pictures were as pretty as the roses out the window, as pretty as the grass when it waved in spring. It took longer to work out the words, but slowly she managed it, matching the sound of the word to its appearance when Duane read her stories.

Back in the kitchen Drusilla told stories of another country, too, but they weren't the same as Master Duane's.

Drusilla told her how, if a man defiled a coconut, a punishment would fall on him; how his life would ebb with daylight till he were colder than a three-day egg. Drusilla explained how her mammy told the future with shells like half eggshells, but that the shells were gone now. So was her mammy.

Drusilla told how if dogs were chasing you, you should take off your clothes, 'cause that way dogs can't smell you; that's the way niggers escaped to the North (Carrie didn't ask Drusilla how she knew that's how they escaped, if they were never brought back). Drusilla knew a woman who'd escaped up North, taking her two chillun with her, but Drusilla closed her mouth after that and wouldn't speak, not even cuss.

Drusilla said that in her mother's country all the men did was fell the trees, while the women cleared the land and brought in food and cooked it and worked for the family. Families were big where Drusilla's mother had been a child. All the family lived together, every family bigger than a whole plantation. There were elephants bigger than a carriage. Drusilla told how monkeys smelt a woman out and bent them over and did their business and how a woman was good for nothin' after that; how toads had poison in their bodies 'stead of blood.

Drusilla told her a story about a toad. The toad was frightened of the tortoise and gave her food, a whole big bowl of food, and the tortoise ate it all quickly then fell asleep, and the toad peered over at the tortoise and poisoned her just by looking at her. That's what witches could do, said Drusilla. Poison you just by looking.

Drusilla told Carrie 'bout Drusilla's father: how as the ship rocked towards America he and another hundred men jumped overboard and were 'gone home to Guinea'. But her mammy, she was left on the ship, an' that's where she had Drusilla.

Men where Drusilla came from gave up huntin', gave up fishin', gave up growin' crops to stock the barracoons on the beach with slaves for the men who came across the ocean. Iffen you were too young, too old, too sick to be a slave they smoked your head instead. That king had a wall around his house made of skulls. That king had women warriors, who ran with giant swords.

Drusilla said her mammy told her that, but that were nonsense. Them white fellas just waved a red handkerchief at the niggers and they upped and walked onto them boats and they just sailed away to be slaves. Drusilla shook her head. 'We niggers surely like red,' she said.

Drusilla said how the Northerners beyond the hills up there, they ate piccaninnies for breakfast, fried with cream and sugar; how there was only one sure escape, and that was into the arms of Jesus.

CHAPTER 12

1850-55

CARRIE (2)

The kitchen was Carrie's home when she was small.

'You, Carrie, if you don't come here you better! Drat that girl, I done call her till my patience is wore out. My craw just gets full up to the neck. Why that li'l heifer is off as fast as a hog can trot. I oughter put her out wit the hogslops. I oughter wear her backside out.'

And Drusilla would cuff Carrie's ear then feed her guava jelly and hold her to her hot bosom smelling of old flour.

In winter the fires burnt high, even when the bread wasn't baking or the chickens weren't roasting. In summer Little Cicero waved a fan over the kitchen table.

'Now see no flies get on that food,' instructed Drusilla, and Little Cicero waved and waved and the wind blew across the kitchen. Some places, said Drusilla, he'd be whipped if he stopped fanning, but this was a good house. House niggers were hardly ever whipped, 'cept for bad sins like runnin' away, just a tickling round the ham bone, hardly even spoiled the meat.

Next to the kitchen was a storeroom, and the back kitchen where the vegetables were washed, and then the house courtyard, and then the outer yard, and then the yard between the slave sheds.

The sheds faced each other. About twenty slaves lived in the sheds. The sheds were wooden, with a door in the middle and a lock on the door to keep the niggers in at night.

The sheds were for the field hands. The sheds had dirt floors and small barred windows up at the top, and there were fleas and ticks and flies, but the ticks were worse, the ticks were from the witches, you got doubly sick from ticks. You got rid of ticks with hot wax dripped on you from a candle; the shock was worse than the sting and then the tick jumped out. Carrie had never had a tick, she didn't know what it felt like, but Drusilla told her. Drusilla told her to take care.

Between the sheds was a big stone-laid area, like the courtyard but dirtier. The field women washed in tubs on Sundays, big wooden ones swollen in the river to hold water, and spilt the hot dirty liquid on the stones, where horses shat when they were led out from the stables. The field slaves shat in the pot in one corner of the sheds; they wiped their arse with cornhusks or leaves brought in to dry.

On Sundays the men played in the courtyard or in front of the cottages in their stiff trousers and rawhide boots. Old Hannibal was the Mont Alba boot maker, though the old men still wore the sandals with a thong around the toe, a pattern their fathers had brought from Africa. They played with a corncob placed on the ground with a knucklebone balanced on top, and a line was drawn and you had to throw a stone to hit the cob.

There was always something happening in the courtyard on a Sunday if you peered out the kitchen door: hair cutting with a long knife, men laughing and talking with the women; babies bound tight on the women's backs and that's what made their noses flat. Lina had never carried her that away — that's why Carrie's nose was straight and long.

Carrie heard the shed bells even far away in the house — 4.30 a.m. to get up, 6.00 for lining up to go out to the fields. That's when the house slaves got up as well and when Drusilla lit the kitchen fire. Then the prayer bell at sunset, and the last bell at 8.00 p.m. for everyone to go to sleep.

There were cottages, but they were down the road a way, with their gardens at the back. The slave cottages were for the grooms, for the foreman, for Cain the blacksmith and Horatio the tinsmith, the brick maker, carpenter, cobbler and the other men who had a trade. Slaves with a trade could have their women live with them, if they wanted, though a slave marriage wasn't legal and could be broken by the master. They could even earn a bit in their spare time, mending boots or patching buggies for people off the farm, and dream of saving up enough to be free for a few years before they died.

The cottages had dirt floors and the wind nosed in the holes, but at least they were rooms of their own.

Out beyond the cottages were the plots of land for sweet potatoes, gourds and kidney beans, Lima beans and peanuts, and for the hogs that rooted for the leavings, after the fields were cleared, or chomped on acorns and wallowed in their sties.

Most of Carrie's life was learning how to roll pastry or peeling potatoes until Lina came to find her, or until it was time to go to their room off the kitchen and wait for Lina in the cold darkness. Drusilla hardly left the kitchen except to go across to the sheds if someone wanted doctoring or to the cottages for midwifing, or to stand on the step and argue with Big Jim.

'You no good yella bastard!'

And Big Jim would laugh and say he didn't have to do but two things, die and stay black, and he weren't doin' neither of them for her.

Drusilla had soft skin and a white folk's nose, though she said it wasn't white folk's but how noses come back where her folks were from, but her ankles were thick under her petticoats and her waist bulged like a corn sack, like a lump of dough after she'd been whamming it and her hair was salt and pepper under her scarf.

'Dis house needs a man for care and assistance, but I done never seen such a one since I was born in de world.'

And Big Jim would laugh as she yelled out, 'Mullet brained, hog bred, mule faced, goat belly! Old hog belly!' and slip inside when she was glazing pastry and he should be choppin' wood, and run his fingers under her backside.

Big Jim was worth a lot of money — a thousand dollars or more — but he was whipped across the face and buttocks and tattooed on his right shoulder when they found him down the road a ways without a pass. Every nigger had to have a pass around his neck, handwritten. Niggers couldn't write so white folks didn't worry about forgery.

Big Jim said when he recovered that he hadn't been escaping, just taking the air a whiles. But his laugh was sourer in the kitchen and Drusilla was quieter after that.

Lina was different from the others.

Lina was still, most times, all except her eyes. Lina watched, careful, in the background, except when it was safe to be forward. She was a tall woman, with generous breasts and purple nipples, a thin waist and buttocks that didn't bulge till they were two hand's span below it, so the line of her body was still graceful in spite of the opulence of its parts.

Lina changed her blouse every day and washed it in the basin on the chair in the room she and Carrie shared behind the kitchen. Lina was the only woman on the plantation to do anything like that. Their room had only one window, above the cornhusk mattress that was their bed. The window was narrow and too high to see out of, but Lina stuck two pegs on the wall above it, and from these she hung her blouse during the day, so it dried straight and clean.

Lina bathed every night, wiping around her private parts with a rag and vinegar, standing in the basin and pouring the water over herself, rubbing laundry soap on the rag until the fat lye smell of it covered the room like the soap slick on her skin, until it washed in a slick into the basin, and Lina scented herself with rose-water that she made from the heavy fat blooms along the courtyard.

Lina's smell changed with the month. Musty on the days she took the rags and bound them across her body with more rags; a saltfish smell the nights after she spent the afternoon with Master Duane. Those were the nights the vinegar was wielded more vigorously so it splashed onto the floor, thickened sometimes with a scum of white.

'Why do you do that, Mama?' Carrie asked, and for once Lina didn't ignore her, or slap her with her long-nailed fingers.

'That's to wash the baby out,' said Lina carelessly. 'Brats will make your stomach sag and your tits droop.' Lina's eyes flashed. 'You remember that, girl. One day you'll need to do this too.'

It was the most Carrie could remember Lina saying to her, though it would be years before she realised what her mother had meant.

Those were the nights Lina slept more restlessly or rubbed herself between her legs, her petticoat hitched in a band around her waist, when she thought Carrie was asleep, as though to finish something incomplete.

Lina scrubbed her teeth every night, with a rag dipped in salt; scrubbed so hard her gums would bleed sometimes, bright red on the deep white. She scrubbed her daughter's teeth as well, and her body. But Lina kept the rose-water for herself.

Lina's nipples were the colour of mulberries and cream. Her breasts were lighter, the hair on her pubis darker, shining, almost straight, and her legs straight and pale below.

Lina laughed in public, never in private. Her temper flared quickly; her fists lashed out, but once they had connected they lost their anger. The way to keep the anger away was not to speak. Carrie learnt that early. Even with Drusilla it was safest not to talk, and certainly not with the strange accent Master Duane taught her that marked her as a darkie with ideas above her class.

Massa Duane was the only white folks in the house when Carrie was young, after his wife died and Miz Elizabeth had married. Which meant Lina was pretty much boss, except when Miz Elizabeth visited, as long as she kept pleasing Massa Duane, as long as she played the role he wanted her to, at least until she grew too old and Massa Duane started looking for someone younger.

CHAPTER 13

1850-55

SLAVERY

Carrie was a slave because her mother was a slave. It was a century of slavery. There were slaves in Australia ('blackbirds') working the sugar; slaves in Africa and Hawaii and New Guinea (blacks there were the slaves of blacks; colour was not a dependable guide to who was a slave owner), in the Middle East, in China. There were serfs in Russia; untouchables in India; Geisha and Ita in Japan.

Slaves in the South lived as well or better than most of the population of the planet. Those were the days when children of six coughed consumptively in factories; dragged carts from mines (cheaper than ponies). Slaves were, in general, well fed and clothed and housed, according to the standard of the day. Violence (except for punishment) was the exception.

A step up from slavery was indentured labour. This was common, in the northern U.S.A. and the rest of the Western world. The participants had worse conditions, often, and less security in illness and old age than slaves.

But slavery had two differences from indentured labour: a slave could be sold (or your child, your father or your lover); and you are different, by caste or race, from your owner.

By the time Carrie was a child no slaves had been imported (legally) into the United States for over fifty years. Surplus slaves from a large estate might be sold to the 'new' farms down south. Sometimes they are bred especially for the purpose. A small 'farm' might make its profit just from a half dozen female slaves. A female slave's value drops sharply after childbearing is finished; a good breeder goes for nearly as much as a good labourer. A man may own a dozen women slaves and only one male; or none; in the parlance of the time, why buy a stud pig when you've got one in the sty.

Colour by the 1850s was no guide to status; many slaves were as white as their owners. In Maryland if you were one-eighth Negro you could call yourself white if you were free.

Carrie was only one-sixteenth Negro. Her skin was as pale as her half-sister's, Miss Elizabeth. But that had nothing to do with whether she was slave or free.

Carrie was classed as a slave; spoke (mostly) with the rhythms and music of her black ancestors, not her white ones.

While Carrie was a slave she would always be seen as black, no matter what the colour of her skin. She had to act like a slave. If she didn't she would be punished, or sold 'down South' to the new and harder plantations, where she would labour in the cotton fields and live in squalor.

At Mont Alba she was petted, well fed, well clothed. She had only to help Drusilla in the kitchen, which was not hard work at all. Even Drusilla's job was easier now that there was only Duane and the house slaves to cook for.

Carrie had never been whipped or even insulted, unless you counted Drusilla's friendly curses. She had been taught to read; if not formally, at least she was read to and was given time alone with the books until she learnt it on her own. Her life was more comfortable than many children in the world then, or now.

But she was still a slave.

CHAPTER 14

1855

MONT ALBA

The fire licked tongues over the wood in the fireplace, small burps of smoke hiccupped into the room — the upstairs Mont Alba chimney always smoked with a high wind, no matter how you swept it.

Carrie sat on a footstool in a fresh apron and watched Master Duane's face as he read. Spit curled in the grey whiskers over his top lip. Carrie was more interested in the spit than the words.

Ay, look again, that line, so black
And trampled, marks the bivouac,
Yon deep-graved ruts the artillery's track,
So often lost and won;
And close beside, the hardened mud

Still shows where, fetlock-deep in blood,
The fierce dragoon, through battle's flood ...

The voice stopped. Carrie waited. She wondered whether to speak. Master Duane liked her to speak; it showed she was listening. Her duty was to listen to Master Duane's words. It was an easier duty than her mother's, perhaps, but still a duty.

So she watched him, to work out what he wanted, this old man with dry lips, remembering pain ...

The kitchen was Carrie's home. She had never travelled further than the slave sheds, but these were still another world on the edge of the courtyard.

Drusilla visited the sheds. Sometimes she took Carrie with her, to learn her, as she said. The sheds were what happened to niggers who got uppity; no candles or lanterns, no water for washin', a stinkin' privy, no laughter and no hope, and ticks to suck the life from you.

In the mornings, Carrie might follow Lina like a ghost through the other parts of the house, as Lina dusted or polished, light jobs only. Lina's real work came in the afternoons when she was summoned to Master Duane.

Sometimes Lina alone would be summoned by one of the bells that jangled over the kitchen door. Lina would go with a straightening of skirts and her secret smile and, as the years went by, a look of relief that she was still being called in spite of growing older. If Master Duane's desire left him, despite all Lina could do, or if he decided on a younger mistress, well, who knew what would happen to Lina then?

Some days Lina would stay upstairs the whole afternoon. Other days she would come down after an hour or so and take Carrie by the hand, checking her face was clean, whispering 'Don't you embarrass me now!' as she drew her up the stairs.

The stairs grew shorter as she grew older.

CHAPTER 15

1856

CARRIE (3)

The afternoon was hot. Heat breathed from the carpet. Carrie sat on Duane's lap as he brushed her hair. His fingers whispered down her backbone and lingered on her rump, then took to brushing again. Master Duane liked touching her now.

'Let's see if you've got hair down there,' he'd say, and Carrie would lift up her skirt, and do a little dance around the room, and Master Duane would laugh.

'When I'm dead, you'll be free,' Master Duane told Carrie. 'I've put it in my will. Come here, girl. Let's see what else you're growing.' His hands ran across her shoulders, and down onto her breasts. He squeezed them like they were plums, considering their ripeness. His breath grew shallower. He ran his fingers up her legs, onto her buttocks, and squeezed those too.

Lina's head appeared at the door. For a moment she frowned, then smiled — at Massa Duane, not Carrie. 'You be needin' me now, Massa Duane?' One shoulder of her blouse had been pulled down, exposing the swell of her breast.

Master Duane hesitated, his hands still on Carrie's buttocks. Then he said, 'Yes, it's time for her to go back to the kitchen,' and Lina's eyes met Carrie's, just for a second, triumphant.

Later, watching Lina undress, Carrie asked her: 'What is a will?'

Lina turned. 'It's a thing that white folks make, sayin' who gets what after they've passed on.'

'Master Duane, he said that he's put me in his will. He'll make me free.'

Lina's eyes brightened. 'He mention me?'

'No. He jus' said, "When I'm dead, you'll be free." Jus' like that.' Carrie spoke in perfect imitation of Duane's words.

Lina took up her sponge and began to stroke between her legs. She simply shrugged. And that was all.

CHAPTER 16

1860–61

EZEKIEL

Ezekiel was an Ibo. Ibos ran away. They were good workers but you couldn't trust them not to run. In the days when a good worker fetched $1300 you'd only get $900 for an Ibo.

Ezekiel had run before. He had four teeth missing in the front where they'd been knocked out for identification if he ran again, and scars across his back.

Ezekiel was as old as Big Jim, nearly, and he watched Carrie from the door of the sheds as she went to the sick house with a bottle of medicine from Drusilla. He watched Carrie going back to the house. The next time Carrie visited the sheds he asked her to meet with him one night.

That time she refused.

The next she didn't.

Why did she go with him? I don't know. Perhaps it was a deliberate refusal to gain security with her body, like Lina. Perhaps she was ignorant of the consequences, though Drusilla had told her often enough in the hot kitchen, 'Don't you be goin' now with no mens.'

Perhaps it was simply the urging of her body, the need to be touched, her body awake from the no longer fatherly caresses of Duane.

I don't know. I don't say it was love either. Carrie rarely talked about Ezekiel. The memory either hurt too little or too much.

Carrie lay with Ezekiel Sunday nights in the yam hills behind the cottages, saying she was fetching kindling or delivering medicines for Drusilla.

Ezekiel ran when Carrie's morning sickness started. (He didn't know about the sickness; that wasn't why he ran.) He didn't tell Carrie he was leaving, he just ran. Drusilla told her, eyeing Carrie across the floury pans.

Carrie waited for a week in case he was in hiding, was going to creep up and whisper to her, 'Carrie, you come escape with me.'

When Carrie realised he'd gone without her she cried in the hot kitchen, her head in the folds of Drusilla's skirt, and Drusilla's hands, soft as butter, soft as lard, soft as uncooked pastry, wandered through her hair.

Drusilla gave her medicine to make the baby go, shaking her head. For once there were no imprecations. This was too serious for swearing.

The kitchen smelt of biscuits baking and ham frying on the claw-footed stove, the kettles sang their song on the hearth, puffs of smoke sent the flour sifting over the table. Carrie drank the bitter concoction, gagged, and forced more down. She held her mouth so as not to spew and drank some more.

Carrie could feel the bitterness in her toes and neck. It tasted of oil, like oil that had fried chicken a thousand times. Her throat began to burn at the oiliness of it, her heart swelled like a million frogs were jumpin' there, the sweat was crawlin' through her hair like snakes in a swamp and the pain was white across her eyes and red in her belly. She knelt with the pain. Then it was gone.

It came back. Weaker. Then weaker again. She lay on the cold floor of the kitchen and vomited.

Drusilla's hands were quiet and comforting.

You only got to take the medicine once, said Drusilla. If it didn't work it meant the baby was latched too tight inside. You take the medicine more than once, you passed away to Heaven.

The baby was still inside her.

The baby swelled inside her and she tied her apron loose. It kicked in the hot afternoons and her face grew thin. Drusilla saw and so did Lina, though Lina never said, just tightened up her lips; tighter'n a hen's arse, muttered Drusilla.

There was no word of Ezekiel.

Sometimes she thought she heard him runnin', so quiet you wouldn't hear him if it weren't for his breathing; a breathing like sobbing, coming back on the wind.

When they caught him — two months later — she wondered if it was his breathing trapped him, if the hunters heard it floating back to them, crying on the wind. (It was the dogs caught him, whispered Drusilla, her face blank and grieving, the dogs that sniffed him down and tore at him, weak and cold with hunger. Dogs, without barking, said Drusilla, with wide wet jaws and blood . . .)

Master Duane paid the slave catcher $300, a third of Ezekiel's worth.

They brought Ezekiel back, his arms and legs chained, dragged him through the dust on his belly, the miles he had run torn off him, the hope he had had torn out of him.

They laid him in the courtyard, and Master Duane ordered all the slaves to watch. Carrie, too. She wanted to cover her face with her apron, but she didn't dare.

Massa Jones, the overseer, drove stakes into the ground, and they tied Ezekiel to those at his wrists and ankles, all naked in the dust, so his genitals spread out between his legs all flat and dusty, not proud and standing like Carrie'd known before.

Massa Jones whipped him longways, then whipped him crossways. His back was ripped into a hundred tiny squares, scars so deep they might never heal, whispered Drusilla, scars that would weep every winter.

When, finally, Massa Jones realised that, no matter how deep the whip bit, Ezekiel would never squeal, though his body was shaking like a wind blew just for him, Massa Jones threw the whip aside and called for salt, and cayenne pepper too, from Drusilla's kitchen. It was Carrie who brought the pepper. With Massa Jones with his whip, with Massa Duane staring from the window, how was she to say no?

Massa Jones poured salt onto the bleeding back, then the cayenne pepper. Ezekiel screamed then. He screamed and then he puked, and Massa Jones smiled, because that would learn the watchin' niggers not to run.

They left him there, all bleeding in the dust. Carrie couldn't move, didn't hear when Massa Jones ordered the darkies back to work, so Drusilla took her arm and led her into the warm kitchen with its smell of yeast and flour.

The sun dried the blood on Ezekiel's back. It stopped running into the dust. Finally Big Jim carried Ezekiel into the sheds, then came to tell Drusilla what he'd done.

Carrie ran down to the sheds herself, that afternoon, when Master Duane was asleep and Lina busy and the shed would be empty. She took a pot of salve for Ezekiel's back in her apron pocket, even though he had run without her, and some corn bread, hoping he could eat. Ezekiel was lying on his stomach on the old grass mattress that was nearly the colour of the dirty floor. He was awake, but he wouldn't look at her, wouldn't say a word even when she asked if she could use the salve. It was like his silence was the only thing he had, something he wouldn't share with anyone, not even Carrie. So she left the pot there by the mattress, and the corn bread, and slipped back to the kitchen, and her heart was grievin', grievin', grievin', for herself or him she didn't know.

Ezekiel hanged himself the next day from the rafters. He used his shirt, pushing his body through agony to get its final rest.

The slaves cried for him that night; heads down by the huts, heads down in the grass. Carrie sat on the step of the kitchen, her face in her apron and sang; words nobody heard, but they all knew they were singing it:

I know moon rise,
I know star rise.
Lay this body down ...

The rows of whitewashed slave cabins with their gardens behind, the slave barracks, the sick house, the overseer's house: all seemed poisoned white by the moonlight. The moon was a white man who'd show up a running slave.

The next afternoon Master Duane felt the roundness of Carrie's stomach, bigger than yesterday, bigger than the day before. He said nothing. He just pushed her from his lap, his lips thin with disgust, and never asked for her again.

Later, when Lina came down the stairs and into the kitchen her right eye was swollen, with a bleeding slash below it, as if she'd been whipped by the riding crop Master Duane still kept on his desk.

'Your fault,' said Lina. She stepped over to where Carrie sat at the table and spat in her daughter's face. 'You fool,' she said, then walked from the room to wash, and spread Drusilla's ointment on her cut, so it would heal without a scar.

Lina never spoke to her daughter again, even in the solitude of their room; the stupid daughter who had endangered the security of both of them by betraying the man with power.

Later, years later, Carrie wondered what had happened to her mother. Lina must eventually have been given legal freedom along with every other slave in the South. Carrie would never know how much freedom her mother had really achieved.

Carrie was fourteen when her labour pains came. She knew she was fourteen. Master Duane had told her when she was ten, and she had kept count since then.

The child was born in the kitchen. Drusilla shoved rags in Carrie's mouth to muffle her cries, and filched brandy from the dining room for Carrie's pain.

The child was black. Her face crinkled in pink wrinkles, black as the crust on Drusilla's brownies, nearly as black as Ezekiel.

A man was shamed if his mistress had a black child. It didn't only tell everyone she'd been sleeping with another. It also meant that the master might have some black blood in him that he was trying to hide.

Carrie wasn't yet Master Duane's mistress, but the shame was still there. It was unthinkable to keep a mistress with a black baby in your house.

If Duane hadn't loved her (probably, possibly) she and the baby would have been sold south to the cotton fields. She wasn't. She was sent thirty miles — her first journey, the first fields and trees she'd ever seen, sitting in the cart with her pass around her neck, her baby in her arms — to Miz Elizabeth's house in town to be a cook, not a concubine like her mother.

CHAPTER 17

1861−62

MIZ ELIZABETH'S

At Miz Elizabeth's in town, Carrie smelt street, not grass; not even the hot dust of summer grass. You could smell your neighbour's drains as well as your own in the city. Even the horses smelt different.

Carrie cooked. She was a good cook, despite that she was so young. Drusilla had taught her well. Pound cake with lemon peel, shrimp gumbo with fluffy rice, crawfish etouffee with fried okra, beef tenderloin so tender it fell apart at the touch of Massa Ralph's carving knife, old Seneca the butler told her when he carried the remnants back into the kitchen.

Seneca was kind to Carrie, especially after he tasted Drusilla's praline sauce recipe, but he frowned on the baby. Babies cried and made bad smells and Carrie had to stop her cooking, sometimes, to feed her.

The baby grew. Carrie was scared to see her growing. When she grew big she would be sold away. Massa Ralph liked his house slaves with pale faces, and this baby was too black.

'You be quiet now,' she'd murmur when the baby cried. 'You be quiet an' maybe they forget you here till you learn som'in' useful.'

The baby was a good baby. Calliope, who didn't like babies, said that she was good. At times, though, her cries could be heard beyond the kitchen, and then Carrie thought she could see Massa Ralph calculating how long it would be before the child was weaned, and she'd be worth taking to the market.

Carrie had thought of running, even before Ezekiel; running to the North where they ate black babies with cream and sugar for their breakfast. She could have passed for white. She could speak white too, good as Massa Duane most times. She might have made it.

But not with a black baby. With a black baby everyone would know she was a slave. She would have needed a guide to tell her the safe houses: the Quakers, the ministers, the miller at Brooks Hill, who might pass you on. At Miz Elizabeth's Carrie had no one to tell her how an escape might be done.

Then, suddenly, war was coming. Everyone talked of it, even in the kitchen. If war came, maybe one day she might be free.

It was illegal for a slave to read about the war; it was illegal for a slave to talk about it. Nonetheless, fat

Calliope whispered under the noise of frying chicken: 'I be surely praying for that Mr Lincoln,' and the fat spurted onto her jowls and hung there, and she stopped, shocked either by her utterance or her burning cheeks.

Things changed with the war. Master Ralph became a Colonel in the Confederate Army, but his slaves still called him Massa Ralph, not Colonel. Then foods like tea and cocoa became scarce as the Northerners blockaded the Southern ports, but those were upstairs food anyhow. It made cooking a bit more difficult, that's all.

Slave prices fell. That was whispered in the kitchen too. No one would be paying much for Carrie's baby now. There was no point to selling her.

Miz Elizabeth went bandage rolling or collecting funds for 'our brave boys'. Carrie kept on cooking, cooking. And then a stranger came. Master Duane's great-nephew, from that place with the new name. Australia.

CHAPTER 18

1863–64

NORTHWARDS

Charles and Carrie left when Charles had been convalescent for two months. They left at night, when Calliope was asleep, when lamps no longer flickered down the road. They were more afraid of Southerners than the opposing army; Charles was a deserter, Carrie an escaped slave.

They walked north. Charles was still feeble, but he could walk. There were no horses available, no carts. Carrie carried the child, as well as a carpetbag she'd taken from Miz Elizabeth packed with the food she'd taken from the kitchen in the quiet hours before they left.

They followed the north star at night, judging direction from the sun by day. Charles tried to mark on the map how far they had travelled each day. The countryside was only vaguely familiar, except for the parts where he had campaigned. It was even more unfamiliar to her. Carrie was more a stranger in this country than he was. Her world had been the kitchens of Mont Alba and Miz Elizabeth's; slave quarters and one brief thirty mile journey.

At first, Charles wondered when Calliope and Aunt Lillian would report them gone. Later he wondered if they had bothered. Perhaps they were glad to see them go. At least there were three fewer mouths to feed.

There were other things for the authorities to think about these days. No one cared too much about one more deserter, another escaped slave, and the rewards for bounty hunters were virtually non-existent.

They walked the byways where they could: old trails, unfrequented roads and bridle paths. It was a march taken by thousands of slaves in the past fifty years, moved northwards by the Underground Railway. Into freedom if they went as far as Canada; a more precarious freedom if they stayed in the Northern U.S.A., to be haunted by the threat of bounty hunters, anti-black riots and repressive laws. In some areas Northern laws were harsher to free blacks than the laws of the South.

It was an empty country. It had been stripped bare three times over: by war, by disease and by fear. Only soldiers and refugees and those who had no other choice travelled now.

Twice they saw the path of an army: ruts and corpses and the stench of blood and shit. Many times they heard voices, horses; army scouts, perhaps, or deserters like himself. Both scouts and deserters were dangerous. They hid from both (her hand over the child's mouth in case she made a noise, her brown eyes watching, terrified).

The child learnt quickly to stay still, to stay silent, to piss standing up, or squatting on the spot, if need be, but not to move. In the months when she should have been learning how to speak she learnt not to speak at all.

For the first week they ate what they carried: cold corn pone, peanuts, cakes she had made and fried in bacon grease. They begged for food at cottages; although they carried cash, Confederate money was almost worthless now. Only gold still had value. Charles did have some gold. He had more sense than to show it.

No door was ever opened wide, but food was sometimes handed out. Yams, milk, more corn pone, cold cornmeal mush. Frightened children peered round the door, men held muskets at the window. But men were rare. Men were either still with the army, or hiding.

It was morning. The dew was cold on the grass next to the blanket; colder on his face. Charles woke and found his eyes thick with sleep, as if protecting them against the dew. He'd been feverish last night, but it was gone now in the cold of morning.

He looked for his companion.

She was watching him.

Carrie had taken off the nigger scarf. Her black hair was pulled back in a loose bun. She wore a dress, not the dark slave skirt she'd worn before. The dress was a light floral, faded but good quality, taken he supposed from Cousin Elizabeth's wardrobe before they left.

Carrie had planned for some time to turn white. There was no need to change her skin or her eyes; just her clothes and her hairstyle and the way she spoke. (She needed to change her manner, too, but it was many years before she properly achieved this.)

As well as the dress and carpetbag Carrie had also stolen two more cotton dresses, soap, petticoats, woollen stockings and a chemise from Miss Elizabeth, and a whalebone corset that she'd wear months later, gasping as she felt her guts implode. She had taken folds of rags and a belt to hold them with, and a muslin nightdress, crisp as meringue, with ruffles and pink ribbon through eyelets of lace.

A hat, a wide-brimmed one with lace and flowers sat on the ground beside her, weighed flat with rocks, still crumpled from packing.

She looked like a white woman. For the first time Charles saw her as a person, not a slave to be left or taken at his whim.

For the first time he felt terror at what he'd done.

He couldn't speak.

The child came from behind a tree, where she had been relieving herself. She could walk by herself for an hour or two at the slow pace that they held. He held out his arms to her. She was still familiar, easier to relate to than the stranger by the tree.

'Xanthippe, here, let me button you.'

The child allowed herself to be buttoned.

Carrie spoke softly, using the English accent Duane had taught her, not Drusilla's accent from the kitchen. 'Her name's Susannah.'

'What?'

'Xanthippe's a slave name. Her name's Susannah.'

'Carrie . . .'

She bit her lip, then held her head high, like she'd seen Miss Elizabeth do. She was playing white, and meant to do it properly. 'Caroline. My name is Caroline. And she's Susannah.'

She waited a moment for him to protest. He was silent. She spoke to the child, using Duane's language, not the musical words of a slave. 'You hear that, child? Your name is Susannah now.'

The child made no response, her brown eyes wide. But she would do as she was told. Slavery and war had created a child of almost unimaginable obedience.

Charles wanted to ask, Susannah what? What's her surname? Then, with a shock, he remembered that slaves took the names of their master. If the woman he travelled with had a surname it would be the same as his. She was Caroline Fitzhenry. The child was Susannah Fitzhenry.

It suddenly seemed impossible for him to abandon them in the North when he sailed for home, as he'd planned. A slave could be abandoned, even an ex-slave, leaving her a few dollars once you'd found her a job cooking in a home or a tavern. He couldn't leave a woman he had travelled with in intimacy. Not with his honour intact. He couldn't leave a woman and a child who shared his name.

Whatever he did in the future, he would have to consider Caroline.

Now they were three refugees, like any others.

Caroline's shoes began to wear. She took them off and hobbled. She wanted to keep her shoes presentable until they reached the North. Charles wrapped her feet in rags, as he had done on his retreat south, then wrapped his own the same. He doubted that his boots would last until they reached the North either.

They walked through autumn. The air tasted cold, the leaves glowed like fire (it still shocked him to see them change; he was used to a few trees changing colour in autumn, but not a whole forest). Sometimes they smelt smoke on the wind. Smoke made them cautious. Smoke could be from a campfire (and any man around a campfire was a threat), or a farmhouse where they might get food. Autumn made the scents stronger, sharper, like the shadows sharp on the ground; or perhaps they were simply becoming accustomed to their world.

There were cottages with smoke sifting from chimneys; farmhouses with crop land overgrown. The worst were the ruins: chimneys black above the ashes, heaps of bricks tumbled into rubbish, orchards dead from fire. Once they came across a graveyard, uprooted by passing soldiers (Northern or Southern, it didn't matter now), skeletons flung among the splintered caskets, their jewellery, if they'd had any, stripped from them. Buzzards hung like bruises in the sky.

Charles showed Caroline how to make ramrod rolls — cornmeal and water on a stick, charred on the fire — when they could find dry wood that didn't smoke. And he would remember the gum tree forests of a few years ago: the profligate wood strewn across the ground; grey wood in red kangaroo grass, brown wood among the ants' nests. And they talked.

The first days were silent ones. What was there to talk about, besides which path to follow next? And besides, she left all that to him; this was her second time in the wide world in her whole life and anyways, she was used to white folks tellin' her what to do.

Once they were away from the roads they had to listen, too. Every sound might be the clue that gave them life or death. Birds singing, even in this empty land; the rustle of a squirrel. The crack of a twig would make them freeze, and glance for cover.

It was harder now that the leaves had fallen. 'I still think they're dying,' said Charles, 'every time I see leaves fall.'

He had been speaking as much to himself, or maybe to Walter's memory — surely he'd said the same to him last year? But Caroline looked up at his words.

'Why, Massa Charles?'

'Call me Charles,' he said hastily. 'Anyone who heard would wonder why you called me master.'

'There's no one to hear.'

Not 'ain't no one' ... He was still astonished every time he heard her speak with a white accent. He'd heard white men 'talkin' nigger' as a joke. It hadn't occurred to him that a slave could be bilingual. 'There will be,' he said. He hesitated, wondering how much she'd understand. 'The trees where I come from don't lose their leaves in winter. They stay green all year round. Not green like these trees though. It's a different green. More blue.'

Even as he said it he realised it sounded ridiculous. But she had seen so little of the world that blue trees seemed no stranger than an ocean, or for that matter a world where she'd be free.

'What's it like, Australia, Mas—' She obediently chopped the last word off. 'It was New Holland once, I think?' She'd copied Cousin Elizabeth's polite conversational style, but she couldn't bring herself to call him Charles.

'How did you know that?' He didn't wait for her to tell him. She was just an audience, not a person yet. (It would be many years before it would occur to him that she might have had a history that held interest as well as shame.) 'It's different. Trees, but different trees. Farms, but they're different too. Our house is by the sea. Up on a hill, but sometimes there's fog around and you'd think the whole ocean had swept in. Sometimes ...'

He glanced at her. She was looking at him intently. How was he to know that in her whole life she'd treasured any information, any glimpse of the world beyond her kitchen?

Whatever the reason, the fascination was genuine. He kept on talking. 'Sheep, that's what we mostly have.' (A pang of grief for Walter and his cows, so deep it almost felt like the flux was on him once again). 'People think that sheep are white, like the fog, but they're more grey, though when you see them moving altogether on the hill it's like a wave, all this way then the other ...'

It wasn't conversation. You converse with equals, when there is respect and interest on both sides. Sometimes she asked questions, mostly to keep him talking. There was no exchange of views, experiences, ideas. It never occurred to him to ask for them; nor to her to offer.

For him his talk was an affirmation that the world he'd left might still exist, still be attainable. Nonetheless it brought them closer.

It was midday. The gnats shimmered in the thick air. Charles' fever had returned. He shivered, though his skin was hot. He pulled the blanket closer round his shoulders.

There was no sound in the forest. Caroline had taken the child away earlier, maybe to look for nuts or berries (Caroline had never seen a berry in the wild, never touched a bush, but she was quick to learn when he had pointed them out to her). Perhaps they'd gone to wash. He hadn't asked where they were going in the weakness after last night's delirium.

He felt the soldiers before he heard them. Their horses first, heavy hooves vibrating the ground. Then he saw the soldiers through the trees, a dozen, perhaps twenty. Blue coats: well fed, well armed Yankees. A foraging party.

He lay quite still. The blanket was camouflage. They were talking, not looking at the ground (if there had been dogs with them he wouldn't have escaped). He tried to listen to their voices, to hear if they mentioned a woman and a child, but the words were indistinct.

He tried to still his mind. The images erupted nonetheless — the child spitted on their bayonets or thrown against a tree, the woman raped. Then the hoofbeats faded, faster than they'd come, the grunt of voices vanished. Charles shrugged away the blanket and tried to stand.

Caroline was back. She must have been quite close. She put a finger to her lips, as though it were she, not he, who had to protect them. The child stood behind her, blank-eyed and silent.

'Did they see you?'

She shook her head.

'They may come back. There may be more.'

She nodded. She pulled the blanket over him again and sat beside him. The child settled in her lap, between her arms, with the high panting breathing that was her substitute for crying. Caroline fed her wild walnuts, cracking them one by one between her palms to muffle the sound and poking the meat into the child's mouth, and pressing some into Charles' fingers too. They waited in case the horses returned.

They didn't. The fever had gone by the evening. The next morning they walked again.

The light stretched between the trees. The days stretched uncounted. He had forgotten to count them in the first week, now he was not sure what the date was. The shadows deepened, purple as bruised knees. Autumn shadows.

The child took Charles' hand as they walked between the trees. Caroline kept walking even when her feet swelled in liquid blisters. She fed half her food to Susannah, assuming — like Moses — that they would eat only when Charles had eaten his fill. Even when Charles protested, time after time, she still waited at each meal for him to gesture for them to eat.

Charles watched her as she walked from light to shadow through the trees, and saw steely determination in her spine. Watching her walk he never doubted that they would make it North.

He didn't know that Caroline walked with three years of planning behind her, that every day she wondered if Ezekiel had got this far, if he had seen that hut, that coppice of hazelnut trees, before the dogs found him and the men dragged him on his stomach back to captivity.

Caroline knew that some slaves had never been found. She was convinced that if they could escape, so could she. At least these days there were no packs of hounds to sniff along their tracks. At least now she had a white man to camouflage her child.

~❦~

It was a cottage like many they'd seen — unpainted, the wood chinked with moss, cleared ground stretching through the trees. There was no smoke from the chimney, though a cow lowed nearby. Somehow it had been missed by the commissariats of both armies, betraying its presence now from hunger or the need to be milked.

Charles told Caroline to wait in the trees with the child. He went to the door, knocked.

There was no answer.

He went around the back.

The cow called across the paling fence. There was no sign of a calf; eaten, he suspected, long ago. The cow was thin, but her bag was swollen. He felt it and the cow kicked out with a hind leg. The bag was hot to touch, too swollen to milk. He felt a moment's comradeship for any creature with a fever like his own, and a pang of homesickness at the musty smell of cow.

Charles left the cow. She had her paddock and her water. With luck she might survive or, more likely, be eaten by the next passers-by. He couldn't bring himself to be her executioner.

He went back to the house. He called (softly, in case there were other ears in the trees): 'Is anyone here?'

He opened the door.

The house smelt of cold soot and illness; a sickness that was almost familiar, almost remembered. He stepped inside. The floor was tamped earth. A plate of unidentifiable food lay on the table. The smell grew stronger. He knew what it was now.

There was a noise behind him. She had come up to the house, with the child.

'What is it? Is there anybody here?'

He turned to her savagely. 'Out! For God's sake, take the child and get out of here!' He thrust her through the doorway and walked back inside to enter the hut's only other room.

The bodies were there. A woman, two children twisted in blankets so he couldn't see their sex; it was apparent, in that one glance, that the children had died first, and the woman later, dying where she rested after tending them.

The three arms out of the blankets and the woman's face showed the unmistakable blisters of smallpox.

He vomited by the doorway, then staggered into the open air. There had been food on the shelves: dried corn, part of a bacon flitch hanging by the fireplace. He left them; it was probable they carried the contagion.

The fresh air helped him. He found his way behind the hut, found the yam hills and the rows of vegetables, and began to grub at the soil with his fingers. Food outside would be safe.

It was a few moments before he realised that Caroline was beside him. She didn't ask what had happened in the house. She simply dug, the child digging beside her and when he leant, exhausted, against the paling fence, she kept on digging until the bag she kept the food in was full.

Later, far away from the dead house, they lit a fire, careless for once of eyes that might see the glow between the trees. They roasted the yams, then wrapped themselves in blankets to sleep. As his eyes closed he was aware of hers still awake. He thought for a moment they were watching him protectively, just as they watched the child.

The sun ranged about the hills now, never sliding high into the sky. Snow clouds darkened the days, but kept the nights warmer; then finally the snow fell, delicately at first, smelling of tin and Christmas, brushing their faces almost in a caress, so Susannah's face shone with delight and her dark hand left off clutching her shawls to try to grab one.

The snow covered the world with freshness, but to him the snow would always have the scent of death, frozen corpses and black blood.

She did not know enough yet to be scared of the snow, or to wonder why his face tightened as he looked at the clouds. It was only as the dampness melted into their clothes that she realised snow could be a killer, only when they huddled in a nest made of packed snow and branches, all their clothes about them, as the air, ground and sky grew featureless with white, that she knew they were a whisper away from death, as sure as any bayonets.

But here, at least, war had shown him how to survive; how to make a snow cave, track rabbits in the snow, make a cup fire of small split wood that would warm your feet when they turned blue and the only warning you had of frost bite was their red blood upon the snow.

They kept on walking.

⁓∰◎

His terror of the future spread. It was like a growth gripping at his vitals, multiplying ...

Home had seemed simple two months ago. Now, as it grew closer, he began to see it more clearly.

To his family at home he would be a deserter. It was something that, to his knowledge, had never happened in all the days of the Fitzhenry family. If it had — if there had been a shame such as his — it had been hushed up.

He had deserted not only his post but his kin; left his great-uncle and his Cousin Elizabeth to what would surely be a hideous fate when the Northern armies swept down on them.

To desert a winning army was bad enough. To desert a country facing defeat was a greater cowardice.

He had taken his uncle's property; not as a man of honour, denouncing slavery, but like a native cat at the henhouse.

He had stolen his uncle's slave, his cousin's food. He had left her husband's Aunt Lillian unprotected in a threatened city, taking both slave and food in a time of want.

There would be no glory to greet him at home. There would only be the shame. He wondered, finally, if there would be forgiveness.

Once more, loneliness stretched ahead of him. There was also the problem of what to do with the woman beside him. Honour was niggling at him by now that he should marry her. (If her skin had only been darker, her manner more servile, he might have felt he was free.)

He was a stranger walking home, but home receded from him every day. The thought began to rise: if he was to be cast out of the family, let it be for something he knew was honourable. Marrying Caroline would cause him to be cast out forever, but it was the honourable thing to do, the right thing to do. He would always have the comfort of knowing: If I hadn't done what was right they would have forgiven me.

Charles and Caroline had been companions, not lovers — not with the child watching; not in the open, where enemies might come on them rutting like animals in a field. Probably, too, with his fever, he might not have been capable. Perhaps the idea of sex with her never occurred to him, though years later she admitted that it had occurred to her.

Somewhere in those final weeks of travel the idea became a certainty. He had lost everything. This was all that he could salvage, a speck of true honour by marrying a slave, even if it shamed him in the eyes of the world. And if he married her, said the smallest voice of all, at least he wouldn't be alone.

As for her: her home was gone. The South was already starving, already blighted with the knowledge of defeat.

In less than two years any security a slave had had in the South would vanish. It was a world that she had rejected, had planned to leave when she could, but it was still the only world she knew; obeying white folks, of existing in the small space they gave her.

She didn't lack courage, only experience. But even with the little experience she had, she knew that marriage to a white man — particularly in another country — would be better for herself and her child than service or prostitution in the North, or common-law marriage to a man of similar caste to herself.

Perhaps she loved him. She had tended him for months. He had treated her with more politeness — though less intimacy — than she had ever known. I don't know if she loved him. I don't know what her expectations of love were.

I know what she felt for him, years later; but she was different then, and so was he.

The road filled with refugees. Now it was easier. They were just three more among the crowd. An old woman with goitre hobbled with two sticks. A child clutched a chicken. They walked beside children with bruised eyes and thin white lips, who had survived the death around them and the flames of burning houses, who walked because that was what they'd been told to do, and no thought of it ever ending.

The roadside smelt again of sickness and fear.

'How long till we get there?'

'I don't know.' He spoke softly in case others on the road heard him, and his accent drew attention to them.

The child hiccupped on her hip. They had managed to buy some hog meat three farms past. (For gold; he'd burnt their last Confederate money three days back.) The fat meat sat heavily in their stomachs.

He heard her take in breath as though to ask another question: What will happen then? She stopped. The unspoken question flowed around them anyway: What will happen when we get there?

So he answered it. 'We'll get a boat as soon as we can.'

'We?'

'The three of us. I'm taking you both with me, to Australia. Don't worry, I've got the money.'

There was no point explaining about bank drafts, he decided. He wasn't even sure if she knew what banks were.

Caroline didn't ask how they would travel: as master and servant, husband and wife, friends or strangers? She didn't ask about Australia either.

Maybe, thought Charles, she had no idea of how it might be different from the world she'd known, or perhaps the strangeness of now was all that she could cope with.

Charles was grateful that she didn't ask questions. It seemed wrong to simply tell a woman that he was going to marry her. It seemed ridiculous though to ask a slave the romantic question, 'Will you marry me?'

He spoke to the child, Susannah, instead. (She hadn't spoken at all for the last two days, though her eyes watched the people of the road. She had said little even when they started. Yassir, Nosir. Now even that was gone.)

'I'll buy you a doll in Sydney. A big doll with a bonnet. That's a promise.'

The child's eyes stayed on his face. She didn't smile.

He wondered suddenly if she were ill, or if she'd lost her mind. Then realised: perhaps she's never seen a doll.

He reached out and stroked her hair. She accepted it. Her scalp felt tense below his hand.

'I'll buy you a dress too. And ribbons for your hair. What colour would you like?'

Her face was blank. Then suddenly he heard her whisper. 'Blue.'

'A blue dress?'

She nodded. She smiled at him for the first time. Then she thrust her head against her mother's breast and closed her eyes.

They wrapped themselves inside the blankets, fully clothed. Caroline curled against his back for warmth, the way they had slept now for weeks past. He felt her breasts against his back. Her breathing shook. He realised she was crying. In relief, perhaps, that someone would take care of her and Susannah? For joy? Why would you cry for joy?

Then tiredness took him, and he slept.

CHAPTER 19

1864

MARRIAGE

Charles and Caroline were married aboard the steamship *Mabel Bailey* as soon as they were out of territorial waters by a Captain who was unaware that he was solemnising a marriage that would have been illegal back in the South where they had come from.

They could have married the week previously, while Charles arranged their funds and passage. But neither knew how to obtain a licence in the United States or how to publish banns, and they didn't want to advertise their strangeness by asking.

Marriage aboard ship was anonymous, safer, beyond the reach of inquiry, no matter how unlikely. Now, with the sweep of the sea around them, there was no turning back.

The bride wore a pale brown dress with a triangle of

cream lace at her throat. Charles had bought it for her two days before. The bridegroom also wore new clothes, to replace those left in the chest at Cousin Elizabeth's. The child wore a dress, a replica of her mother's, with shorter skirts and pantaloons. They all wore new shoes that pinched their feet after months of spreading their toes in rags.

They had a cabin to themselves. The banker's draft had been honoured. There was enough money to see them to Sydney in comfort.

Charles walked on deck and smelt the scents of three years before: salt and smoke and oil, and the faint cigar of another passenger. Another sort of terror gripped him. His wife waited for him, and the duties of a marriage bed.

Charles Fitzhenry was twenty-one. He was also a virgin. The confines of life at home had left no room for experimentation. The youngest housemaid, Jane, had also been his nurse. All he had ever done with Sally was kiss her lips.

Any leave he had had from the army had been spent at Cousin Elizabeth's. There, probably, he would have lost his innocence if Cousin Ralph had been home to show him the way to the local bordello, or even the slave quarters. But apart from the first few days Ralph had not been home when he was. If he had gone to a whore, he thought desperately, she'd have shown him what to do. But although the lines before the whore's tent in camp had been two hours long, he'd never thought to join them. He would not sully a noble cause with whoring; and later, when the cause had lost most of its nobility, his bowels had left him too weak for more than a passing urge.

Charles had never seen a naked woman. He had been taught to hide his own body: to void his bowels by opening the flap at the back of his underdrawers, rather than expose the whole of his nakedness to the air. His body was a private thing, to be washed behind a screen in case a servant entered, to be touched and smelt and savoured only by himself.

It was a regime that created sensualists, ascetics and just the plain repressed. Charles was all three.

His sensual pleasures had been private ones: the smell of the wind on his face; wave spray like a thousand splinters; the smell of his farts like a hot fog; his private knowledge of the soft skin around his penis.

As for sex ... he was a farmer, and knew all about procreation and the deeds of animals. Now, like any bull tethered at the rear end of a cow he had to do it too.

It would be easier, he thought, if he loved her. He had always expected to have longed for this moment, to have imagined it a thousand times. Now there was only tiredness and fear, and the weakness of two years' privation and his illness.

He went down to their cabin.

The cabin had four berths. The child slept in one. His wife was already in another. He could see the frill of the nightdress at her throat. (It was the first time he had seen her in a nightdress — they had slept in separate rooms at the boarding house.) She lay between the sheets. (He didn't know that at the boarding house she had slept under both sheets until she worked out where she had to fit.)

His guts knotted. He blew out the candle. He undressed slowly, hoping there wasn't enough light from the porthole for her to see him. He found his nightshirt by touch, slipped it over his head, then shrugged off his trousers and underdrawers. He pushed his clothes aside and crossed with bare feet to her berth.

He heard her move aside for him. He slipped in beside her, bumping his head on the berth above, hoping she hadn't noticed the ignominious crack.

The sheets were cold. The boat creaked. He could hear the wash of waves. He could hear his wife's breathing and the faint snort of the child in sleep. His wife wasn't asleep. He knew the sounds she made in sleep, an intimacy even before they were intimate.

She felt warm. She felt smaller now he was close to her, fine boned like a rabbit. Warm as a rabbit too.

He tried to summon up everything he'd heard. He lifted her nightdress, felt. Her knees were hard, there was more flesh above them than he expected. There was hair, a lot of hair. He hadn't expected so much hair. She opened her legs and shifted slightly towards him. He lifted his nightshirt, rolled on top of her and pushed. It was warm there, incredibly warm, but it was no use, he couldn't. Whatever was expected he couldn't do it. He rolled away from her and lay in the blackness watching the deeper black of the bunk above.

She moved properly for the first time. He could hear her breathing change. It was almost a croon. Almost as though she were amused. With this, at any rate, she was in familiar country. She wriggled. He tried to interpret the wriggle then realised she was taking off her nightdress, folding it behind the pillow. She turned and worked on the buttons of his nightshirt.

She was smaller without her nightdress. She felt almost fragile, a surprise to him after her courage and resolve in the past months. He touched her waist tentatively, felt the surprising curve, so much softer than a waist in stays, a different shape entirely. He felt her ribs above her waist, the soft weight of her breasts, small with hard nipples. Her breathing changed again.

She touched him now, his chest beneath his nightshirt, a caress like you'd give a child, soft fingertips against his nipples. He felt her breath and her tongue on his skin, her mouth on his neck, kissing his cheek up where the skin was hairless by his sideburns, kissing his lips, small sucking kisses that demanded nothing, light as butterflies, cool as moths.

His hands curved around her breasts. Her hands moved down to his flanks, found his privates, smoothed them, soothed them, cupped her hands around him, stroked again. He felt a moment's shock that she should be so knowledgable. He had forgotten the child, what must have gone into her begetting. Extraordinary astonishment to feel another person touch him.

He was on top of her, somehow, his knees pressed into the flock mattress, the sheet creased around his waist. There was moisture now, thicker than spit, not hair. He felt himself sucked deeper. It was almost like a mossy well, but too warm for moss; almost like something half remembered, something of security and pleasure. He was riding through the trees at home, the wind was in his hair. There was no need to think. The whole world was movement, bodies, sweat. It was a burst of pleasure that blotted out the future.

He lay beside her. The boat rocked. He could smell the sour wood smell of the cabin — many years accumulation of body smells in a small space. Her body seemed to have grown into him, an intimacy of darkness and of flesh. He thought he had been asleep. This was so quiet it could be sleep. It didn't matter.

Her hand moved, took his hand, pulled it between her legs. The space was hot and wet. The bed smelt strange with the smell of semen, familiar, if shameful, and another smell, of her, of them both combined. She pressed his hand, instructing it, until he caught the rhythm, then froze, shocked, as she began to writhe against him.

The animal part of him responded as the civilised part held back. (She was a Negro, the civilised part of him remembered. Negroes were nearer to the animal, weren't they? Much closer to the beast than him. Surely no

135

white woman would act with urgency like this.) She slipped on top of him, slid her legs down either side of his body, pushed down around his upright penis, keeping her head low to avoid the bunk above. She rode him with her lips pressed close to his, her bottom (too narrow, too muscular for beauty) arched above him.

In the morning she dressed before him and took the child up onto the deck. He lay where she had left him, his body relaxed, his mind numbed (perhaps if he had gone to school he would have been familiar with what had happened last night from pornography, have at least visited a brothel. Nothing had prepared him for hands that woke him in the night, as though she'd never heard of reticence or shame).

She said nothing at breakfast, as usual, even to the child.

The fears of his marriage, of his homecoming, were still there. But now he remembered the woman in the night.

It seemed to him that the country he inhabited was like the land of war. There were no known rules; there were no familiar paths at all.

This couldn't be love. Each time, each culture, has its own vision of what love is. For Charles, love was his parents' marriage, or his Aunt Euphemia's, or Cousin Elizabeth and Ralph. Love was romantic novels. Love was poetic passion. Love was laughter and moonlight. Love was sonnets and despair. Love is what you feel towards an equal.

No one saw his wife as a slave now, except for him.

—♨︎

Months later: They had disembarked at Plymouth — no thought this time of travelling to the family estate and Sir Roland — and almost immediately boarded another ship for Sydney.

Out at sea a crowd gathered at the sides of the ship to watch porpoises dart through the spray. The ship lurched and shuddered, more ungainly than the porpoises, but Charles and Caroline and Susannah were used to it.

Charles and Caroline walked arm in arm. They were used to this, too, after the initial awkwardness. Caroline walked with a swaying of her skirts, her body held upright in her stays, just like every other woman in the first-class cabins on board. She wore her gloves and hats as though she were used to them. (Her high lace collar hid a bite on her neck. Each morning Charles felt embarrassed at himself, but he had begun to accept that there was another law at night.)

Susannah — Zanna — peered between the adults, too short to see over the deck. A sailor laughed at her. 'Here you go, missy!' He hauled her up on to his shoulders.

Charles looked at her, then looked at Caroline. Without thinking he asked, 'Who's her father?' (or perhaps he had been thinking this for months).

Caroline looked at the porpoises, not at him. 'His name was Ezekiel.'

'A slave?'

'Yes.'

'Where is he now?'

'He died.'

Jealousy was sharper than the salt spray. Charles tried to tell himself it was disgust at a black prick burrowing where he had been, and went below.

~∰◯

The ship burped dark smoke. Soot smudged the cheeks of the passengers when the wind was blowing hard. The nights retained their intimacy. The days took on a routine. Caroline slowly learnt to take a bed for granted, knives, forks, to sit without too much self-consciousness at the dining table with other people with white skin. The ship continued to New South Wales.

Caroline left behind her mother (how would Lina survive in a world where her bright body was too old to win a new life, where the security she had won was gone with the days of slavery, the wealth of the people who owned her?), and her memories of Drusilla, Ezekiel, Moses.

Caroline would never know what happened to them, though she could easily have found out. She need only have written to Cousin Elizabeth. (Her daughter did write that letter, years after Caroline died, and Cousin Elizabeth's daughter replied. Cousin Elizabeth had survived the war and the reconstruction, and died at ninety-three, a matriarch with fifteen grandchildren, fifty-seven great-grandchildren and two spaniels, her memories of the glorious war well brushed and tidied up to tell to her descendants.)

After the war was over Cousin Elizabeth had no power over Caroline. If Caroline had returned to the United States she would no longer be an escaped slave, once slavery had been abolished in the South as well as the North, although she would still be discriminated against as a Negro unless she hid her background. Even Charles could no longer be imprisoned as a Confederate deserter.

But neither of them ever wrote to Cousin Elizabeth, or to Duane. I don't know whether it occurred to either Charles or Caroline to write. The past was another world for both of them.

As the ship chewed into each wave, moving closer to Australia, it was a world they would both keep tightly packed away.

CHAPTER 20

1865

AUSTRALIA

The Captain announced at breakfast that later in the day passengers should be able to make out the coast of Australia.

Along with most of the other passengers, Charles and Caroline waited on deck, staring at the crack between the sky and ocean. It seemed impossible after so many days at sea that a landmass could insert itself in that thin space.

Somewhere across the grey water was Charles' home: the neat stone-walled paddocks, green hills and blue–green trees. It was so vivid he could almost smell it over the taste of salt.

He knew there could be no true coming home.

He had already written the letter to his father, even

though it couldn't be posted till they docked. But he wanted to confess at once, to get it over.

Charles hadn't minimised his sins in the letter. He admitted he had deserted the Confederate Army, that he had escaped to the North with a slave woman and her child, and married her.

He didn't tell his father his wife's name. He didn't say that she looked like a white woman either. If they wanted to assume his wife was as black as coal, let them.

He also didn't say that his wife was his cousin. I'm not sure, in fact, if either Charles or Caroline ever made the connection, even after Charles realised they shared the same surname.

In the letter, Charles told his father that he and his wife and her child would stay in a small hotel in Sydney until he heard from his family.

Was it possible that he still hoped he might be forgiven? That his father might say, 'Come home, my son. Whatever you have done we still love you.'

Surely Charles was more realistic than that.

Charles had lost his inheritance. The prosperous acres, the house on the hill, the family money. He had lost his family, his heritage.

In return he had Caroline, silent and bewildered, except at night. He had Susannah, with her dark skin and shadowed eyes. Even if Zanna's skin had been white, she was a far cry from the plump ideal of a laughing, ringleted Victorian child.

His health was poor. His mind was battered from two years of war. As he looked out over the rail I don't know if he saw any future at all.

Chapter 21

1865

JAMES FITZHENRY READS HIS
LETTER

James Fitzhenry sat at his breakfast table and glanced at
the mailbag.

The mail had arrived last night, but it had been late
when he came in. They had been branding the calves in
the lower paddock, and he only wanted a bath, and
then his whisky, before a late dinner with Emily and
George.

After dinner he had left the bag on the hall table
where Campbell had placed it. There was no hurry. The
letters from solicitors, the gossip from Margaret or
Euphemia in Sydney, the catalogues for Emily could all
wait until tomorrow. The only letter that mattered
would be one from the boy, and there had been none
from Charles for over a year.

He'd told Emily not to worry, refused to reveal the horrors that sometimes woke him in the night, lying between the well ironed sheets that smelt of lavender from Emily's garden. James remembered the smell of swollen bodies split open by the crows, the scenes in India that no woman could or should ever know, and especially not Emily. He had never thought that the American war would be like that, when he agreed to let the boy go. He'd thought it would be like the American War of Independence — raids and gallantry — not the war the boy described.

It was important that Emily not find out how bad things were. Women were different. Soft little things, and childlike. Women must be humoured, sheltered.

So he'd told her not to worry. The boy was safe. Although few letters could get through the blockade, important ones did, somehow. If Charles had been killed they would have received a letter from his commanding officer, or from Duane or Cousin Elizabeth. If Charles were held prisoner in the North he would certainly have been able to send a letter.

The blockade had done more than deprive him of news of his son; because of the blockade the only news of the war came from the Northern papers. What had once been news was now mostly propaganda. Nowadays the Australian papers were full of Southern atrocities, inhumanity to slaves and Northern victories. The Southern cause was no longer glorious. The Confederate Army was monstrous, inhuman ...

He didn't believe them. Who would believe what one enemy said about another? How could the Australian papers print such lies? He didn't read the news of the U.S.A. to Emily these days, but he cut the articles out nonetheless and kept them filed in the second drawer of his desk.

Chicago, April 16.

Letters received detailing the capture of Fort Pillow now give a more appalling description of the fiendishness of the rebels than the telegraph. Many of the wounded were shot in the hospital and the remainder driven out and the hospital burned.

The morning after the battle the rebels went about the field to shoot the Negroes who had not died from previous wounds. Many of those who had escaped from the works and hospitals, who desired to be treated as prisoners of war as the rebels had promised, were ordered into line and inhumanely shot down.

Of 350 coloured troops not more than fifty or sixty escaped and not one of the officers in command of the coloured troops survives. General Chalmers told the correspondent that although it was against the policy of his government to spare Negro soldiers and their officers, yet he had done all in his power to stop the carnage; at the same time he believed it was right. Another officer said our white troops would have been protected had they not been found on duty with the Negroes. The rebels suffered heavily and their wounded filled three hospitals ...

It hurt that the papers could twist his son's heroism and make it evil. It was a slur on the whole family. The

Fitzhenrys took heroism for granted. But to be a hero you had to be on the right side.

At least the war would be over soon. The South had lost, despite its wealth. No army could win a war without supplies, without guns and powder to fire them. And then the boy would come home. They could forget ...

James Fitzhenry stared out the window. No, you didn't forget. But you could pretend to, as he had pretended. It should have been such a glorious small war. Not this: the lies, the slurs, the humiliation of defeat ...

But Charles would soon be home. He would marry, take up the reins of the property. George was a good lad, but he didn't have Charles' ... depth ... to him. James Fitzhenry wondered sometimes if a man only ever had one son who kept the family fire alive.

The smells of breakfast still clung around him as he opened the mailbag: grilled bacon, kedgeree, a baked ham studded with cloves, comb honey from their own hives, lime marmalade and ginger marmalade, porridge in the silver porringer. On the table toast crumbs marred the white damask tablecloth, shiny with starch. The butter, impressed with the family crest using the wooden pats brought from England decades before, still weeped whey in the butter dish. This morning's milk was cold in its chilled silver jug. He was firm on that; yesterday's milk would do for cooking if it was still sweet, but milk for porridge had to be today's.

James Fitzhenry pulled out the Sydney papers, with

more lies probably, the local paper ... and suddenly he stopped, and felt his heart pound so hard his hand began to shake.

There was a letter in the boy's hand. Not Duane's, nor Elizabeth's, nor a stranger's. Charles was alive, or had been months ago when the letter had been posted.

How had he got the letter through the lines? Or had the boy been captured?

Then he saw the postmark. Sydney.

Why had the boy written, when he could have been home before the letter arrived? Why was he in Australia, when his comrades were still fighting?

James Fitzhenry opened the letter slowly, as if his body knew the evil before he read it.

The letter was short. There was no need to cross the lines. Two pages, written clearly (though the boy's hand had changed ... the words were thinner, somehow the writing of a much older man).

The page blurred as he read. He had to read it once more and then again, before his mind could absorb the words.

It was impossible. His son could never act like that.

He read the letter again. This time he believed it. He sat there at the table and the world faded around him, the cattle calling to their calves, a burst of laughter from the kitchen ...

James Fitzhenry put the letter down.

His first thought was for Emily. How could he keep this from her? But no, she had to be told. Then life would go on and on and on, and that was the hardest part of all.

He went to the sideboard, took out the whisky and a glass (smudged, said his mind automatically; Esther skimped on polishing; he'd have a word to Emily), pulled the curtains and stood looking out.

It was a strange grief. Not for himself, not for the loss of his son (for his son was gone, more finally than if he'd died). The pain was at what his son had lost — property and family name, the stone walls Campbell was finishing around the orchard, the tennis court (he had put it in for Emily; not that she played, but it was good for parties) — the ancestors he'd shamed ...

He'd have to make arrangements. Write to Sydney. He'd give Charles and his ... wife ... an allowance of sorts. It was only right. He wasn't a hard man, he would be fair.

It was cold. He hadn't noticed it before. His hand was shaking, blue against the darker blue of the curtains. Autumn was high time to light a fire in the mornings. He'd tell Emily.

He'd have to tell Emily. What words could he use? Even though the boy had no thought of he and his wife (the pain bit deeper) being received, Emily might argue, might want to see them. His son, the deserter, and his nigger wife.

The thought slashed through his brain.

He wondered if Duane knew, and Cousin Elizabeth and Ralph. Should he write to them? Or just (this would be better) pretend the boy had vanished, and never mention him again.

Grandchildren. Black. Thank God for George. He thought of George, obedient and dull. George would never be a hero. He'd never bring shame to them either. Should George be told? A part of the story, perhaps. Not all. Not yet. Margaret and Euphemia in Sydney — would they find out? The boy would have to leave Sydney, go somewhere the Fitzhenry name wasn't known.

How could Charles have done it?

He took another whisky. If there were tears on his face they must be gone before he had to face his wife. Tears for his son. My darling son, my lovely son: if only you were dead.

CHAPTER 22

1865

MRS MERRYWEATHER MEETS
HER NEIGHBOURS

It was Phil who told her they had come, sitting at the kitchen table with his napkin tucked into his shirt while he ate his currant tart for supper.

Mrs Merryweather had made that tart herself. Lily was a good girl, for all she was a darkie, but she didn't have Mrs Merryweather's way with pastry. And, anyway, making pastry kept your hands soft. Mrs Merryweather's hands were softer now than they had been ten years ago, when she still worked outdoors.

'New people've moved in down the road,' said Phil in that slow way he had. If Phil was to tell you the bull was out and ready to charge the sulky he'd still take half a day to do it. 'Day before yesterday it were. Bill

Driver told me this mornin'. He met the new bloke too, taking the cart back to town.'

Higgins' was down the road a mile or two. Old man Higgins had built it for his mother-in-law and, when she'd died, he'd put it up for rent. But who'd want to rent a house, with no more than a paddock, so far from town?

For a moment Mrs Merryweather was affronted that it had taken three days for Bill Driver to think to mention news that important, but then she remembered he'd been fencing down the back paddock, which excused him. 'Did he say what they was like?'

Phil shrugged. 'A gentleman by the look of him. Sickly like. Wife too.'

'No children?' She glanced at her Frank, in his neat shirt and braces just like his Pa's. He was at school most days now, five miles away down the road.

Phil shook his head. 'Didn't mention any. Just the wife, that's all.'

Mrs Merryweather swallowed her disappointment. She'd have liked kiddies about, and not just as company for her Frank. 'I'll call on them tomorrow then. Tell Bill to harness up the sulky. Oh, and mind that fence down in the bottom paddock. Bill said the lambs were getting through.'

Phil was a good man, none better, but he needed getting into order. They'd still have only cows if it were up to Phil, which would be a crime the way the price of wool had soared.

Cattle was what they had started with, twenty years ago, both of them fresh off the boat, apart from six months working at Higgins'. Phil would have worked for Higgins all his life, but that wasn't what she'd travelled for; six months on the boat and drying his hankies under her blouse to get them flat, and the weevils in the biscuits though old man Merryweather had paid enough for their passage. She'd asked him for their passage money when she told him she'd decided to marry Phil.

Old man Merryweather. She wondered if Phil would ever get called that. His father had smelt of snuff and strong tobacco and thirty years of wood smoke in his coat.

She'd expected argument. There wasn't any. Old man Merryweather just chewed on his pipe, and winced when he hit his broken tooth at the side, and looked at her, and nodded, not even surprised it was her who broke the news to him and not his youngest son.

Phil's father was no fool. She might have been six years older than Phil, but that was what Phil needed, a strong woman to look after him. And what future was there for them in England? The farm was too small to support yet another family.

They'd bought 'Burgoon' the first Christmas they were here, with what they had and what the bank would lend them. (She wished they'd come out just ten years earlier, when there were still grants to be had for an able-bodied man, but Phil would have been twelve then. If wishes were horses we'd go for a ride, she thought.)

It had been a hard year, that first. The flies like she'd never seen before, and the wind flowing through the slabs of the hut. She caulked the holes with clay, until the clay shrank and she had to redo them, and after that she didn't bother with the wind through the walls, she was that tired. There was that much else to think of.

The creek flooded the first year and took one of the corn paddocks. They'd camped all night for weeks by the rest of the corn, taking it in turns to keep the 'roos away. They'd got the crop in finally, working like blackfellas for ten days straight, and put in another crop straightaway. She was still new to the country, but she had guessed from the warmth of the ground that the season might stretch to two crops.

They kept both paddocks in corn the second year, ploughed a third paddock in pumpkins and started ringbarking what would be the west paddock, and her with a babe in her arms by then and another in her belly and the trees like a green sea down the hillside.

She had lost that one. That was when they were clearing the bottom gully, ringbarking one side while they burnt the other. Hadn't even noticed, she was that tired, until she'd felt her skirts wet around her. It was a quick one, though, there was that to be thankful for and she hadn't sickened. She reckoned it was when you didn't bleed much you went bad.

They'd bought the cattle then, with the money from the corn. Agnes was born and the price of wool rose, so she got Phil to buy some sheep the year that Toby was born.

It was the next year that Agnes died of the diphtheria and young Toby, too. Then she'd lost another two months before it was due. She had known she should take it easy, but there was the shearing and Phil had fallen sick the same as Toby; it was months until he recovered. She'd had to check the fences round the corn herself.

She'd felt the pains three miles out and cried, not for the pain but for the loss. She'd lain on the hot ground and cried till the ground by her head felt as wet as by her legs, but it was no use. The babe was too small to live. Even if the Queen's surgeon had galloped through the bush right then, he couldn't have helped.

Three children lost in one year; sometimes she thought the pain of it would kill her, but it didn't, of course. She kept on going.

There'd been nine years without children then, not even the monthlies, no rags to hang on the line. That bit was a blessing anyway.

She'd turned herself on the land as though to revenge herself for the barrenness within, as though by changing the land and making it fruitful she might change herself. She'd ridden to the sheep and cattle, hacked the suckers on the ringbarks faster than any man, raised the trees in the orchard from seeds and slips. That orchard and the eggs and wheat and the paddocks of potatoes she'd made Phil put in the first year of the gold rush had been their making. The miners brought the money in then; not the sheep you couldn't get a man to tend. There was money in food for the miners.

Then Frank. She'd given up hoping by then; thought she'd had the change, that maybe it came to you early when you lived as a man. It wasn't till her breasts swelled again that she realised she was expecting.

Phil was wanting to follow the miners, so like a man, all for the glory and no thinking it through. There was no money looking for gold, she could see it easy. And there was Frank now to hold Phil close to home.

She hadn't lost her energy with Frank's birth, but it had changed. She hadn't ridden a horse since she felt him quicken. The sulky was good enough. She'd looked at the slab hut when she felt him in her, had seen the holes that no amount of chinking ever plugged, the dusty floor, the tracks the bush rats made under the table. She resolved there'd be a new house to bring her baby to.

She'd supervised it all herself, every nail. It had been hard to get nails in those days. The drays were full of stores for the miners, not building materials, and most men had gold in their eyes. Even those who'd lost their stake were certain they'd make their fortune the next time they held a pan.

She walked out on the road herself, pushing her belly in front of her (in the old country they'd have hidden it in shawls, but you didn't have time for that out here) and argued with the men trailing back from the diggings with empty hands and bellies. Offered them work enough to pay their way back to Sydney, or to stake them in another set of diggings if they must.

Frank was born in the new house. The old one was a bunkhouse for the stockman.

The town grew with the gold, and when the gold shrank to a few mines the town was still there, a fixture, smaller but more settled. It was a good life she'd had to offer Frank when he came gulping into the world, not screaming like the others, as though he knew she'd prepared the world for him and was slightly overwhelmed.

The flesh began to gather on her body, as it knew now it was anchored in one place, with Frank. But as her body slowed her mind began to scurry. Phil was a good man, none better. She'd watched the tears run down his face as he sat with her, the night before they'd buried Agnes.

But Phil never thought beyond his breakfast, and the poddies to round up afterwards. And if you wanted a future from your land you had to think in terms of next year, and the next.

Sheep or cattle? No question there. War meant uniforms, and uniforms need wool, no matter that Crimea place is across the world. Fences or shepherds? No question there neither, with no men to be had; but fencing must be planned for and ...

It seemed her mind worked faster these days as her body slowed.

She smiled at him, her blond haired, red nosed son, with his look of happiness just like his dad. Frank'd bounce with joy over a butterfly still.

She passed him the cream, then changed her mind and poured it on his tart herself, and a good helping for Phil too. A good supper in a good day, and a good year. Every year had been better'n the last since she'd had her Frank.

~◦◦◦~

Mrs Merryweather picked a bunch of flowers to take visiting; pansies and calendulas and the winter jasmine that liked the cold.

If she hadn't been what she was, if she'd had girls, perhaps, not Frank, she might have chosen differently when the money came easier, and bought fine furniture or silver spoons. But she'd put the money into the farm, into good fences and decent rams and a solid house.

The only luxury was her garden: roses that thrived in the hot summers, just like her Frank, and daffodils under the apple trees. She ordered bulbs from Sydney whenever she saw a new shipment advertised, and flower seeds. Phil might blink if he knew how much she spent on her garden, but Mrs Merryweather did the accounts, and what Phil didn't know wouldn't hurt him.

Mrs Merryweather wore her Sunday dress and her second-best bonnet with the pansies, but not gloves, because she wasn't that sort, never would be, and anyway the reins would stain the gloves.

She drove the cart herself. Many women got their menfolk to drive them, but not her. The flowers bounced beside her, with a pumpkin in the back and a half side of mutton wrapped in hessian (a bit bloody at the edges, but thank goodness the flies were still asleep) and one of her cheeses, three months old and at its best, she reckoned, if you didn't like them strong. Frank wouldn't eat a strong cheese.

It was a quick trip. She could have walked it at a pinch, but not with the pumpkin and the mutton, and you had to be neighbourly. She wasn't one to arrive at a neighbour's empty handed.

It was good to have neighbours again. There were few enough gentlefolks around here still and none so near. Transportation wasn't far in the past and as well as the ex-convicts there was riffraff from the Californian goldfields still. Mrs Merryweather panted for some gossip in the kitchen.

~❦~

The man came to meet her at the gate ... what was his name? Phil had told her; a funny name — Fitzhenry. He must have heard the cart or perhaps he'd been sitting on the verandah. He was sick, or had been, she saw that at a glance. Not just his thinness, or the fever red that stained his cheeks. There was a look about him, as though he wasn't there at all.

He hefted the mutton, though, as if he were used to carrying fresh meat, so it didn't drip down his back or smudge his waistcoat.

She apologised for the bloodiness of the mutton.

'It'll have set by tomorrow. Phil only killed it yesterday. I'd have brought last week's but we've eaten the best of it, there's only a forequarter left.'

'We'd have been happy with a forequarter. How much do we owe you?'

She nipped that one in the bud right away. 'As though we'd take money from a neighbour for a bit of meat.'

He accepted that. He was a gentleman, you could see that easy. A real one, not those 'gentleman-once' who came round cadging.

'It's very kind of you then. But later on we'd like to buy some, if we may.'

'Well as to that, you'd better take it up with Phil next time you see him. But a bit of meat is neither here nor there, not between neighbours.'

They were at the kitchen now. He'd had to bring the meat there, of course, but Mrs Merryweather wasn't the sort you left in parlours.

The girl was at the stove. (You couldn't call her a woman, for all she was a wife.) She was as thin as he was, but there was a bloom to her, and her hair was good (Mrs Merryweather always reckoned a woman's hair was the first thing to dull when you were poorly), dark and shiny and neatly parted and fixed in a bun at the back.

The girl's eyes fixed on the flowers. You'd have thought they were the crown jewels. She stammered as she took them.

'That's nothing. You're welcome to more any time. Or seeds or cuttings as you've got the fancy,' she said, planting a kiss on the girl's cheek, because the girl was so young and her Agnes would have been her age, if she'd lived, and because of her happiness at the flowers.

The girl didn't kiss her back, not even a press on the shoulders. Mrs Merryweather was almost offended for a moment, then, stepping back, she saw the girl's eyes were filled with tears. Her lips were tight as though she was trying not to cry.

Wherever the girl had come from Mrs Merryweather reckoned there'd been precious few kisses going begging for a penny.

Mrs Merryweather had brought tea, in a twist of paper, in case they hadn't any, but they had, so she kept it in her pocket so as not to offend them. The girl ladled it out from a brown canister, new. They'd have bought that in Sydney before they came.

Mrs Merryweather put the pumpkin to one side where they would see it for their dinner, not to make a point of offering it, then sat firmly at the kitchen table to make it clear she wasn't parlour company (you could never have a good talk with anyone in the parlour). The man sat beside her. The girl served the tea and scones fresh from the oven, then stood back as though uncertain. She only came to the table when her husband gestured for her to sit too.

It was strange. It wasn't that she was scared of him — Mrs Merryweather had seen wives scared of their husbands before, you couldn't mistake it — just that she was a stranger somehow, in a way Mrs Merryweather couldn't pin down.

The husband glanced at his wife, and then at the plate of scones. The girl said 'Oh!' and then, 'Would you care for a biscuit, Mrs Merryweather?'

'Well, I would,' said Mrs Merryweather, 'though they look like scones to me.'

The girl looked stricken. Her husband said to her, 'That's what we call biscuits in Australia. Scones,' and smiled at her reassuringly.

'Biscuits or scones, you've got a light touch with them,' said Mrs Merryweather. 'I always say you've got the touch or you haven't. I'd guess your pastry's as good as these,' all the while helping herself to butter (she'd have to bring some jam down next) and thinking, well, I guessed she was foreign. But from where?

There was another strangeness as well, but she couldn't put her finger on it. It wasn't just his illness. Maybe it was the girl's silence. When she did speak it was careful and very low, as though the sound of her voice frightened her each time.

'We're a good way from Sydney here,' said Mrs Merryweather hopefully. There's nothing like stating where you are to get people to say where they are from.

The girl nodded.

'Caroline's from the United States,' Fitzhenry offered, seeing Mrs Merryweather was expecting more.

'Just off the boat?' she guessed. And Caroline nodded again. (Later in bed, Phil snuffling beside her, a thought occurred to her. Wasn't there a war or something over there? Maybe they'd been mixed up in it. But he'd probably been after gold, that was more likely. That's what they all did over in America. It would explain the look of him too. The starved, desperate look of so many miners, great hopes and lost them all.)

A child cried from the next room. Caroline Fitzhenry glanced at her husband. He nodded, she stood, and stepped into the small room by the kitchen where the slavey would sleep if they'd had one. She came back with the child on her hip, then sat her on her lap. The child glanced at Mrs Merryweather, then hid her face in her mother's bosom. She was three perhaps, or maybe four; younger than Frank, and smaller too.

And she was black. Well, not black exactly. Brown skin and deep brown eyes, but it were a shock, Mrs Merryweather couldn't deny it, her so neat looking and him such a gentleman, and there was the child, dark as you please.

The man — Fitzhenry — was looking at her, waiting

for her reaction, and the girl had her head bent to the child, as though she didn't want to meet her eyes.

Well, you had to say something, thought Mrs Merryweather.

'Our trip out was more'n twenty year ago. I remember the time we had of it. I was sick the first six weeks,' said Mrs Merryweather. 'It must have been a hard trip for you, and you with a young one.'

The child glanced up from her mother's lap. A pretty child, a girl. Her black hair curled just like Agnes' ... Mrs Merryweather glanced again at the parents. Was there a touch of tarbrush in them? They said it came out darker in the children. But they didn't look it ...

'She's your first?' she asked. She just said it to get them talking, but it didn't, they froze again. Caroline looked at her husband without speaking and he answered for her.

'I adopted her, back in the United States,' he said.

Mrs Merryweather blinked. In her experience that meant that the child was born on the wrong side of the blanket. But what man would adopt his black mistress's child? What wife would put up with it? Maybe they did things different over there.

The silence was growing uncomfortable.

'What's her name?' asked Mrs Merryweather quickly.

'Susannah.'

The child looked up at her name. 'Let me hold her then,' said Mrs Merryweather, stretching out her arms. 'Have you got a dolly to show Auntie Merryweather then, Susannah?'

The child blinked, as though she wasn't used to being spoken to by strangers. But she nodded and slid off Caroline's lap, ran from the room and came back a moment later with a china doll, all frilled dress and velvet bonnet over her gold hair.

'Isn't she a pretty one!' said Mrs Merryweather, hauling the child, doll and all onto her lap. 'But not as pretty as you, is she, dear?'

She lifted her eyes to see them both staring at her, husband and wife. So what if the child had more than a touch of the tarbrush? Mrs Merryweather's fingers itched to plait blue ribbons in her hair.

Later, walking in the garden with the child's hand in hers (not that you could call it a garden yet) and the husband indoors (she hoped he'd have a good lie down, he was that peaky) she tried to get the wife talking, without much success, till suddenly the girl stopped and vomited neatly in the wattle regrowth over the fence.

The smell was sharp in the cold air.

Mrs Merryweather looked at her consideringly. 'How many months gone?'

For the first time the girl looked as though she knew the answer.

'Four, I guess.' Her accent was different out here, away from her husband. Slower, longer, as if there was a tune in it, a foreign tune, but careful.

'You don't want to overdo it then,' said Mrs Merryweather. 'I lost my second that way and my third. Don't you go lifting stuff and have a lie down after lunch. It's a pain that eats at you for the rest of your life when you lose a baby.'

A shadow passed over the girl's face, froze and was gone.

'Staying here for it?'

She looked blank.

'Some folks go into town or even down to Sydney. I never had much patience with that. The house gets out of order when you're gone.'

'I guess I'll be staying here,' the girl said slowly.

'You've no family? No, of course not, not round here. Well, I didn't either, and neither do most of us these days. Your hubby hasn't anyone?'

The girl shook her head. Mrs Merryweather would have liked to ask why they came here then: no job to come to, no family and the house not much to speak of. She suspected that the answer might be: no reason, just that the Sydney agents advertised a house, a distant place that they could afford, better than the Sydney boarding house where he was embarrassed by the loudness of his nightmares and she bewildered by the city's size and noise.

She took the girl's hand in hers and patted it. 'You tell me now if I'm interfering, but it's good to have neighbours out here, good neighbours. Binsons, who were here before you, he was off on contract most of the time and she was no better than she should be. I'm that glad you've come.'

Tears came into the girl's eyes again. It struck Mrs Merryweather that she was the loneliest creature that she'd ever seen.

A blue wren leapt from the broken fence, darted for insects at their feet.

'Those blue boys. You could step on them and they wouldn't notice. I want you to promise you'll come up if there's anything you need. You promise? You send your husband up when your time comes. Never mind about the doctor. I'll send Phil for him or Jones. Men aren't much use at times like these.'

Mrs Merryweather shrugged. 'I've been through six, though there's only my Frank living. I'll bring Frank next time. He's at school. You won't want him under your feet while you're settling in, but he's a good boy, Frank.'

The voice didn't quite hide the pride in Frank.

'You come up any time you're feeling low. It gets to a woman sometimes, times like this, being by herself, no family. Men are no help when you're down, not that I'm saying anything against Phil, he's a good man, and I can see your hubby's one too, but it's not the same, is it? I can tell you, I've done it all.'

The girl was quiet. Then she smiled. It was as though, said Mrs Merryweather to Phil, as she plaited her hair for bed, a lamp was shining from her face.

'Why, thank you very much, Mrs Merryweather,' she said, formal as though it were a dinner party and she the Duchess of Middlesborough. 'I would love to come.'

They went inside and the girl woke her husband (if he was asleep, which Mrs Merryweather doubted, he looked too fine-drawn to get much sleep) and he came down the passage to see her out and harness Budgy for her. He smiled at his wife as he came and that put the lid on it for Mrs Merryweather; no woman would be afraid of a man that smiled at her like that.

But it underlined the strangeness nonetheless. It was a reassuring smile, and what was there to reassure about in the visit of a neighbour?

They both stood at the gate to wave her off and, when she looked back, they were still there, small figures dwarfed by the trees, by the road, by everything about them, and it struck her that if the girl was lonely, so was he.

~❦~

In bed that night, smelling the starch of Phil's well ironed nightshirt as she straightened his nightcap which he would leave off, he'd get arthritis, same as his father if she didn't watch him, he surprised her.

'Reckon he's got a touch of nigger in him, then? They say it comes out darker in the children.'

She considered. 'Doesn't look it.' She tried to think what a nigger looked like. There'd been none among the miners.

Nigger was African, wasn't it? Not like blackfellas or the Chinee, more like Maori, maybe. There'd been a

Maori family at the diggings, settled over at Jeratgully. Good people; adopted two white kiddies after the floods. Even the Chinee weren't as bad as they made out, though you couldn't say so to Phil, he was that down on them, she thought drowsily, halfway to sleep. And it would be nice to have good neighbours.

Phil's hands were lifting up her nightdress.

'If you're going to do that, Phil, then blow the candle out, there's such a thing as decency,' she said and turned to him, lifting the fresh nightshirt from his body, so he could dip into her warm flesh that smelt (still) of sweet apples.

CHAPTER 23

1865

MRS MERRYWEATHER

After a while she didn't know how she had managed without another woman to talk to. You couldn't count Lily, for all that she was a good girl. What was there to gossip with Lily about, apart from how many eggs the hens had laid and whether to roast the leg or the shoulder for lunch?

It had got so that Phil would ask every morning, should he harness Budgy up? There was always something to take to the family down the road. They were buying their milk as well as their meat from the farm now.

As for gifts of Burgoon eggs and vegetables ... Mrs Merryweather just wished there had been someone growing a few potatoes and a cabbage or two twenty years ago, she'd been that parched for a bit of green.

'Even ate the pumpkin tops,' she admitted to Caroline one morning (you couldn't call a girl that age Mrs Fitzhenry, and Caroline hadn't asked her to call her by her first name, so Mrs Merryweather called her Caroline in her mind and nothing at all when she spoke to her).

'What were they like?' Her voice was slow and careful, as though she was trying not to sound too Yankee, thought Mrs Merryweather, though she didn't sound like Ned the Yank who had worked on the house for a while when he got sick of the diggings. Hers was a different voice entirely, slower, prettier, and not just that hers was a woman's voice and Ned's had grown hoarse yelling over the mining cradle.

'Pumpkin tops? Bit like a dishrag you've left so long it's gone crunchy.'

Caroline smiled — it was something she didn't do often, and Mrs Merryweather had yet to hear her laugh — and passed the shortcake over to her. It was good. All that the girl cooked was good, but different; it was amazing what two cooks could do with the same eggs and flour and butter.

Strawberry shortcake and strawberry butter and the buttermilk biscuits that were scones, but with currants sometimes, or walnuts.

'Though they should be pecans really,' said the girl.

'What's a pecan when he's at home?'

The girl blinked.

'What sort of tree do they grow on?' said Mrs Merryweather patiently.

The girl hesitated. 'An ordinary tree, I guess.'

City girl, thought Mrs Merryweather, but she didn't think it unkindly.

She and Phil had come to Sunday dinner at their place once. Only the once, because you needed to get a shovel to get Phil to Church, much less to a neighbour's afterwards.

She could see Phil lifting the food carefully with his fork, because it was different, not Phil's usual roast mutton and potatoes. But it was good; what Caroline called fried chicken, a sort of fritter with gravy and cream in it, and apple pie, and the girl's bread was white and light with a crust on it like a drover's dream. Better'n her bread, Mrs Merryweather had to admit, and Frank had lapped up the fried chicken like there was no tomorrow.

And afterwards biscuits she called cotton blossoms and cats' tongues to take home. There was always a parcel of baking to take back whenever Mrs Merryweather came visiting, and you couldn't refuse it, it was what neighbours did for each other. She'd brought them eggs and cabbages, hadn't she? And besides, the girl blushed with happiness every time Mrs Merryweather said that Phil had praised the walnut pie, or that Frank had finished up the last of the pralines.

Today she'd brought a basket of figs, half split with last week's rain and a few bees still sipping at their sweetness. The girl had said she'd make preserves of them, whatever that meant: like a jam, she supposed. Mrs Merryweather was just reaching for her third piece of shortcake (she'd had to lengthen her apron strings since the Fitzhenrys arrived) when she noticed the sweat on the girl's face.

Mrs Merryweather eyed her sharply. 'How long you been having them?' she demanded.

'Since dawn. Not bad till now.'

'Waters broke?'

'Not yet.'

Mrs Merryweather nodded. 'Well, your man can take Susannah up to the farm right now, and Phil will go get . . .'

'No!' The girl's voice was sharp with alarm.

'You don't want your man to go? Well, that's natural, I'll take her and . . .'

'No. Zanna stays here.' The Southern accent was stronger now.

Mrs Merryweather glanced at the child making sheep from bits of dough on the floor. You forgot she was there sometimes, she was that quiet.

'It's not the place for a child . . .' she began.

'Please,' said the girl.

There was no point arguing with a woman when her time had come, and maybe they did things differently where Caroline came from. But it was still strange. They never took the child to Church either. One or the other stayed with her at home. Well, that was natural, not wanting to parade her darkness in front of everyone. But the farm — that was different . . .

'Well, Phil can get the doctor then.'

'No doctor,' said the girl. The sweat was gathering on her top lip again and her fingers were white as they grasped the table.

'But ...' Mrs Merryweather stopped. She hadn't had a doctor for Frank and look how that had turned out. But Frank hadn't been her first.

'No doctor,' said the girl again, and Mrs Merryweather gave up the battle. Time enough to call the doctor if things went wrong, and when things went wrong when you got to this stage, Mrs Merryweather reckoned, it was never quickly.

She got the girl to the bedroom, stripped the bed and put the towels on it and clean cloths, as she made it up afresh. The waters broke as she was doing it, which meant the mess to mop, and the girl's legs too.

She made the girl change into a nightdress — 'Not your best one, mind' — got her into bed, then called Charles — he'd been asleep, she reckoned — to bring some twine inside, tied it for a pulling rope between the bedposts, and got the water warmed. Then she thought to send him with a message up to the farm to tell Lily to serve the cold meat and the pickle for dinner and cook up some potatoes. (They'd have to make do with cold meat for once, and bread and cheese for supper, if it went on that long.) To make up a baked custard, too, to serve with the stewed pears already in the larder. And not to let Frank have more than two slices of plum cake when he came home from school, three at the most, and to make sure he drank his milk.

Husbands, thought Mrs Merryweather, were best away at times like this, when you didn't have to worry about them too.

Then she made some bread and milk for Susannah, sitting quietly at the kitchen table, listening not speaking.

'Your ma will be all right,' said Mrs Merryweather reassuringly. 'And you know what? Tomorrow I reckon there'll be a baby brother or sister for you.'

She wondered whether to tell Susannah that Mr Merryweather was bringing the baby down from the gooseberry patch at the farm, but she looked into the child's dark eyes and for all that the child never said anything she somehow doubted she would be believed. At least with Susannah there wouldn't be questions after …

And then back to the bedroom again.

The pains were coming strong, she could see by the way the girl pulled the rope, but the girl didn't make a noise, though she must be busting, thought Mrs Merryweather.

'Let it out, love, there's none to hear,' said Mrs Merryweather, taking a cloth and wiping the sweat from her forehead. Well, only Susannah, she amended to herself, which is why she'd wanted the child up at the farm; there weren't any hens here so she couldn't tell the child to go get the eggs, or to count the new apples in the orchard.

Another contraction. The girl gasped. Blood showed at her mouth where she'd bitten her tongue. As soon as she was still again, panting, gasping, Mrs Merryweather dashed for the door. 'Zanna, you go look and see if your pa is coming back. Wait for him out by the gate, mind, and knock at the door soon as you see him.'

The child slipped off the chair obediently, her boots tapping on the wooden floor. Mrs Merryweather hurried back inside, and lifted the nightdress. 'Scream, girl, scream,' she ordered.

The girl shook her head.

'Scream! A good strong scream makes a good strong baby!' Which she'd made up on the spot, but never mind, it worked. The girl opened her mouth.

It wasn't much of a scream; like it got choked halfway through.

'Louder!' ordered Mrs Merryweather, crossing her fingers that everything was going all right. She could see the top of the head, and if it wasn't right now there was no time for a doctor to make it so.

The girl screamed again, louder, and then a proper scream, on and on and on. It was as if she were screaming for all the years she'd never screamed at all, a deep-down scream that made Mrs Merryweather catch her breath, sure that things were wrong.

They weren't. The girl screamed and pushed and the baby shot out onto Mrs Merryweather's waiting hands, all red and glossy white and shiny just like Frank had been, so that Mrs Merryweather had to fight back the tears before she could even get a grip, and pull the baby to her. And realised she didn't even have her apron on.

She'd have to soak the dress as soon as she got home, and what would Frank think, her coming in, all muck and blood ...

'Please,' gasped the girl, her hands out towards the baby. Another push. The afterbirth oozed out onto the towels.

The baby gave a startled squawk and blinked around the room.

'She's a knowing one,' said Mrs Merryweather. 'Never seen one that knew what she was looking for before.' Mrs Merryweather tied the cord and snipped it with the kitchen scissors. She wiped the baby down a bit and wrapped it and put it to the girl's breast and watched her shove the nipple expertly to its mouth. And suddenly Mrs Merryweather's suspicions coalesced into a certainty: You've done all this before, my girl, she thought, and Susannah has more than a look of you. Adopted, my fat foot.

The girl looked up, her eyes sunken and shadowed, her face glowing.

'She's perfect,' said Mrs Merryweather, 'just perfect.'

The girl nodded, her fingers stroking the baby's cheek. A white-skinned cheek, Mrs Merryweather noticed. Maybe Caroline had been worrying what colour it would be. Perhaps that was why she hadn't wanted the doctor, she thought, with sudden insight.

A knock on the door. It opened a crack and Zanna whispered, 'Mama? He's back.'

Mrs Merryweather twitched a towel over the blood

and afterbirth and pulled the door wider. 'Come in, child, and meet your sister,' she said.

'Annie,' whispered the woman on the bed. 'Her name is Annie.'

Mrs Merryweather stilled. Had they known her name was Anne? The girl met her eyes, and smiled, despite the white face, the smear of blood on her cheek.

Mrs Merryweather pressed a kiss on the top of Zanna's head as the child stared wide-eyed at her baby sister. 'Off you pop, pet,' she said. 'You go tell your pa.' As the child went out she twitched the towel off to gather up the afterbirth.

'Going to plant it?' she asked. 'Under a tree or a rose maybe,' she added. 'It's said the child will thrive while the tree has leaves.' Not that it worked for Agnes, she thought, or Toby. Their trees were roof high now. But a thriving tree could be a comfort to a mother nonetheless.

She smiled down at the girl. 'I'll do it for you,' she said. 'Now I'll send himself in to see his daughter, and get them fed for you and maybe you'll have a bite to eat as well. Then I'll send Lily down to help ...'

'No. Please,' said the girl.

'Well, I know she's a darkie but she's a real good girl.'

'No!'

Mrs Merryweather gave in. She had an inkling that what with Zanna's dark skin and all, maybe the Fitzhenrys weren't too comfortable with a darkie in the kitchen.

Later, setting two plates of mutton chops and mashed potatoes in gravy — her brown gravy, not the milk gravy she'd had here before — in front of Fitzhenry and Zanna, she said, 'Phil'll be off to town tomorrow. Want him to take a letter to the mail? There're people you'll want to tell, I reckon.'

'No. There's no one. But thank you for the thought.' He hesitated. 'I don't know how to thank you. Not just for today. For everything, Mrs Merryweather.'

'No thanks needed,' she said briskly, then added honestly, 'I reckon I'll be getting more joy from that babe than anything I could be given and that's a fact. Now you eat your supper and I'll check on them both and you can harness Budgy for me.'

The man hesitated. 'You'll be her godmother?' he asked.

Who else? thought Mrs Merryweather. 'Oh yes,' she said, 'I will, indeed.'

They were sleeping, mother and child, dark hair against the pillow. Mrs Merryweather lifted the sheet carefully to check on the bleeding, but it was nothing much, and she had a bit of colour in her face.

Not a bad time of it at all, considering, and a deal shorter than most. The girl was lucky.

Mrs Merryweather blew a kiss to Annie and shut the door.

CHAPTER 24

1866

ZANNA AND THE COLOUR OF
RAIN

It was warm in the kitchen. The kettle bubbled on the edge of the stove, fogging the windows, so Zanna could hardly see the rain outside.

Rain fascinated her. Rain stripped the colour from the world, and left it grey. How could something that had no colour itself make a change so profound?

Colour was important. The most important thing in the world. Hold the toast against the fire, Mama would say, until it's gold, that's right. If you held the toast against the flame too long it turned to black. Black toast was burnt. Occasionally she wondered if some time long past her skin had been burnt as well, to turn it as dark as that.

Annie gabbled on Ma's knee, her face stained with the bread and milk Ma was spooning into her. Annie's skin was like the bread, all soft and pale, and hers was like the crust. They would have to be careful with Annie, she thought, to make sure her skin didn't blacken too.

After breakfast Mama cleaned, and that was colour as well: wash the plates so they were blue and white, not streaked with food; scrub the floor and rub the sink, so it gleamed white; polish the furniture in the parlour so it gleamed black and shiny. Black was the right colour for tables and chair legs; black was for useful things, like Lily who helped Mrs Merryweather over at Burgoon, like Zanna helped Mama.

It rained while they had breakfast; it rained while Mama swept and while she dusted; it rained while they all sat at the table and ate their omelette and creamed beans. After that Annie had a nap, and Mama too. Mama napped every day now, because another baby was coming. She'd overheard that when Mama talked to Mrs Merryweather and they didn't know that she was near.

It was too wet to go outside, so she sat on the back steps, her back against the kitchen door, and watched the rain stripe the trees, the grass, the flowers Mrs Merryweather had given Mama to plant, the rosebush whose flowers were pink in sunlight, purple today, the daisy bushes that today seemed more blue than white.

No, rain didn't take colour away, she realised. Rain changed the colours, and those colours gave rain a million different shades as well, a rainbow in each raindrop.

Other children are told that rain is grey. Zanna watched its true colours with eyes of isolation.

The man she called Papa came up the path from the dunny. His face was streaked by raindrops under his hat and the brown of his coat streaked into many browns. He looked at her looking at the rain and smiled.

'Gentle Annie,' he said.

She shook her head to show she didn't understand.

'The rain. People call it Gentle Annie.'

'Gentle Annie,' she repeated. She smiled as Papa went back inside the kitchen. The rain was a friend now. They had been introduced.

'Zanna! Where is that child? Zanna, you come inside! The wet will rot your bones!' Mama spoke with music in her voice, the way she never spoke when Papa was near. He must have gone back into his study, to read or doze.

Zanna opened the door and stepped inside.

Inside the kitchen the ironing blanket was spread on the table by the stove. Mama was ironing: camisole ribbons and thick white aprons; starched petticoats and the shirts folded on the chair; tablecloths with broderie anglaise; flat thick sheets already in the basket. She hummed as she ironed, a tune with no words. She placed the cooling flat iron down on the hot stove and took up the other, rubbed it with beeswax, and bent to the ironing again. Baby Annie sat in her high chair by the table and waved a stained spoon.

For a moment Zanna was jealous of Annie. Annie had the same name as the rain. But the jealousy faded.

Annie belonged to Papa, as somehow she didn't. Annie deserved her name.

Zanna looked at her mother's face instead. It looked happy. This needed to be checked often, as sometimes it wasn't. Not sad precisely, but her face clouded, as though she were seeing things that Zanna only dimly remembered: the sweat and turnip smell of a bulging woman carrying a piglet down the road, one of hundreds trudging north; all of them scared, but none as scared as her.

When you were scared you had to be quiet; terrible things happened if you made a noise, all the more terrible for being unknown. It was good to be quiet. When you were quiet you were safe.

Were there other memories? Another place where frogs cried, another kitchen with another smell? They were closed off memories. With a child's certainty she knew there was no one she could ask.

Sometimes in the afternoons Mama spread the *Sydney Illustrated News* over the kitchen table, and made strange marks on scraps of brown paper from the medicine box, though never when the man Zanna called Papa was near. Zanna didn't understand the brown paper. There was better paper in Papa's desk. (It was only years later that she realised Mama was secretly teaching herself to write.)

Other afternoons Mama wandered from room to room. Mama smiled as she touched things: the four-poster bed with the turned posts, the kitchen chairs with apples painted on the back, the chesterfield with the pale silk cover, the looking glass, and the chest of blankets. Even the wooden clock and the hardwood kitchen table. Even the oilcloth with its bright blue pattern, and the brown teapot and the china on the shelves. Mama wasn't cleaning or dusting; simply touching. It was a ritual as private as the markings on brown paper.

The man she called Papa mostly lay on his sofa, or read or wrote in the front room that was his study, though he also tended the woodpile down the back, and curried down the horse and took it to town.

Once a month Papa went to town with Mr Merryweather to bring back bags of feed, sacks of flour and sugar, and ham in an oiled cloth and other things as well: lemonade and ginger beer packed in a candle box, sweet and frothy when you pulled the corks; baker's bread; lengths of material for pinafores or overalls; fish in a box of salt; preserved ginger, and sweets in a twist of paper. Once there was a Chinese doll in a silk dress and a rattle for baby Annie. ('When's your birthday, Zanna?' Mrs Merryweather had asked kindly, but she couldn't say.)

Once Papa brought back a letter and sat with it for hours.

But today he simply went to his study to doze after the omelette and the hot rolls with Mrs Merryweather's butter and Mama's peach preserve. Mama ironed and Zanna stood by the ironing board and sprinkled the clothes with water for Mama, avoiding the tadpole that swam in the bottom of the bucket.

After the ironing Mama fed Annie again, so Zanna was free to take the book of paper — the precious blank pages that appeared in her Christmas stocking last year — and one of Mama's pencils, and sit on the front verandah to make her shapes.

The verandah was a good place to sit. You could see right up the road; the dust songs in summer that meant carts or buggies or sulkies. You could see the paddocks opposite, too, with their brown and white Merryweather cows, their round pools of droppings that made ripples as they dropped from the cow but dried to a thick hard pad. Mama used a thick pad to bulk her hair at the back (an idea copied from the *Illustrated News*). You could turn the cow pads over and small brown insects scurried off in fright.

You could see the dunny down the back from one edge of the verandah too. Zanna didn't like the dunny. There were spiders in the smelly depths and the rim of the can left a cold red mark on your bottom. Chamberpots were only for the evening, so most days she waited till she could slip through the fence and squat in the broken light and feel the pattern of warmth and shade flicker on her bottom.

Through the trees the land dipped down a bank, with nettles and ferns and a creek singing on its stones. The creek was marshy at the edges, full of fat mosquitoes and green grass, the only brightness the flicker of the red bellies of the snakes and the shy glint of sunlight on the water.

She could ignore the mosquitoes, especially when she was clad in woollen stockings, and the snakes ignored her. It was possible to be quiet here, among the shadows and to watch.

Until a year ago all she did was watch. Then from nowhere came the pressure to take this with her, back inside. Next morning she brought a pencil and a scrap of paper on to the verandah and sat there, trying to translate the things she saw on to paper.

It wasn't easy. She had been trying now for almost a year, but still the shapes eluded her. Maybe the pencil was the problem. If only she had paints, like Frank Merryweather, perhaps she could mix the colours into shapes ...

You had to make so many lines to make a shape. Sometimes she felt it was impossible to take images with so many sides and place them on paper so the light flowed, and colours almost appeared, all with a pencil.

She had no idea the problem was a strange one for a six year old. She had no knowledge of the efforts of other older artists attempting to do the same thing. She had never seen a reproduction of an Old Master, as any art that cost more than a guinea was called. All she knew was the magic of images that grew on paper, images that were always less than the scene in front of her, gradually understanding that even as they were less they could be more.

The door opened behind her. The man who wasn't her father said: 'Zanna — let me see.'

She handed him the paper. He looked surprised. 'Zanna, this is very good. Who taught you to do this? Your mother? Mrs Merryweather? Frank?'

She shook her head. It had never occurred to her that anyone else might try to make colour with pencil lines too, or that it would be possible to teach it.

'It's very good indeed,' he said, and smiled at her. She smiled back. For one moment it was almost as though she belonged to him, and she was happy.

Later, that night, she was in bed. The starched sheets rustled as she moved, were cold against her toes. They were fresh sheets. After a few days they'd be softer and seem warmer, and her hair wouldn't slide so much on the starched pillow.

'I'll pick up some paints for her next time I'm in town.'

It was Papa's voice. Mama answered, but her voice was too quiet to be heard.

Then Papa spoke again. 'I suppose she should be sent to school. But people might talk.'

Mama's voice again, then Papa's. 'It's for your sake as much as hers. I just don't know how they'd take her. If she wasn't quite so dark ... If the school refused to have her it would mean all sorts of problems for Annie, for the next one when it comes. It would be a precedent the school would have to follow. We just can't risk them being tarred with the same brush.'

There was a pause. 'If I could afford a governess ... but with two children ... three ...'

Zanna looked at the back of her hand, dark in the moonlight, darker than Papa's and Mama's and Annie's. She knew already why he never took her to town, although she knew with a child's certainty that one day he'd take Annie.

She wanted to run to him and beg to be held tight. She didn't. She lay on her white sheets and thought of colour. Moonlight colours, colours of the night, colours of skin and hair and eyes. The whole world is colour, she thought, if only you could reason the pattern out.

Burgoon Road
August 1867
Dear Mother,
This morning my son was born, and as I gazed on his small limbs and red pinched face my heart swelled with an unbearable grief that You will never see him.

We have called the boy John Roland, even if he is never to know the family from which his name has come, and that too grieves me more than I can say.

My health continues poor. My strength deserts me at the least exertion and at times I wonder if I shall ever have hope again ...

(The letter was never sent.)

CHAPTER 25

1871

ANNIE

Even at six years old, Annie knew her family was different.

The first difference was their name, Fitzhenry, which sounded like a sneeze and embarrassed her at school. Other families had sensible names like Merryweather, Ferguson, Taylor, McDonald, or properly different names like the Lee Paks.

Papa was different too. Papa never smelt of sweat, or hair oil, like Mr Merryweather on Sundays. Papa smelt of spice and smoke from the cigars he bought once a month at the stores in town.

His hands were different as well.

Papa's hands were soft and white. Other men's hands were brown and calloused. Few men had a full ten fingers and even fewer had ten fingernails. Papa's hands had calluses across the fingers from holding the reins, but despite the rider's calluses he rode very little. Where would he want to ride to, except to town?

And that was different.

Other men worked, even Tiger Sam when he wasn't drunk and dancing with the fairies. Papa slept a lot in the front room they called his study, and his only task was to ride to town once a month to collect the letter that came every fourth Tuesday and to bank the draft inside.

After he had done his banking Papa would buy tobacco and four cigars, one for the next month of Sundays after lunch. He'd buy bull's-eyes for her, gobstoppers for John Roland and a newspaper. Sometimes he'd buy a length of dress material for Mama, or scented soap. Sometimes, when he remembered, he'd buy paints for Zanna, or special paper for her pictures. But he never bought Zanna bull's-eyes or gobstoppers. It didn't matter, though, as Annie always shared hers with Zanna.

Zanna was another reason their family was different.

Zanna had brown skin, the colour of milky cocoa but nicer, and more interesting than Annie's because Zanna's palms and feet and other places weren't cocoa-like at all but pale in some and dark in others, a whole universe of differently coloured skin. Annie could study Zanna's hands for hours on the back step, when the rain made the frogs croak and it was too wet to hunt for cicada shells down by the creek.

Annie wished that her skin could be different colours like Zanna's, but not a cocoa colour. Cocoa colours caused problems, though as yet Annie wasn't sure exactly what these were. Maybe she could be green, or blue . . .

Zanna could make a butterfly come alive on paper. She drew magic dragons with the washing-up suds on the window. The suds slowly slid down the glass, making the dragons fat and droopy, so that Annie and John Roland laughed and laughed, until finally the dragons sagged too far and disappeared.

Zanna was her sister, but she also wasn't, because Zanna was adopted. No one else Annie knew had a sister who had cocoa skin, or who was adopted.

Zanna never came to Church. There was always some reason: she had to watch the roast for Sunday dinner or the wind had teeth and Zanna had a cold. But Zanna's cocoa-ness was a shadow that followed the family even when she wasn't there.

There were other mysteries in Annie's family: Mama's voice, which wasn't like other mothers' voices. Sometimes Annie thought Mama sang her words, they were so pretty. The song was sweetest when Mama was in the kitchen, for it was in the kitchen that Mama was happiest and most relaxed. Her words would slur then into one long, slow, happy song. At other times, when she was with Papa, for instance, her voice became all clipped and sharp like his.

Mama wouldn't have a slavey, like the other families at school who paid a girl pennies to help with cleaning, to hang the washing out and to iron. Mama did the work herself, with Zanna's help: dipped the tablecloths in starch to make them crisp and shiny after they were ironed, dusted the paper flowers she'd made from patterns in the paper. Sometimes, when Papa was in his study reading or asleep, Mama would trail her fingers across each surface in the parlour: the china dogs upon the mantelpiece, the urn with peacock feathers, the curved legs of the tables, as though she were celebrating each possession, rejoicing that it was still there.

Mama baked apple teacake, buttermilk and walnut cake (should be pecans, said Mama sadly, nibbling the nuts as she cracked them and fished out bits of shell), cotton cookies made of crushed nuts and meringue, apple fritters with a fringe of melted sugar, flapjacks, and *pain perdu* — last week's bread dipped in eggs and milk and sugar and orange juice and fried in the blackened skillet she hung on the wall by the stove. And milk bread, and raisin bread, potato bread; rolling, rolling at the dough each Tuesday and feeding the yeast to make the bread on Mondays.

'Drusilla always fed the yeast Mondays,' said Mama, as though she suddenly remembered a long way away.

'Who was Drusilla, Mama?' asked Annie.

'Drusilla,' said Mama dreamily. 'Drusilla was ...'

And then she saw Papa standing at the kitchen door. He'd come in for a light for his cigar.

'Drusilla was no one,' said Mama, in the high sharp voice. 'She was no one, hear?' And she handed Annie a broom and told her to go and sweep the steps.

Later, Annie thought she heard her father crying in his study. But that couldn't be right, she knew, for grown-ups never cried. She thought that for two more years.

The five of them lived in the house that was too big for a labourer, and too small for a gentleman — Mama and Papa and Zanna and Annie and John Roland. John Roland had been a baby not so long ago, which had been interesting, as Annie had got to feed him prunes and apple, and sing him songs. But almost every family had babies, so John Roland wasn't *really* interesting, like Papa or Mama or Zanna.

Zanna buttoned Annie's boots until she learnt to use the button hook herself, and tied her bonnet ribbons and mended her hem when she trod on it. Zanna was silent, as though her lips were buttoned as tight as her boots. Even when she laughed at John Roland making faces around the dunny door it was silently. But Zanna had always been like that, so Annie didn't think it strange.

When she was six she thought the world would be like that forever.

~∰©

Being six meant Annie went to school. Not a real school, such as John Roland would go to when he was older, because he was a boy and would learn to become a gentleman, whereas she would just be Annie, which seemed a better fate by far. Annie's was a little school: three hills and a gully distance through the bush and Merryweather paddocks, or a dusty hour by road and sulky.

School smelt of whitewashed walls and stale cake, and musty orange peel from the satchels out in the sun. Needlework in samplers lined one shelf and copybooks lined the other to show to parents.

The school was run by the three Taylor sisters, in the front part of the house the sisters had inherited when their father died. The sisters were paid in pennies: one for Annie and one for Frank and one for Janie Taylor and all the rest of them, one for each day they spent at school. There was a Government school in town, where you didn't have to pay in pennies, but that was too far away. (The town wouldn't swallow these houses on the outskirts for another two decades.)

The schoolroom was divided into two, with two blackboards, and scratchy slates and muddy inkwells on each desk: 'infants', where Annie sat, and 'big ones', where Frank Merryweather sat in lordly splendour at a desk by himself like the other older boys.

Miss Frances taught infants after she'd washed up the breakfast dishes and before she had to slip dinner into the oven. She did the washing on Monday mornings, so on washing mornings one of the big girls had to read to the littl'uns until she'd finished. The washing flapped on the line, propped up by wattle poles to catch the wind. When it was dry Miss Frances left the spelling and the pothooks to go and take it in.

Miss Emily and Miss Serena gave the big ones lessons. Their lessons were more interesting than Miss Frances', so Annie listened to them when she could,

'Good morning, children!' swished Miss Emily, wiping crumbs from her bosom as her skirt swept the dust from the floor.

'Good-a-morning teacher!' they chanted as they ambled to their feet in desks too small for most of them. (Annie's had a heart carved on it, and initials, though not of anyone she knew. She wondered if, one day, someone would carve her initials into a desk.)

'Ah Father we chart in Heaven, allowed be Thy name ...'

'Twelve inches one foot, three feet make a yard, six times six is thirty-six, the Magna Carta signed in ... what year was it again, Serena?' whispered Miss Emily, heard by all the class, who giggled.

'Sit up straight. You too, Bill James, I'm looking at you. Harry McCarthy, you will come to the front of the class immediately!'

The sharp whip of the cane on Harry's fingers, and on Annie's sometimes, but not often. She liked school.

(Sometimes when she read at home she saw her mother watching her with an expression of joy. It was a look she didn't understand until years later.)

'Miss, Miss, Miss, can I go round the back?'

Two identical dunnies sat side by side down the back path. One said 'Girls' and one said 'Boys' and there were two rows of lemon trees up the paddock, planted where the last two dunnies had stood. The dunnies moved when the pit was full and fruit trees planted to take advantage of the fertile depths.

Playtime. The boys clustered like bees around a circle in the dust and shot their marbles *crash!* against each other, or clambered, yelling, on to the slip rails to oversee the girls. The girls sat and talked or skipped in the worn grass of the front yard. Yes, Annie liked school. It was more interesting than at home, with her mother and Zanna busy with the housework.

By the time she went to school Annie could already read, from the years spent looking over Mama and Papa's shoulder as they read to her, but no one noticed, especially not Miss Emily. Annie was made to do pothooks on a slate. Her pothooks were so clumsy that it was months before she was asked to form a letter, even longer before a word was scratched on the slate for her to sound out, and even then she failed. She had read the first chapter of *Rob Roy* by herself the night before, but she had no idea how to sound out a word letter by letter.

But she learnt other things. She listened to the big class as she scratched her pothooks. She learnt about the Magna Carta and King John burning the cakes (or was it Robert the Bruce? Or Alfred?). She learnt about the Good Queen who sat on the throne (how wonderful, she thought, imagining a throne with gold and jewels that the Queen sat on to have her dinner, though the dunny seat was called a throne sometimes, which confused her at first).

Best of all, school meant that Frank Merryweather called for her every morning on his pony. School meant clutching Frank's broad back and smelling the starch in his shirt mixed with the smell of the pony and the scent that was just Frank, and sometimes on the way home Frank would stop to show her the lyrebird's nest in the gully.

'See that platform? The bird glides down from there. Lyrebirds don't like flying much,' said Frank.

'Have you ever shot a lyrebird?' breathed Annie. Frank could shoot rabbits and wild ducks. He brought a pair of wild ducks down to their place just last week, and Mama roasted them with bacon and apples.

'Nah. There's not enough eating on a lyrebird,' said Frank, helping her up on to the pony before he climbed on himself.

As the pony trod between the trees and ferns, Annie thought, It's good being six.

Chapter 26

1872

THE NIGHT OF THE
BUSHRANGERS

The bushrangers came halfway through Annie's second year at school.

She didn't see the bushrangers, but everyone talked about them at school and Church, and for three weeks Mr Merryweather drove her and Frank to school in the sulky, instead of letting them go across country, in case the bushrangers should kidnap them, though John Roland snorted and said, 'Who'd want Annie?'. For those three weeks Mama bolted the back door every night, instead of leaving it open for the breeze and the mosquitoes.

The bushrangers had held up a coach on the Friday. On Tuesday the troopers arrived at the Fitzhenry home, three of them, on panting horses that they tied up at the gate. The sergeant wanted to know if Mama had heard anything strange in the night. She hadn't, but she served them tea and fresh buttermilk cake with lemon icing.

The vicar had his tea in the parlour, when he made his annual call on his parishioners, and Papa gave him a white envelope at the end of the visit as he collected his hat at the door. But the troopers took it for granted that they would eat in the kitchen, and John Roland and Annie sat at the table and watched them eat, gazing at their shaggy whiskers and their uniforms and their hot rank smell of horse, while Zanna refilled the teapot, and if the troopers took her for the servant no one corrected them.

Three cups of tea and most of the cake later Papa came in. He'd been up at the farm when the troopers knocked at the back door and Mama asked them in, and now Mama started guiltily, as though she had done something wrong, but Papa just smiled and sat down at the table.

Papa and the troopers talked of the bushrangers and the weather and politics, none of which Annie knew about or cared about. Their words only became real when Papa nodded at their muskets, leaning against the kitchen wall.

'I used one of those or very like it. May I see?'

The sergeant nodded.

Papa brought the musket to the table, and examined it. 'Cut-off Enfield.'

The sergeant nodded, his mouth full of cake.

'Ours were American muskets.'

The sergeant swallowed. 'When was that, sorr?' (His voice sang like Mama's, but not the same tune. Scottish or Irish maybe.)

'America. The Civil War,' said Papa absently, still examining the Enfield.

'Please,' asked Annie, fascinated, 'what was the Civil War?'

The Sergeant grinned at her, showing his yellow teeth spotted with cake. 'The North fought the South, missy, to free the slaves.' He nodded towards Mama. 'That where you met your missus then?'

'Yes,' said Papa.

'Thought I knew that way of speaking,' said the Sergeant. 'Back when I was searching for the gold, you heard a lot like that.' He lifted his eyebrow at Zanna. 'Brought the darkie back with you, did you?'

Papa hesitated. 'She's my adopted daughter,' he said.

'Adopted, is it?'

The Sergeant looked closely at Papa, then at Mama, as though to compare Zanna's skin to theirs. But Mama and Papa's skin was a pale shade of tan — like all Australians who are ever in the sun — and Zanna's was clearly of a different race than theirs.

The Sergeant nodded again, but warily now. It was clear that — buttermilk cake or not — he mistrusted anyone who adopted a darkie.

'Dumb, is she?' he asked. Annie wasn't sure what he meant, but Papa shook his head. She didn't know what his expression meant. Regret? Embarrassment? Pain ... yes, certainly pain, but for himself or Zanna — or Mama, whose face had the tight blank look it sometimes got — Annie couldn't tell.

'No,' said Papa, as Zanna froze with embarrassment by the stove, 'Susannah can speak. She just doesn't speak very often.'

The troopers left. Ten days later they found their bushrangers, and duly shot two of them and took the third captive, and a week later everything was back to normal.

CHAPTER 27

1872

HEROES

It all made sense to Annie. All fathers are heroes, at least for a time, and hers was a hero too. He had gone to America to fight the slave owners. He met her mother when he was fighting there. Perhaps she soothed his fevered brow when he was wounded (Annie wasn't sure what a fevered brow was, or how you soothed it, but it seemed a necessary activity when women met men near battlefields).

And Zanna ... Zanna had been a rescued slave ...

It was only a coincidence, of course, that Miss Emily should start to read *Uncle Tom's Cabin* to them two weeks later. But children never really believe in coincidence. To Annie it all seemed part of an inevitable pattern.

The afternoon was hot, which was why Miss Emily was reading, instead of scratching on the blackboard with her chalk with the sweat trickling down into her stays. Thunderclouds massed on the horizon and cicadas yelled from the trees. But despite the heat, and the mottled flush of her cheeks, Miss Emily read the words clearly and with all the passion it might never occur to her to give to another person. It was evidently one of her favourite books, and Miss Serena listened as well, as she crocheted an edge around a duster cut down from an old skirt of her sister's. (Miss Frances had one of her sick headaches and had gone to lie down.)

Sarah Feehan put up a hand.

'Yes, Sarah?'

'What are slaves, Miss?'

'Slaves are ... slaves are ... they were poor unfortunates, Sarah, who were bought and sold so they must do what their master says. That's why the Civil War was fought, to free the slaves.'

Annie put up her hand.

'Miss, Miss, my papa went to fight for the slaves, Miss.'

Miss Emily looked at Miss Serena. They would have taken this with a grain of salt — and possibly a few strokes on the hand — if any other child had said it. But they had heard Annie's mother's accent, after Church. They must also have heard the gossip about the mostly invisible Zanna.

'Really, dear?' said Miss Serena, with the studied casualness that adults use to coax information out of children. 'And is that where he met your dear Mama?'

Annie nodded importantly. 'Papa fought for the North. He freed the slaves too! And that's when he met Mama. And Zanna.' She hesitated at this, aware that she was going beyond the crumbs of information Papa had given the troopers, but the way the class was looking at her was too exciting for her to stop. 'Zanna was a slave and Papa rescued her and he ad— adopted ... her and brought her to Australia.' She glanced at Frank, just to make sure he was watching. 'My papa killed hundreds of evil Southerners with his musket. Hundreds and hundreds.'

'Really?' said Miss Serena, weighing this up with what she knew, or guessed. The sisters glanced at each other, storing the discussion for later, over their roast mutton and stewed apple. Miss Emily said, 'That was very interesting, Annie.' And went on reading.

Annie was queen for an afternoon. Janie Taylor offered her a bite of her liquorice. Even lordly Frank gave her a ride back home on his pony, which he hardly ever did now that she was old enough to walk home by herself. Then in the way of children it was all forgotten.

One Saturday afternoon a month later there was a knock on the front door. Papa was in the parlour, re-reading the paper he had brought from town last Tuesday; Mama was darning socks; Zanna was playing knucklebones with Annie and John Roland out in the passage. The bones flew up. Zanna nearly always caught them all in her long-fingered cocoa and cream hands, but Annie couldn't catch more than one … two … three. She was just going for four when the knock sounded.

Mama started and patted her hair, nodded to Zanna to put the kettle on and stir up the firebox in the kitchen stove, and walked down the passageway.

It was Miss Emily.

Miss Emily wore gloves, the lace ones she wore at Church, and her best bonnet and a lace shawl, even though it was so hot Annie had taken her stockings off. (She hoped Mama and Miss Emily didn't notice her bare legs under her skirt.)

Miss Emily sat on the edge of the sofa in the parlour, her back straight and six inches exactly from the back of the sofa, her knees together. Annie sat tucking her skirt around her legs so no one saw her bare ankles above her buttoned boots. There was no sign of Zanna. Although no one — especially not Papa — had ever told her to stay away when they had company, some things do not have to be said aloud, especially to children.

Mama brought the tea in, on a tray covered with a square of cloth she had embroidered with crochet lace around the edges, and teacake, with melting butter and the scones that Zanna had the wit to mix up quickly when she took John Roland to the kitchen.

'How lovely it all is,' said Miss Emily, nodding at the paper flowers in the ginger jars. 'You have quite an artistic hand, Mrs Fitzhenry.'

Mama beamed as though she had been given jewels, and glanced at Papa to see if he had noticed.

Papa looked wary. He sipped his tea. The cup rattled ever so slightly on the thin china saucer. Papa's hand shook often when he had his fevers, so Annie took no notice.

Mama looked ... joyous. She always did when they had visitors, and Annie wished that they came more often. The possessions Mama stroked in the afternoons seemed finally to have a purpose when visitors admired them: the silver candlesticks, the polished mantelpiece, the fan of lyrebird feathers bound together with lace and silver paper.

Miss Emily put down her teacup. She cleared her throat. She hadn't come just to eat Mama's teacake, excellent though it was. 'My sisters and I were wondering,' Miss Emily smiled at Papa, 'if you would possibly consider giving a little talk to our Ladies' Guild next Thursday. All quite informal, of course, a cup of tea afterwards, we would be so grateful ...'

'A talk on what?' asked Papa.

Miss Emily looked startled. 'Why, your experiences in the war, of course! Dear little Annie was telling us all about it.' She tittered lightly. 'So exciting. Did you actually meet any slave owners, Mr Fitzhenry?'

'I beg your pardon?' said Papa.

'In the Civil War. When you were fighting the secessionists. So romantic ... you too, Mrs Fitzhenry, of course. We would love to see you, any Thursday you care to join us.'

'I beg your pardon,' said Papa again. 'There's some mistake.'

'But ...' For the first time Miss Emily sent a wary glance at Annie. 'You mean you didn't fight in the Civil War?'

'Yes, I fought,' said Papa. 'I fought for the South.'

The silence crashed through the room.

Miss Emily picked up her teacup. It was clear she had no idea what to say.

Mama sat there frozen, her hands in her lap. She didn't even offer Miss Emily more teacake, as a more experienced hostess would have done.

Annie wondered what to do. Running out the back door seemed the best solution, then keep running, so she never had to go back to the school.

Miss Emily sipped the last of her tea as the silence deepened, crumbled the rest of her cake, and rose to go. 'Thank you so much for the tea, Mrs Fitzhenry,' she said. 'And please, any time you would care to ...' Her voice died away.

Papa escorted her to her buggy.

By the time he came back Annie was helping Mama with the clearing up, brushing cake crumbs into the dustpan.

'Annie, I'd like to talk to you,' said Papa. 'In my study. Now.'

Annie had never been beaten (that made their family different too, she had discovered at school), but she expected it to happen now.

Papa closed the door.

'Sit down,' he said.

She sat.

'Annie.'

'Yes, Papa?'

'There are some things ...' He looked out the window. His face was pale. 'Some things are hard to explain,' he said at last.

At first she thought he was referring to her crime. Then she realised he was talking about himself.

'I need to explain,' said Papa, 'but not today. One day. Just ... just don't ever mention at school what I tell you. Some things are private, Annie. Only for the family. You understand?'

'Yes, Papa,' she said, though she didn't.

He waved her out of the room.

No one had yelled at her, or punished her. But she was crying so hard she could barely make it to her bedroom.

CHAPTER 28

1873

PAPA EXPLAINS

It took him three weeks. One Saturday, Papa said, 'Come for a walk, Annie.'

Annie glanced at Mama. Mama was washing up, with Zanna drying and Annie putting away, while John Roland had his afternoon nap. 'Don't forget your bonnet,' said Mama. Mama was careful about how much the sun touched her children's skin.

It was dry along the road. The dust smelt of sheep droppings, and horse. It was almost a month since it had last rained. They walked towards the distant town, not towards the farm. Papa was silent for the first half hour, and then he began to talk.

'I was young,' he said.

'My age?' asked Annie.

Papa gave an almost-smile. 'Older than you. But still young. Things seem very simple when you're young. I thought — I thought the Southern cause was right.'

'But how could it be, Papa? The slaves ...'

'It wasn't about the slaves,' said Papa. 'Or it didn't seem so then. It was a war about States' rights. About a way of life. Although it wasn't like that when I got there. No, that isn't true. It was, but there was more.'

None of which made sense to Annie. She tried to head him back to the most important part.

'Papa?'

'Yes?'

'How did you meet Mama? Did she nurse you while you were wounded, like Miss Nightingale?'

'A bit like that,' said Papa finally.

She nodded. 'Was ... was Zanna a slave?'

He hesitated again. She counted six long steps in the dust before he answered. 'Yes. Zanna was a slave. But she's your sister now. You must not mention that she was ever a slave. Things in the past can hurt. You promise, Annie? It's important. Don't mention it to Mama, or Zanna or John Roland. It's a secret between ourselves.'

Annie nodded. She liked the idea of a secret with Papa. It made Zanna more exciting too. A freed slave for a sister.

It wasn't as good as a father who had fought for the North, of course. But it was good enough. Exotic, exciting. The story made sense again. She was too young to think there might be gaps.

'Papa?' she said.

'Yes?'

'What you did was right, wasn't it? All your fighting? Miss Emily was wrong?'

Papa stopped walking. 'No,' he said, 'it wasn't right. It wasn't wrong either. It just wasn't simple, the way I thought it was.'

'But you were right to fight?' Annie was determined to keep her hero father.

Papa was silent. Annie thought he was listening to the lyrebird singing deep in the gully beyond the wattle trees. Finally, he said, 'I thought war was heroic. It isn't, Annie. There are heroes sometimes. But war is simply war.'

He took her hand, and began to walk.

~❧~

No one at school ever mentioned Annie's lies about her father. Perhaps the Misses Taylor weren't sure quite what to make of them. Her father *had* fought in the Civil War, after all. Perhaps they were wiser, and kinder, than Annie gave them credit for; it was, after all, an understandable mistake that Annie had made about which side her father fought for.

She never again mentioned Papa's exploits. Her friends at school forgot about them. Luckily, there were more interesting things to talk about that Monday: a dead rat in the water tank; the brown snake that slid into the girls' dunny at morning tea and was not seen to leave, even though the whole school sat around the dunny and watched for it. Was it hiding in the hole, ready to sink its fangs into their naked bottoms?

At lunchtime Miss Serena ordered the boys to dig another hole; at 3 o'clock the whole school clustered around the dunny and lifted it to its new spot.

By the time school broke up at the end of the year Annie had almost forgotten the embarrassment she'd felt.

Chapter 29

1875

JOHN ROLAND GOES TO SCHOOL

When he was nine years old and Annie ten John Roland was sent to school. A school in Sydney, not the Misses Taylor's house over the hills. Papa had been teaching him every afternoon, proper boy-type subjects like Greek and Latin, as well as his letters, but now he was old enough for a real school, said Papa.

Real schools cost a lot of money, but were worth it, said Papa, for John Roland would learn to be a gentleman, and how to make his living when he was grown up.

'Why can't he have a farm, like Frank?' asked Annie.

Papa smiled. 'Farms cost money,' he said.

'More money than going to a real school?'

'Much more,' said Papa dryly. 'A proper farm does,

anyway.' So it seemed there were real schools and unreal ones, and proper farms and ones that weren't. Annie hoped the Merryweathers' was a proper farm, then felt ashamed of her disloyalty. What farm could be better than the Merryweathers'?

The new school meant uniforms, made for John Roland by Mr Clarence the tailor in town, so Papa had to borrow the Merryweather buggy to take him in for fittings. Bags were packed — dusty leather suitcases fetched down from the top shelf of the linen cupboard.

John Roland shared his gobstoppers with Annie, on the front steps the day before he left.

'Do you want to go?' she asked.

Annie wasn't sure whether she wanted him to or not. He was her brother, and company of a sort, but he always got the parson's nose when Mama fried chicken; with him gone she could have it.

John Roland stretched his legs and inspected his new boots.

'Don't mind,' he said loftily, taking his gobstopper out to inspect it. Gobstoppers changed colour the more you sucked. Annie's had started off green and now it was red, with yellow peeping through.

'Will you write to me?'

Frank had an aunt who wrote to him. She had once sent him a ten shilling note.

'I might,' said John Roland generously. He plopped his gobstopper into his mouth and felt the back of his head. It had been trimmed by the barber in town.

Annie gazed at him. Papa had told her John Roland would be back for holidays, but those were months distant and, besides, a friend might ask him to visit with his family instead of John Roland coming home. Something in Papa's tone told her that this would be desirable.

'I wish girls went to school,' she said.

John Roland ignored this.

'I shall play cricket,' he said.

'Like Frank. Frank plays cricket.'

'Not like Frank. Properly.'

'What's properly?'

'In white trousers. On a proper pitch.'

Annie glared at this disloyalty. 'Frank could have white trousers if he wanted to.'

'No, he couldn't,' said John Roland. 'Frank will never go to a proper school.'

'He could if he wanted to.'

'No, he couldn't,' said John Roland. 'It's an exclusive school. For the sons of gentlemen.' He sounded like he was quoting.

'Is Papa a gentleman then?'

'Of course he is,' said John Roland. 'Frank's father is just a farmer.'

The tone made it an insult, but as Annie could think of nothing better than being a farmer forever, she didn't bother replying.

Mr Merryweather drove his cart down from the farm to take Papa and John Roland to the train the next morning — the Merryweathers' buggy wouldn't hold the three of them and John Roland's suitcases and big chest too.

Somehow, riding to the train in a cart didn't fit with the idea of gentlemen that Annie had read in Papa's books, but she didn't say anything to John Roland. This was partly because she loved him, even when she didn't like him much; mostly because she had decided that, yes, she was going to miss him.

The light was just turning from velvet to dark grey when she heard the clop of the hooves. The lamps were lit in the kitchen, and in John Roland's room as well. Annie ran to the front door and peered out.

'Frank has come too!'

John Roland nodded, as though the larger audience suited his new grandeur. He was a bit white-faced, but otherwise calm.

Annie grabbed the smallest of his bags as an excuse to run to the cart. 'Hello,' she said.

'Hello, young lady,' said Mr Merryweather, as he always did. 'Are you coming along?' Frank just grinned at her.

Annie shook her head.

'There's no room,' said John Roland from behind one end of the large trunk as Papa edged the other end down the stairs.

'Yes, there is,' said Frank unexpectedly. 'She can come if she wants to, can't she, Pa?'

'Of course you can, missy,' said Mr Merryweather.

Annie glanced at Papa.

'You'll need to change,' he said. 'Your bonnet, too.'

She ran.

Mama and Zanna moved in the puddle of lantern light as the horse clopped into darkness, but within five minutes Annie realised it wasn't dark at all, despite the stars still in the sky. The white dust of the road shone ahead, and the trees cast moon shadows, and she was warm between Frank on one side and John Roland on the other, her feet cramped by the trunk and suitcases. Papa and Mr Merryweather, his bottom wide as a potato sack, talked of rain and sheep up front.

This was the third time in her life that she had been into town. It was the first time she had been there in darkness, and seen the islands of light.

Small islands, at first, and not so different from home. Cottage parlours with pianos, lit by candles on the mantelpiece or by a lamp; kitchens with curtains left open for the breeze, the bright sear of red as a stove door was opened to receive kindling to boil the kettle, the inhabitants slowly and sleepily getting ready for the day.

'Look at that cat,' said Frank, and pointed at a cat asleep on a kitchen windowsill.

The houses grew thicker: light, dark, light, dark. The cart rattled through town, its springs complaining of the ruts. Past the Oddfellows Hall, the stores, the new Town Hall, and over the creek, the water darker than the dawn.

'What's that?' Annie whispered, awed, as an even more enormous island loomed closer.

'The Commercial,' said Frank, as though she should know what a Commercial was.

They drew closer. The Commercial was a hotel, the largest, grandest one that Annie could imagine, three storeys high and lit up, the brightest light she'd ever seen, apart from the sun, which didn't count. She expected the sun to be bright.

The Commercial's travellers would be preparing for the train, like John Roland. They would be eating white bread rolls off thick white plates, with silver-plated cutlery and silver pots of tea. At another time, she would see it lit a hundred times brighter, every room streaming light into the street. Even now its light sucked the starlight from above; candlelight from the candelabras in the breakfast room spilt into the gutter, along the wooden footpath.

Annie had never seen such light. She craned her head and watched it as the cart rattled down the street.

The next island was the station, long and low, the light from the Station Master's office lighting the ferns and geraniums in boxes along the front.

They were early. Papa and John Roland and Mr Merryweather carried John Roland's trunk into the office.

'I need a wee,' said John Roland suddenly, displaying his first sign of nerves. He dashed for the station restroom. Frank and Annie stood on the platform, ostensibly to guard the other bags.

'That's where the train comes,' said Frank, pointing along the rails.

'I know,' she said. 'I've seen drawings in the newspaper.' But Frank just grinned.

The sky turned pink and yellow. A rooster crowed and then another. Annie gazed at the rails and wondered if she should show Frank how she could balance on them, but luckily she didn't, because Papa and Mr Merryweather came out to join them, then John Roland returned.

There was noise behind them now. The clop of other horses; Sam neighing; the challenge barking of dogs. More passengers came onto the platform. A small queue grew at the Station Master's bench. A porter came out, yawning, with luggage on a trolley, and she recognised John Roland's trunk.

She peered down the railway line. It all looked far too empty, far too small to ever contain a train. Then a noise grew in the distance, smoke billowed dark into the air and the train was at the station before she had time to appreciate its magnificence, all steam and groans and metal.

Doors were flung open. People scurried everywhere.

'I'll write,' said John Roland, though it wasn't clear if he promised Annie or just the station as a whole.

'You be good for your Mama till we get back,' Papa said to Annie. He and John Roland climbed into a carriage while the train sat there, snorting mildly, and was tended by men in greasy uniforms. Papa waved from the window, then the train drew off, slowly, slowly, then faster.

John Roland leant out of the window, waving wildly. Annie ran along the platform till the train was a small snake in the distance, and John Roland and Papa were gone.

'Well, we'd best be heading back then,' said Mr Merryweather.

Frank sat in front on the way home. Annie hadn't expected that. She sat by herself in the empty back of the cart and watched the houses, less interesting in the morning daylight, and the dogs beginning to explore the day.

The cart dropped her at the gate. Neither Mr Merryweather nor Frank seemed to expect to come in. She wandered back into the empty house and down the hall into the kitchen to tell Zanna all about it.

CHAPTER 30

1875-76

THE QUIET HOUSE

Papa returned from Sydney three days later.

Always, it had been Papa and John Roland studying Latin grammar in the study, with only brief afterthoughts for her. Now she had Papa's full attention.

Life took on new patterns now. Porridge in the morning, the volcanic glug of the pot on the stove, with syrup and cream then scrambled eggs; a lunch packed that was always so superior to every other girl's, she was the Queen for ten minutes every lunch hour — praline cookies, sandwiches with the crust cut off, tongue and mustard, lamb with chutney, almond wafers no thicker than a threepence that melted on your tongue, as though her mother had an unimaginably high standard that must be adhered to.

School, a separate world except for the reminders in

her lunch bag; home to orange cake and telling Zanna all about it. Outside the shadows would thicken in the bush behind the kitchen; the frogs begin to yell under the tank, and Papa would emerge from his study to say, 'I feel like a walk. You coming, Annie?'

Every dusk, almost, he walked; and every time Annie came along. But each time he asked, as though one day it might be different. And each time there was the thrill that an adolescent feels: he has chosen me over Mama.

It was only years later she realised why he walked at dusk. Partly for its coolness; in those years his face was often flushed with fever; he found any extra heat insupportable.

But mostly it was because the hours of a man's work were over. This was the quiet time, the relaxing time, when he need no longer feel self-conscious if a buggy passed or man on horseback, to wonder why a man his age walked instead of worked.

Often they walked in silence, listening to the thud of their footsteps in the dust, the last trill of the cuckoos, the first mopoke song down in the gully.

Once they found an old sheep cast on its side, unable to get up, and Papa righted it; he talked about lambing and the problems of long wet fleece for hours, it seemed. In those years she took it for granted that Papa, who tended no animal except his horse, would know more about sheep even than Frank.

These were the best of times, in Annie's opinion. The slow rhythm of walking, the softness of the shadows, seemed to relax some barrier in Papa. He talked about the pony he'd ridden when he was her age, and a beach where he found bits of coral bleached by a thousand miles of tides. There were just the two of them in the world, at these times, her and Papa.

There was something about walking, the rhythm of it, that made the house behind them disappear. Back there Papa belonged to Mama, to the routine of breakfast, cups of tea and supper, or his secret world in the study where he must not be disturbed. Here there were just the two of them in the universe.

'Papa?'

'Yes.'

'Have you ever met a ghost?'

Papa laughed. 'Not that I know of, Annie.'

'Papa? If you met a ghost, what would you say?'

'Good morning, Sir,' said Papa. 'You must be polite to a ghost.'

'I would ask it what Heaven was like,' decided Annie. 'So I'd know what to expect before I get there. Papa, why are there ghosts?'

Papa frowned. 'I don't know that there are.'

'But there *are* Papa. Johnny Middleton's pa saw one.'

Years later, Annie would remember Papa's whiskers twitch at this, realise he is trying to find a way to say that Johnny Middleton's Pa finds his ghosts at the bottom of bottles of rum. But all he says is 'Did he now?'

'Johnny Middleton says,' persisted Annie, 'that ghosts come when someone's killed. But I think if I was killed I'd want to get away to Heaven not stay where it happened. Papa? Don't you think that is right?'

'I think,' said Papa slowly, and his face was serious now, 'that sometimes a horror can stay with you all your life, so no matter how much you want to you can't get away. So maybe ... maybe it happens after death as well.'

Annie thought about that. 'No,' she decided. 'If I were a ghost I'd only stay for nice things, not horrid ones.'

The whiskers twitched again. 'Good thinking,' said Papa. 'I hope you carry out that philosophy.'

'Yes,' said Annie, and she nodded.

He never talked about the war. But almost, Annie thought, it was as though his memories melded into hers, like the shadows merged with each other as it grew dark, and the war became hers as well.

In those years, too, she realised, she came to think of man as a companion, a habit that would mark her marriage, and contribute not a little to its happiness.

The lamplight would be a shock as they walked through the door, another world of light and smells of mutton fat and furniture polish. The cutlery would gleam on the white cloth Mama put on fresh each night. The cruet would be polished. (Only later would Annie discover that the first time they had eaten in this house Mama had assumed she'd serve Papa and stand back, and eat only when he had finished; that it had taken years to feel at ease sitting at the table with them all.)

They would talk of her day at school, the last letter from John Roland. She took it for granted that her parents had no life that wasn't centred on their children.

Sometimes Papa read aloud to all of them, sitting in the parlour after dinner, articles from the newspapers he bought in town. Other days, when the fever gripped him so that his eyes grew shadowy and his cheeks a hot dry red, he asked Annie to read instead, stories from the dozen or so books kept in his study, smelling of leather and new paper.

When John Roland had been home he and Papa had shared a world from which the rest of the family was excluded; a gentleman's world, which Papa had been part of, and that John Roland would inherit if he did his lessons and learnt his Latin and didn't speak like the farm boys who lived nearby. But now Papa could relax and enjoy his family as they were. Years later, when Annie remembered her childhood, the contentment of those evenings still glowed in her mind.

John Roland didn't write, or not to her alone. He wrote to Papa, letters for the whole family, and Papa read them at the dinner table. 'Dear Papa, I am well ...' Letters obviously copied out from a letter on the blackboard.

But he was lordly enough when he returned for the holidays; skited so much to Frank that even Frank, loyal Frank, refused to take him possum trapping two nights in a row. The third night, though, he forgave him. Annie heard them go yelling down the road and envied them and was angry at them. She was older than John Roland and should have been allowed to go too, even though she was a girl.

This time John Roland made the train journey back to school by himself. Annie considered refusing to go and see him off, but the temptation to see the town was too great. Anyway, he'd taught her to play marbles properly the day before, and had made her a slingshot, even though he said a girl shouldn't use one, so she forgave him.

CHAPTER 31

1877

MEMORIES IN THE NIGHT

She had been asleep. For a moment she didn't know what had woken her. Then she heard it: a shout from the bedroom next door, almost a scream.

The screaming stopped. She heard her mother's voice soothing, and then her father's.

Silence. Now she could see the owl on the branch outside the window. Was it going to catch a mouse? Janie Taylor had seen an owl catch a mouse and rip its head off. Annie was so interested she forgot to go back to sleep. She was drifting off (the owl stubbornly not moving, or disembowelling anything) when she heard footsteps down the hall.

Her father was in the kitchen. Somehow she knew from the texture of the sounds that it was him, and not

Mama. She tiptoed out, to find him sitting at the kitchen table.

He was shivering, although the night was warm, but Annie was used to her father shivering from the recurrent fevers that attacked him. She slipped into a chair beside him, and only then noticed the pan of milk he'd placed on the banked-up stove.

'I heard yelling,' she said at last.

He nodded. Annie wasn't quite sure if he really realised she was there. In some strange way it was like the two of them were still asleep.

'It was the dream again,' he said, as if Annie already knew about the dream. As in some way she did, she realised, remembering other cries that woke her in the night. 'Always the same one. It's the morning before the battle, and everyone knows the way, but I've got lost, I can't find it. Everyone knows the way but me.

'Strange,' said her father, 'you'd think I'd dream of far worse than that, but that's the horror of it, you see. Waiting. Knowing the battle's waiting. Knowing that unless I find the others the battle will never end. I'll wander searching for it forever, while they keep fighting, fighting . . .' His voice shook, and then was silent.

The milk began to rise in the saucepan. Annie stepped over and picked it up. Her father, it seemed, had forgotten it. She dropped cocoa and sugar into a cup, poured in a drop of milk, stirred, added the rest of the milk and handed it to him. He took it absently, and sipped it.

'That's good,' he said, surprised, as though cocoa and hot milk had never occurred to him. 'Thank you, Annie.' He seemed to have noticed her at last.

'Charlie?' It was her mother at the doorway. She hesitated, then said to Annie, 'Go to bed now, girl. You need to sleep for school.'

As Annie left her mother sat in the chair that she'd vacated, silent, waiting for her husband in case he wished to talk.

In the morning when Annie woke up the saucepan and the cup had been washed. Nothing was said about the night.

How do you cope with a grief that can never be mentioned? Dreams are the only outlet, and the long evening walks towards nothing at all.

Sometimes it seemed to her that she had two fathers, the one behind the study door, the one who screamed at night, and the polite friendly one who sat at the dinner table, whom her mother watched with careful apprehension.

What was war, anyway? It was difficult to imagine. The school readers made it sound like the heroes just stood there and the enemy were 'vanquished', whatever that might mean. Disappearing, most like, into a sort of dew, while the heroes 'took the field'. To Annie's ears that sounded like a picnic; the heroes galloped onto the field where the enemy had been, and spread their blankets and took out their baskets and helped each other to raspberry vinegar and rock cakes and egg and bacon pie.

Somehow from the look on Papa's face it hadn't been like that at all. The only conflict Annie had ever really seen was in the hen yard, two roosters savaging it out, or the Merryweathers' dogs after a bitch. But surely that dust and barking had nothing to do with war. War was glorious. It had to have been glorious, to have attracted her Papa.

CHAPTER 32

1878

DINNER AT THE COMMERCIAL

So life went on.

Frank Merryweather left school. He and his pony no longer made the journey every day, but somehow the way over the hills had become shorter, and Annie didn't mind the walk.

John Roland came home for holidays, and then went back to school. Mrs Merryweather visited, as she had every day or so throughout Annie's life. Annie progressed to Miss Serena's class.

When he was ten John Roland's weekly letter informed them that he would visit a friend in the next holidays, instead of coming home. The friend's family property had horses, tennis parties, cricket ...

Mama cried a little over the washing up. Papa looked

pleased, as though his son's world was expanding while his shrank.

Annie wasn't sure what to think. She missed her brother vaguely, when she thought about it, but his absence meant more attention for her. Besides, her life was more exciting than it had ever been.

Annie now had friends, more important to her than a brother, or Frank Merryweather, who after all was a boy. Sarah Greenwood, Mary Henderson, Jane ...

Papa bought a buggy. The Fitzhenrys no longer rode to Church with the Merryweathers. Then, for Annie's thirteenth birthday her father took her to dinner at the Commercial Hotel.

She wore a new dress, bought from a Sydney catalogue. Unlike her friends' mothers, Mama had no knowledge of sewing, apart from rudimentary darning and the embroidery she'd taught herself from the ladies pages in the newspaper.

Annie wore gloves and a blue hair ribbon, and her first pair of evening slippers. The buggy set off in daylight but the sky was fading as they passed the first houses of town and, by the time they reached the hotel, it was as she had first seen it — an island of light, brighter than ever.

The town had other hotels, of course. The hotel by the railway station for the accommodation and refreshment of less affluent travellers, and hotels where you'd go to attend land auctions, or for singing, dancing, fighting or whores.

The Commercial was different. The Commercial was the place for Saturday night dining, for balls and celebrations. It had the only dance floor in town, so highly waxed that dancing slippers could glide across it, a hotel that burnt wax candles every night of the week.

Papa pulled on Traveller's reins. Some instinct made Annie keep her seat, until an ostler took her hand to help her down then took Papa's place in the buggy.

'Where's he taking it?' she whispered.

'To the stables.' Papa placed her hand on his arm and they walked up the steps into the hotel's embrace.

Annie gazed around and tried to disguise the fact that she was gazing. Women in dresses cut so low that she could see their ... she wasn't sure of the polite word to call them. Surely not the name the boys said in the school grounds.

The women looked glossy, as if they had been groomed by the ostlers before being allowed to take their places in the yellow ponds of light. For a moment she thought she could smell flowers, then realised it was perfume, that sudden flush of perfume as a woman enters a room hot with candlelight.

The waiters served them onion soup from fat tureens. It wasn't as good as Mama's onion soup. A thin film of fat floated on top, which Mama would have mopped off with a slice of stale bread.

Then fish on a silver platter, and the long and shining roasts wheeled in on trolleys with men wearing gloves to serve them, and she had roast beef for the first time in her life. When Mama bought meat from the butchers, it was pork or chicken, and the meat that Mr Merryweather brought down from the farm was always mutton, bloody in its hessian bag.

The starched napkins were stiff as cardboard; the waitresses had tall caps and black ankles; the silver candelabras glittered brighter than the light they held and the shadows flickered dark under the tables.

Later, there was a plate of fruit, gleaming as if they were wax, not real — oranges and deep red apples. A plate of dates and marzipan and raisins, nuts and sugared cherries. Laughter flew like swallows winging across the room.

It was the closest Annie had ever been to paradise; the closest she had ever felt to her father. This was even better than the walks along the road.

Had Papa's home been like this? she wondered. From the scattered references Papa had made about his childhood, on their walks, she knew that his youth hadn't been spent in a small wooden house.

Papa poured a trickle of white wine into her glass. She sipped it and felt the room buzz.

'Papa?'

'Yes?'

'Why don't you go home again?'

For a moment he didn't understand. 'We will go home. After dinner.'

'I mean to your other home. The one where you grew up.'

Her father put down his wineglass. 'I ... quarrelled with my father, Annie.'

'Can't you say you're sorry?'

Her father stared at something that wasn't there. 'I have. I am sorry. More sorry than I can ever say.'

'But why then?'

'Because ...' For a moment Annie was sure he wasn't going to tell her anything. But he did; after all, he had no one else to tell. 'Because what I did was unforgivable.'

'What was it?'

'I married your mother,' said Papa, and gestured for the bill.

The dust clouded the spokes of the buggy, pale in the moonlight, as they drove home. Papa was silent. So was Annie.

What was it that made Mama unacceptable to Papa's family? Young though she was, Annie had read enough and heard enough to know the basic reasons why some women were unsuitable to be made wives.

Religion was the first. Mr McDonald wouldn't even speak to his son, who had married what he referred to as 'a harlot of Rome' and Papa called a 'Roman Catholic'.

But Mama came to Church with them, the same Church as the Fergusons, who were wealthy and respectable.

Her foreignness? But Papa's great-uncle was an American. Surely there was nothing wrong there.

It must be because she had no fortune, Annie decided, just like in the penny novels Jane's mother read and she and Jane borrowed when Jane's mother was out. Papa's father had wanted Papa to marry a rich woman, maybe one who owned the property next door. Mama was poor, but proud, and Papa fell in love with her when she nursed him in the war and so he married her . . .

It made a satisfactory romance — well, almost. Parents aren't the best of romantic figures, but at least it had all happened a long time ago.

The buggy drew up outside their gate. The house was dark, except for a lantern hung on the gatepost and the yellow light of another lantern shining from the kitchen.

'In you go,' said Papa. 'I'll give Traveller a brush down before I come in.'

Annie handed him the lantern. 'Papa?'

'Yes.'

'You love Mama, don't you?'

She was more drunk on moonlight than the few sips of wine she had had at the hotel. She almost expected Papa to begin a novel-like protestation about how he gloried in every tress of Mama's hair.

But instead he seemed to think about it. 'Yes,' he said at last. 'I love your Mama, Annie. Now go inside.'

She was thirteen years old that birthday. Looking back, it was the last day of her childhood.

CHAPTER 33

1878

RETURN

The noise woke her from dreaming of clouds of budgerigars smothering the trees. She'd always hated budgerigars; was glad the flocks of shrieking birds only visited the district occasionally when the lands out west were dry. There were so many of them, and what if they decided to land on your head and suffocate you?

The budgerigars faded, but the noise remained. It was a strange noise; almost like an exhausted dog, a wuffling, panting noise.

Annie pushed off her sheet and pulled her nightdress down respectably and peered out the window.

She expected to see a lost dog, lifting its leg on their fence post. But there was nothing there.

She was fully awake now. The noise came from the

porch. The wood floor was cold under her toes. She opened the front door a crack.

It was John Roland.

He lay against the steps. At first Annie thought he was sick, even dying. He breathed in soft gasping pants, like the dog she had thought he was. But then he saw her and sat up and she realised he wasn't sick; he had simply been running, or staggering. His face had the bone-staring glaze of exhaustion.

'Johnny!' she said. She'd never called him that before — always John Roland — but that's what everyone called the Johns at school. Johnny. And that was the word that came from her lips.

He stared at her. She wasn't even sure he saw her, just the open door. He pushed himself up and she saw his boots were scratched and dusty and there was crusted blood about his nose.

'What's wrong?' she cried.

He didn't answer. He pushed past her into the house. She automatically looked for his baggage, but there was none, and as sleep finally cleared from her head she realised he had walked — or run — all the way from the midnight train.

She turned and watched him walk down the corridor to the kitchen. With every step he banged his hands against the wall, *bang, bang, bang*, making whimpering noises at the same time.

Someone murmured in her parents' room. The door opened. Mama looked out, her lace cap over her hair.

'John Roland!' she cried and held her arms out to him.

At this her brother stopped. He stared at Mama, as if she was a snail on Mr Merryweather's cabbages, like a dog baring its teeth about to fight. 'Get away!' he screamed.

Mama took a step back. Papa was there suddenly, fastening the cord of his dressing gown. 'Son! What is it?'

'Don't let her touch me!' John Roland backed down the corridor, as Zanna appeared in the kitchen. John Roland shrank from her as well. 'Go away! Go away from me!'

'Don't speak to your mother like that ...' began Papa, then stopped. He looked at Mama.

'Go back inside and dress,' he said quietly.

'But, Charlie —'

'Go back inside.' Papa nodded at Annie. 'You too.'

Annie stepped into her room. But she didn't shut the door and, as Papa moved down the corridor, she followed him.

Zanna clung to the doorjamb of her room off the kitchen. She looked at Annie and held her arms out, as though Annie was still the baby she cared for. Annie ran to her and felt her arms around her.

Neither their father nor their brother noticed them.

John Roland's face was red, or white; or was it drained of colour? Annie had never seen a face in so much pain as he stared at his father.

'Why didn't you tell me my mother was a nigger?' he screamed.

And then he sobbed.

--✻○

Annie could never quite remember what happened after that.

She remembered John Roland sobbing, Papa clasping him so hard it seemed his bones might break. She thought Papa was crying too, but she couldn't bear to look, so she helped Zanna light the stove, then took the kettle out to the tank to fill it.

When she brought it back into the kitchen Mama was there, still in her nightdress, not looking at Papa or her son; so carefully not looking, making scrambled eggs in the skillet and frying ham.

Annie made the tea; poured it; put a cup for Papa on the table and one for her brother. Mama's face was blank, as if any emotion would crack it irreparably. She put the eggs and ham on a plate and touched her husband's shoulder.

'Make him eat,' she said. Then she took Annie's hand, and Zanna's, and led them out of the house and down the road in their bare feet and their nightgowns.

She didn't speak. Nor did Annie. There was only one word in her head, over and over: nigger, nigger, nigger.

But that was impossible. Mama's skin was white. Her own skin was white. If Mama were a nigger her skin would be brown, like Zanna's ... like her sister's ...

Annie looked at Zanna, and for the first time saw beyond the colour of her skin, saw the shape of her face, the mouth, the chin just like Mama's, like hers ...

For the first time Annie realised that Zanna was truly her sister.

It was the most momentous moment in her life, and totally ignored; the three of them just kept walking, walking, walking. Zanna didn't even look at her, this new real sister she had suddenly discovered. She just kept shooting glances at Mama, her face holding the same blankness that Mama's held at times. As Mama's was blank now.

Did Zanna know that Mama truly was her mother? Did she know the blackness in them all? Tell me, Annie wanted to scream. Tell me what you know! But somehow she knew that Zanna's silence would be absolute if Annie asked her.

They were almost at the turnoff to the Merryweather house — and Annie was just starting to worry that someone might see them, ask why they were wandering in their nightwear and bare feet — when Mama turned, still without speaking, and they headed back.

The sun was rising and was now shining in their eyes. It was an excuse for them to water. It felt good to be able to cry, thought Annie, without admitting what she was crying about.

The girls followed Mama into the house. There was no sign of John Roland. Papa sat at the kitchen table, staring at the cold cup of tea in his hand. He looked up at them.

'He's sleeping,' was all he said.

'That's good,' said Mama, in the nightgown dusty at the hem. 'That boy needs sleep.' Or some such. Her accent was stronger than Annie had ever heard it this morning. She nodded to Zanna. 'You be going on with the vegetables for lunch, you hear. And you,' to Annie, 'you be getting ready for school. See, it nearly seven o'clock and you not ready yet.'

Annie had never heard her speak that way, the accent and rhythms so strange. Papa didn't seem to notice. He just sat there with his cup of tea.

Zanna fled out the back door to the vegetable garden. Annie went to her bedroom. She dressed, throwing the dusty nightdress in a corner. She wanted to trample it, as though it had caused all the trouble. She gathered up her satchel. She went to school. The morning passed.

When she came home Papa was packing up to leave.

CHAPTER 34

1878

ACCUSATION

No one ever explained to Annie what had happened to John Roland. Maybe she just absorbed the story from the air like children seem to do.

It was simple enough: a new boy had arrived at school. In his letter home one week he had mentioned his new friend, John Roland Fitzhenry.

The boy's parents knew a Fitzhenry family. Naturally enough they asked if John Roland was related to the family they knew. Their son asked John Roland what his father's name was, and John Roland replied.

The parents had heard of Charles Fitzhenry. He had married a Negro slave when he deserted the Confederate Army in America, and had brought her home to Australia, where his family, quite rightly, had nothing more to do with them. It was enough to have the word spat at John Roland during prep: 'Nigger boy! How dare you show your nigger face in here?'

It was a monstrous allegation, but John Roland believed it. He already knew his family was different. Every other boy that John Roland knew had uncles, aunts, a history, not an emptiness that no one mentioned. And there was Zanna too.

John Roland stole away from school that night. He wandered Sydney weeping for a day and night, then caught the next day's train, to walk, run, stagger his way back home to cast his accusation at his father.

CHAPTER 35

1878

CHARLES FITZHENRY LEAVES
HIS WIFE AND DAUGHTERS

Annie was thirteen when her father left, though she didn't know then that he was leaving them.

She spent the morning of John Roland's return at school. Somehow the shock of his return, and her parents' reactions, had all shrunk down to the word 'nigger'.

She knew what 'nigger' meant. 'Nigger' meant black, but a certain type of black — not Aboriginal black or Maori black (there was a Maori family in town — the father had come in the gold rush). It meant American black. Zanna's black.

Mama was American, but she wasn't black, but even at thirteen Annie knew that colour can fade in a generation. She had heard the schoolyard legends of the black mother of a white baby who turned black overnight when she was twenty-one; of the white mother who gave birth to a black baby because her great-grandmother had been Aboriginal and 'colour comes out in the end'. (Annie was too innocent to think of the more likely explanation for the unexpectedly dark baby.)

According to Joey Ferguson you could always tell if there was black in your family. Your palms would be lighter than the backs of your hands. (They had all checked their palms. According to that test they were all black, so then Joey said it was a different sort of pinkness in the palm that showed how black you really were.)

Joey had said you could tell by the legs too, Annie remembered. Blacks have skinny legs. If the tops of your legs were as skinny as above your ankles, then you were black for sure.

Annie tried to feel her legs under her skirt, but the desk got in the way. She put up her hand. 'Miss!'

'Yes, Annie?'

'Can I go out the back, Miss?'

A weary nod.

She fled out the cottage door, round past the laundry, down to the dunny, shut the door and held up her skirts in the darkness. They bunched up too much to see her legs, especially with her petticoat, so she gathered the material and twisted it behind her, then looked down.

Her legs weren't skinny. They were quite plump, in fact, from butter cake and Mama's pineapple fritters and the buttermilk biscuits with strawberry butter that were like scones but better. It was too dark to tell whether the tops were much fatter than the calves.

Did Zanna have skinny legs? Annie tried to picture Zanna on bath night. Surely Zanna's legs were much like hers.

She let her skirts fall and sat on the dunny lid to think.

Suppose Mama was a nigger. Would that mean if Annie had a baby it might be black? How could she marry any man and let that happen?

How could any man understand that Zanna was black and the kindest, cleverest person Annie had ever known? Zanna could make a crow come alive on the page, a cow that was so cowlike it didn't need to moo. But a black baby ...

It couldn't happen often, could it? If it did, then John Roland and she would be black, like Zanna.

She thought of more things, sitting there in the hot, smelly dark, but the main ones kept floating over and over in her head. She might have a black baby, and she didn't know who her Mama was at all.

Annie waited in the dunny till she heard the yells that meant it was lunchtime, then slowly walked over to the kitchen, where the Taylor sisters were sitting with their cups of tea and cold sliced mutton and chutney. She knocked on the doorjamb. 'Please, Miss?'

'Yes, Annie?' said Miss Serena.

'Please, Miss, I'm not feeling well. Can I go home?'

Miss Serena looked at Annie carefully. But no doubt she was pale enough and, besides, she'd never wagged school before. 'Certainly, Annie. Do you feel well enough to walk home or would you like me to send one of the boys to fetch your father? Or,' reluctantly, 'my sister could hitch up the buggy if you like.'

Annie shook her head. Miss Serena looked relieved. 'Off you go then,' she said.

She took the shortcut over the hills, as she always did; it took almost two hours to walk to the school by road. As she walked up the gully from the creek below the house she could see John Roland with Traveller, giving him a can of oats.

She climbed the steps into the house. Her parents' bedroom door was open. Papa knelt on the floor, packing clothes into a carpetbag.

Despite the clothes in the carpetbag, and the tin of oats he'd asked John Roland to feed to Traveller, Annie assumed her father was simply packing to take John Roland down to Sydney; to pick up his clothes, to find him a new school, perhaps, where no one knew the name Fitzhenry.

She didn't know he planned to head north, not south. The further north he and John Roland travelled, the further they'd be from anyone who knew the Fitzhenrys. There was also the fact, though she only realised it years later, that her father was tired of idleness. He had finally regained his strength after his illness in America. Up north, where labour was scarce, he could find a farm manager's or overseer's job in the new lands opening up in Queensland.

She wanted to stand there by the bedroom door and scream at him, 'Am I going to have a black baby, Papa?', but something about the silence in the house was too oppressive, so she didn't speak at all.

She walked down the corridor to the kitchen instead. Zanna stirred a pot of Irish stew on the stove, made from the mutton chops that Mr Merryweather had brought down the day before. Zanna glanced up and smiled. It was the sort of smile she'd given Annie when she was small and had fallen and scraped her elbows. It meant: No, things aren't all right, are they, but I'm here and I'll comfort you.

Mama stood at the table kneading bread, though it wasn't her breadmaking day, pummelling the dough over and over, as though to rid herself of words that couldn't be said.

'There's cake in the tin,' said Mama, as she said every afternoon when Annie came home from school. Mama didn't even seem to notice she was home early.

Annie didn't want the cake, but she cut a slice of pound cake, which Mama always made with cream cheese as well as butter. (In years to come Annie would make that recipe at least once a month. It made the best textured and moistest pound cake she ever ate.)

This afternoon though it wasn't tasted at all. Annie sat crumbling the cake while Mama pounded and Zanna stirred, until John Roland came in.

His eyes were still shadowed, but he had washed and changed into a shirt of Papa's (Annie hadn't realised how much he'd grown). He nodded to Annie, ignored Mama and Zanna, and went down the corridor to his bedroom.

He hadn't much there — a few shirts, and old trousers good enough for going shooting with Frank Merryweather, but not to take to school. Later Annie discovered he had also packed the books from his mantelpiece.

The front door opened. Mama left her bread dough and hurried down the corridor. Her voice came from the porch. Her voice had a pleading tone Annie had never heard before.

'At least wait until tomorrow. It'll be dark soon.'

Papa said something, too low to hear. Annie glanced at Zanna. Zanna took the pot off the stove and rested it on a board on the bench with a towel over it to keep off the flies as it cooled, and took Annie's hand as they ran down the corridor, just as she had when Annie was small. By the time they reached the porch Mama and Papa were standing by the buggy. John Roland was high up on the seat with his bag beside him, while Traveller swished his tail and his tongue searched for the last of his oats around his teeth.

Another two carpetbags lay on the tray below the seat.

'At least take some food,' pleaded Mama, wringing her hands in the folds of her skirt.

Papa shook his head. 'We'll stay in town the night. That way we'll get an early start.'

For a moment Annie thought he meant that he and John Roland were catching the early morning train, which meant the buggy and Traveller would be left at the Station Hotel, to be collected when Papa returned. But then Papa said, 'I'll write. As soon as we're settled somewhere, I'll let you know.'

She would never forget the way her father looked at her mother then. He looked at her as if she were a stranger, as well as his wife. It was a helpless look.

And Mama? Mama just stood there, slim and dark haired, hiding her anguished hands in her skirts. Mama never seemed to expect anything in those years, not in daylight at any rate. She took what Papa offered and never asked for more.

Annie wanted her to scream. She wanted her to yell, 'Don't go away. How dare you go!'

Annie wanted to scream too, but on that day she didn't know her mother's story. She just knew that whatever her mother was or had done, Annie was her daughter. Annie was 'nigger' too, and that's why Papa was leaving her.

A nigger could demand nothing.

Papa kissed Annie, hesitated, then kissed Mama on the cheek, not on the lips. Mama gazed at John Roland. Annie crushed Zanna's hand at the agony in Mama's eyes, staring at her son.

But John Roland just sat there in the buggy seat. He

didn't move to kiss Mama, or Annie or Zanna either. By then shock and sleeplessness had left him almost unaware of where he was, or who he was with. (In later years Annie wondered if he might have kissed Mama if he had known what was to come.)

Zanna stood with Annie's hand in hers and watched, as she'd watched birthdays, Christmases, all the celebrations she'd never really shared. She never spoke at all.

Papa cleared his throat, seeming desperate to say something, but the words that couldn't be said were too heavy on his tongue.

'The chimney in the kitchen needs sweeping,' he said at last. 'You'd best get Kenny Hooper. Phil Merryweather'll see you right with him.'

Mama nodded. The dark hair slid over her face. She tore her gaze from John Roland and looked at Papa.

'Billy Toogood'll be up to do the wood on Tuesday. The bank draft is due next week. Bishop at the bank will see to it. I'll have a word with him tomorrow before we leave.'

Mama nodded again. Papa searched for something else to say to her. Was this was all he had to give to her, these last pieces of advice? He shook his head and turned to Annie instead. 'You be good for your mother now,' he said.

Annie nodded.

'It's not ...' began Papa, then stopped. 'I can't be living in idleness,' he said to Mama. 'You know that, Caroline.'

Annie waited for him to say he'd send for them, wherever he was going. But he didn't.

He bent and kissed Annie, hesitated, finally kissed Zanna, and then Mama once more.

Annie watched him step into the buggy, shake the reins. Traveller broke into a trot.

Neither Papa nor John Roland looked back.

CHAPTER 36

1878

ANNIE WONDERS

In the years after that Annie often wondered why Papa only took John Roland with him, and not her.

For a while she assumed he liked John Roland best and, anyway, sons were more important, everyone knew that. Later she tried to pretend that John Roland had been hurt more than she had, so Papa had to take him away before he was hurt some more.

It was only as an adult she accepted that her father had done a reasonably sensible thing. If the secret of her mother's past became known in the district, it wouldn't hurt Annie's marriage prospects; she was obviously destined to be a local farmer's wife, none of whom would worry overmuch about a faint touch of tarbrush in her ancestry. She'd even take her husband's name. In another six years, or ten perhaps, she'd no longer be a

Fitzhenry. Her parents' history could no longer shame her.

John Roland, though, would have to make his own career. The monthly cheques would cease on Charles' death, though there might be a small pension for his wife.

John Roland needed better schooling than he'd get with the Misses Taylor. This meant a town, and Sydney was now out of the question.

Perhaps her father also reasoned that a girl needs a mother more than a boy does. Annie would be happier at home than in a boarding school, or keeping house for him wherever he ended up. Which, she supposed, was true enough.

It still hurt, though, even when she was an old woman, when she remembered her father driving off in the buggy with her brother, leaving her behind.

CHAPTER 37

1878

CARRIE (4)

Caroline wandered round the house. Her skirts swished as they brushed against the doors. She had always longed for swishing skirts, skirts that shone with starch, petticoats that rustled. Later she would go to the kitchen; start serving out the stew, start talking to the girls about something, anything, just so it would seem that life went on, though a portion of her life was broken. It was as if the wind was flattened out of her. She hoped that by the time the stew was ready her breath would have come back.

The bed was empty; the four poster she had polished every Wednesday. There would be his smell on the pillow; the stains on the sheets from the night before, when it still seemed that the life she'd claimed might go on forever. But she'd got no time for symbols. She would just scrub the stains all the harder in the wash.

She touched her garnet brooch, a photo in a silver frame and a cut-glass vase on the mantelpiece.

He was her first possession.

Now he'd gone.

He had said he would be back. Somehow, the stating of it implied the opposite, and they both knew he might not be; that she and the girls were to stay in the wooden house, not follow after him as any other family did.

She wished she had known how to plead with him not to leave. She wished she could have pinned him with her body to the sheets she'd ironed and starched and hung by the stove for an hour to freshen.

She had thought that in the past two years, learning to talk — both of them — sitting by the whispering stove, he had finally started to be hers.

She wondered now if that was why he left.

No one ate the stew, though the three females pushed it round their plates. Mama washed up and Annie dried, then Zanna read to her on the back steps, as she had when Annie was a baby. Zanna was kind to Annie that night.

Zanna knew what John Roland and Annie were feeling. Zanna had known it all her life.

Later that night, after Annie had gone to bed, she

heard Mama in the parlour. She slid out of bed and peered through the door.

Mama hadn't undressed. She drifted across the parlour, back and forth. Her long fingers touched things: the garnet brooch on her dress that Papa had given her last Christmas; the photo in a silver frame; the cut-glass vase that perched on the mantelpiece. Mama had always touched things. But now it was as though she touched them to remember rather than to reassure.

Later Annie heard Mama crying in the quiet night.

Annie told the Misses Taylor that Papa had gone to Queensland to work, which was true, as far as it went. At least it was the Queen's land, she thought. The Queen would look after Papa there.

Annie didn't mention John Roland. If the Misses Taylor assumed he was still at boarding school, she let them.

It was strange, suddenly knowing that Zanna was really her sister, not adopted at all, but it was good. She and Zanna belonged together now.

It was out in the vegetable garden, pulling up carrots and picking rhubarb for dinner, that Annie finally asked Zanna, 'What do you remember?'

Zanna sat back on her heels, the rhubarb stems held in her apron. 'You mean back then?'

Annie nodded.

Zanna seemed to look far away. 'A kitchen. Black faces. Walking, always walking. Being hungry.'

'You knew you were a slave? And Mama, too?'

'Oh, yes,' said Zanna, and her voice was like Mama's. 'I surely knew.'

'You never said,' said Annie stupidly.

Zanna was silent. Then she said, 'It's like a game, is all. You know the rules, even if no one ever says. Specially if no one says. It's all fine as long as you obey the rules. Keep on smiling, keep doing what you're told.'

'Is that what it's like to be a slave?'

'I don't know,' said Zanna. 'I was so young, you know. I don't remember slavery much. I meant now.'

'But you're not a slave now.' All at once Annie was aware of all that Zanna had never had: the gobstoppers, the visits into town, school, the stories read just for her at night.

And suddenly Zanna looked freer than Annie had ever seen her, as if a cage had been lifted with Papa's departure.

'Maybe not,' she said. 'Not now.'

⁓❀⦿

These days no boots dried by the stove, no shaving brushes stood in the mug in the laundry. There were no silver-backed hairbrushes on the toilet table in Mama's room, only Mama's brush, in tortoiseshell, a gift in a velvet box the Christmas before last.

John Roland's room, the house's second best bedroom, remained untouched, the door kept permanently shut. Mama was the only one who cleaned it. Sometimes Annie heard her crying in there.

Things changed with Papa gone, but though Annie missed her father desperately, to her surprise they were good changes, not bad.

In many ways their household was more normal now than it had ever been. Many families had a father droving, shearing, hunting the last of the gold. It had been Annie's father — not her mother, or even Zanna — that made the family different; his accent, the unconscious way he bore himself all called 'here is a gentleman'. He wasn't even a drunk, which would have explained his flight from his own class.

Now he was gone, and to Annie's friends there was nothing but interesting exoticness in her mother's accent, especially given the quality of the cakes that always waited for afternoon tea, and the fact that Annie's mother never questioned anything they did, but smiled as they sprawled on counterpanes, tried on her corsets and stuffed handkerchiefs into the cups, as though every aspect of her daughter's friends made her happy.

And Zanna? It wasn't unknown for households to have a young black servant who had almost become one of the family, but never quite, of course. And though Annie spoke of Zanna as 'my sister', which was going perhaps a bit too far, it wasn't as though she expected them to invite Zanna to their houses too.

They started to have visitors. The first, of course, was Mrs Merryweather, who seemed to have smelt on the wind that Papa had gone (or, more likely, one of the farm workers who lived in town passed on the gossip that the buggy had been seen heading north).

Mrs Merryweather had never been comfortable with Papa, with his white hands and upper-class voice. But Mama had always been her pet. Now, for the first time, it became a friendship of equals.

Instead of Mrs Merryweather always driving down to them, the Fitzhenrys now visited the Merryweather farm, strolling up the road for Saturday lunch, or Sunday lunch after Church. Zanna came to the farm as well, and sat at the table in spite of her dark skin.

At the Merryweather table everyone sat together, including Billy Zachary, the fencer who had black skin. (Lily had married years ago, and the Campbell's Agnes had taken her place.) Everyone ate in the kitchen at the farm — the dining room stayed neat and empty except for Christmas time and funerals.

Zanna now came to Church as well. They sat with the Merryweathers, so everyone who wanted to gossip with Mrs Merryweather had to talk to Zanna too.

Mama grieved for Papa and her son, but she seemed freer. She laughed more loudly, spoke more carelessly. Annie began to realise that when Papa had been home Mama had considered every action, every word. She had tried to imitate an upper-class wife for Papa.

Now, in their community of farmers, tradespeople, ex-convicts — few, if any, of whom had a totally respectable background (there were even rumours about a touch of the tarbrush in the Fergusons; how old Mr Ferguson's Ma, back when the family first got their land grant, had been a half-caste) — she was able to be herself or find out, at last, who that self might be.

Once she even danced around the kitchen to the beat of a lyrebird call out the window and laughed when her daughters stared at her, then made them join in, holding their hands and jigging them around the table.

With Papa gone Mama began to talk to her daughters, as she showed them how to feed the yeast in its old chipped cup on the windowsill, how to clean the silver spoons that had been dipped in soft-boiled egg and tarnished. Though Zanna still rarely spoke, she listened, as Mama's stories fed her memories.

Mama never spoke of slavery, at least not by using the word outright, but with Papa gone she could claim her past, instead of trying to pretend it had never been. And besides, it was safe enough to tell those stories now. She knew both daughters had learnt too well that some things were not to be mentioned beyond the kitchen door.

Slowly, Annie began to piece together her mother's story, and Zanna's and Papa's, in those conversations around the kitchen table. Stories of Drusilla as she learnt how to roll pastry; tales of Miz Elizabeth as she stirred the pot for pickles; the memories of the journey north as she and Mama and Zanna rubbed the skins off the walnuts to make Drusilla's pounded pepper sauce. Stories that came from so far away they didn't seem to hurt anyone, except at night when Annie heard a whisper through the darkness, 'black baby, black baby, black baby . . .'

There were other visitors, not just the Merryweathers. The bank manager, who made a special visit with his wife to explain the new banking procedures to Mama, and every month after that the chief clerk visited to bring them cash, until eventually Mrs Merryweather showed Mama how to handle the Merryweathers' buggy.

The instant freedom delighted her, and after another three months of bank drafts Mama bought a buggy of her own (or rather, Mr Merryweather bought it for her) and a poor sad horse called Billy Bob (well, he's quiet at least, said Mr Merryweather), who managed to pull the buggy to town and back, or up to the Merryweathers' farm, where he'd stand swishing his tail sadly as though it had all been too much for him.

Now that the household had a horse and buggy — and the garden growing into weeds and a new hole needed for the dunny — they could afford more help. Old Mr Griffith came two afternoons a week to do the necessary, and after Mama discovered that she could pay another human and manage to give him orders, she finally agreed to have help in the house.

On Mondays, Ethel came to do the washing. Ethel was nearly toothless; she dipped the bread into her tea at dinner time and refused meat. Her hands were as pleated as tripe, her arms long enough to fold a sheet by herself.

On Wednesdays one of the O'Reilly girls came to do the ironing — Mama's standards were always of the house she had grown up in, where every camisole ribbon had to be starched and ironed — and on Friday to polish the house for the weekend.

Caroline had never handled money; but in this she was in good company; many girls, women, wives of a certain class rarely handled money; household, even dressmaker's bills were settled by their husbands. Even Mrs Merryweather only laid down who was to be paid what, and didn't handle the coin herself; what she needed Phil bought, or Frank.

Caroline had never made a major decision in her life, apart from lying with Ezekiel, and leaving Cousin Elizabeth's. Where they lived, how they lived, except in details of praline cake or orange tea bread, and even then she deferred to him ... was a matter for her husband, and while this too was not so unusual the reason for it was: in so many things she had no idea of what was usual at all.

Or hadn't. She'd learnt, of course, over the years, even in the relative seclusion of their family. And now she was to find out how much she knew.

Decisions, she found, were addictive. The power to evaluate, to say, we will do this ... she liked it. Today I will not plant zinnias, but a camellia bush; would I care to go to the concert next week? Certainly. A tennis party after Church ...

She hesitated about that. She had never learnt to play tennis; had never even seen it played on the court next to the Church; they always left after the service, before the picnic and the tennis games so precious to families who only travelled from their farms once a week to Church, except for sale days.

But now she stayed, she watched; her daughter coached her at home, and finally a triumph, she played a tennis match. Not well, admittedly; but enough to feel the sun upon her face and laugh as she fluffed a shot, and finally to know that she was free.

Mrs Merryweather persuaded Mama to join the Church choir. It seemed Mama had a 'voice', once she gained the courage to bellow properly. She had always sung lullabies, or in the kitchen, in an almost-whisper.

Ladies called for afternoon tea, and Cathleen O'Reilly would serve the coffee cake, the beignets dusted with icing sugar, the ladyfinger biscuits, while Mama sat there flushed and ladylike. Her Americanness was feted nowadays, as she gave recipes for blackberry cobbler, butter-oatmeal cookies, mint juleps in the summer and tea punch.

And suddenly she found herself arguing about the post-prayer meeting supper: *not* tomato sandwiches, as they always went soggy, and they must have something savoury as well as cakes. Egg and bacon pie, perhaps, or devilled eggs; no, not lamb sandwiches with chutney, you know how the flies get to the cold meat and in a sandwich there might always be that nasty wriggling surprise ...

And ladies who had had fathers and grandfathers — real ones, not just a transfer of seed — who had never worn a pass around their necks or wondered where their baby might be sold, they did what Mama said, as though she had every right to say what should be done. Mama's accent was educated, her dress was good, the family had independent means, and besides, no one made an orange cake as moist as Mama's, with sugared walnuts on the top.

Mama could order servants now, hold her own in discussions for Church suppers, but she still couldn't command her husband to come back, couldn't write to her son and claim him as her own. Was this a remnant of the time when white folks gave in Mama's world, and white folks took away?

Or had Mama made a choice, some sleepless four a.m., to let them go, if that was what they wished; that the best she could do for her son was to wait for him to make the first contact, if indeed he ever would. Annie never knew, could never risk her mother's pain to ask.

The word that John Roland had hissed across the room — *nigger* — hadn't been heard again inside the house walls. In time Annie almost managed to forget it, except for those whispers in the night.

And Zanna? Well, that made it all the easier to forget, for Zanna was no longer there.

CHAPTER 38

1878–80

ZANNA (1)

The Fitzhenrys' house had been perched on an empty road, with only the Merryweathers for neighbours. (The Merryweathers had bought Mr Higgins' farm the year Annie was born, and gave their foreman the Higgins' house to live in.)

Now town was growing closer. Houses trailed along the road from town, as the town grew larger and more prosperous. The houses hadn't quite reached them yet, but the year Papa and John Roland left they came close enough for the baker's cart to jolt the extra half mile along the road to bring the household bread three times a week, so Mama's baking became limited to cakes and her cat's tongue cookies and her cotton blossoms with their layer of meringue.

The butcher came too — or the butcher's apprentice,

at any rate, Sammy Hudson, son of a Maori goldminer who had stayed when the gold was worked out. He was a tall boy, big across the shoulders and a lazy grin that seemed to take in half the world.

Sammy came Thursdays, with his enamel tray under his arm, filled with sausages and slabs of pork or beef — Mama never had learnt to like mutton — and he stayed to drink tea and eat the pumpkin pie that Zanna made from Mama's recipe.

Somehow after the first three weeks the orders were rearranged so Sammy arrived at lunchtime, and could be easily persuaded to sit and eat with them; then rearranged again so he came to them at the end of the run, and stayed and stayed until his horse grew impatient standing in the road while Sammy talked and talked and Zanna listened and sometimes even laughed aloud, and Annie stared. Who would have guessed that Zanna could imitate how Mrs Beeson snored in Church, how Mrs Bingely gave a special snort before the most malicious of her gossip, and all just to make big Sammy grin?

The next thing Annie knew Mama drove Zanna in to town to buy her a party dress, because there was a dance . . .

It seemed natural to Annie that Sammy must love Zanna. It was impossible for anyone not to love Zanna. And it was true that Sammy was growing to be the biggest, best looking man in town, with muscles like a Hereford bull and a laugh that shook the hall. But still . . .

'He said he'd hang my paintings in his shop one day,' said Zanna softly. Zanna still painted, all afternoon sometimes until Mama had to call three times to get her to help with dinner.

'In a butcher's shop!' Annie tried to imagine Zanna's streaks of light and colour — Zanna could make trees move even when they were painted on a page — hanging above the chops and sausages.

'No. In a special room next door, just for my paintings, where people can go and look at them. He said he saw a room like that down in Sydney, when he went there with his pa. He said when he looks at my paintings he sees the whole world like someone has washed its windows. No one ever said anything like that to me before,' she added softly.

Zanna and Sammy were married in the Church in town, with a party at the Church hall, and soon after Sammy started a butcher's shop of his own — helped by the monthly Fitzhenry bank drafts, but it soon became quite prosperous — and it did have a room for Zanna's paintings. Zanna transformed into a busy town wife — with more than a touch of the tarbrush admittedly, but dark skin looked so much paler dressed in respectability — a member of the sewing circle, the Church Ladies' Guild . . .

Every gossiping shop wife in town liked Zanna. Zanna was the perfect audience, who always seemed to agree with whatever had been said, and if at times she didn't, she had learnt to mimic the gossips perfectly, and it was her husband or her sister who heard her laugh.

And Zanna's paintings were ... well, not pretty, you couldn't call them that. They were striking and after a while people realised they liked them. (And years later people realised they still remembered them; her vision twisted into the mind, so they were remembered more vividly than the real scenes that they pictured. In later years two of Zanna's paintings would hang in the National Gallery in Canberra. Ironically, Zanna's would be the only Fitzhenry name to gain public recognition.)

Even the Mayor's wife had one of Zanna's paintings on her walls. Zanna could hardly be called black, after that.

CHAPTER 39

1879–80

ZANNA (2)

The shadows were lengthening as Zanna walked down the street, but the sweat still dribbled down her stays. She had never bothered with stays until she married Sammy, but now, as he said, she had to do things right.

The shopping basket cut into her arm, although she'd only bought butter which they'd run out of this morning, and a pound of sugar, to keep them going until the grocer called again. Sammy had been on at her that morning to hire a slavey to do things like fetch last-minute groceries. (He never saw how she winced at the word.) Sammy knew about her history, of course, but it never occurred to him that the word still hurt. In Sammy's mind you fought for what you wanted, with fists or whatever way would work.

'So what if some white girls won't work for darkies? We put an ad in the paper and wait for one that will.'

Sammy grinned. 'I'll be takin' on an apprentice soon, and a boy to take the money, the way business is going. Don't think there'll be any lack of takers there.'

She wanted to say that working in a shop was different from a white girl working for two people with dark skins in their home, but Sammy saw things his own way, or not at all, and anyway, maybe he was right.

'Take it on the chin, girl,' said Sammy cheerfully. 'You got to get these whiteys used to you tellin' them what to do.'

She smiled at him, her dear husband. Despite the pugnacious words, in an hour he'd be all politeness, beaming at the customers, doing his bit to buy a bit of whiteness for their children. She kissed him in that tender spot below his ear — the only spot of Sammy that was always soft and unprotected — and he beamed at her.

Sometimes, just sometimes, Zanna thought of her father, the shadowy Ezekiel, dragged back from freedom, whipped till his sides were red with blood. But it was difficult to see Ezekiel as her father. If he'd ever known of her existence she suspected he'd still have run, leaving her behind, still have hung himself to escape in the only way he knew was sure.

The only part of her she really knew was the mostly white part, her mother's part, so it seemed right, somehow, that she should try to achieve whiteness too.

And Sammy? It was different for Sammy. Sammy's dad could tell you stories of battles and heroic explorer ancestors in their giant canoes, and every one of those heroes was black. Sammy's ma had been a poor creature, according to Mrs Merryweather, for all that she'd been white. She'd died at Sammy's birth, as though she hadn't the energy to cope with father and son both. If there'd been stories from the white side of Sammy, they'd died with her.

Sammy didn't see it as turning white. For Sammy it was claiming the world he wanted, winning it just like his hero ancestors, as though this was a battle too.

Sometimes, thought Zanna, it seemed as though it was. It had looked so simple when she married him. Sammy had established his foothold in the world of white, and he'd carry her along with him. How could she have known you had to fight to keep that foothold every day?

And if at times she wondered if her family might have made this battle easier if they had acknowledged her a little more as a child — if Annie had taken her just sometimes on outings with her friends, if resentment ever bubbled at how much her sister had been given that she had not, including the years with a father — Zanna had been trained in her early years to disappear, so no one would notice her to sell her, or soldiers rape and gut her.

It was no wonder that in later years her family had been able to forget about her too. At times she wondered if she disappeared even from herself.

But no one could doubt Sammy's solidity. And with him she was solid too.

Yes, she thought now, she'd have to put the ad in for the girl. Sammy was right, she couldn't put it off. A cartload of firewood rumbled past close to the hitching rails under the fig trees and the horses skittered at the dust and noise. The driver's boots dangled beneath the seat, yellow as the dust he passed above. A dog peed under the fig tree at the corner. Its urine pooled on the hard ground. Over at the Post Office, Jim Rogers was pulling down the shutters.

Zanna walked past Wilson's Wholesalers (a stock of timber for every need; handsome and convenient cottages of two, three and four bedrooms furnished and erected in one month; American farming implements) and Ezra Jones, Bookseller, with the advertisement for Holloway pills in the window and a display, not of books, but violin strings and bridges and a half-strung violin — Ezra Jones played at the Church on Sundays; then Herrings, Quality Drapers; and finally, their shop, Hudson's Fine Meats, and beside it the door with the small sign above it 'Paintings', with the bell above the door.

Zanna stepped inside and heard it ring above her. Theoretically, if a customer entered she would hear it beyond the swing door that led to their rooms behind the shop, and come out to see what the art lover wanted. But although a surprising number of the paintings had been sold they had all been bought by Sammy's customers, wandering from one shop to the other, and they'd paid Sammy ... she'd only ever heard that bell ring twice, perhaps, except when she walked through the door.

She was just thinking about that, had just put the basket on the table, when the door did jangle. She went out, her gloves and hat still on. 'Mrs Henderson! How can I help you?' Not a painting, she thought. Not this one.

Mrs Henderson smiled a touch too brightly. 'Mrs Hudson. Thursday morning, a tennis party, and luncheon afterwards ... perhaps you would? Meant to ask at Church but quite forgot ...' The smile stayed in place. 'Or don't you play?'

'Thank you,' said Zanna quietly. 'I would love to come. Yes, I do play tennis.' How hotly had this invitation been debated, she wondered, by the Henderson set?

Mrs Henderson glanced around. 'Quite delightful,' she said brightly. 'Painting lessons, for my Charlotte ... do you ever? Till Thursday then.' The feather in her hat brushed the doorway as she jangled out.

Zanna went to the kitchen behind the swing door. It was a small room, with a parlour and bedroom attached. Next month they would move to their new house. Mrs Henderson's husband had been the builder. How much, she wondered, was the tennis invitation due to that?

She poked sticks into the fire, watched them flame, shut the firebox and moved the kettle to the heat, checked the lump of beef slowly roasting in the oven, dried the potatoes that had been soaking in cold water and pushed them into the hot fat.

She would put the ad in for a servant tomorrow. She would go to the Hendersons' as well (and check the rules of tennis with Annie before she went. She'd only played at the Merryweathers', and that wasn't even a proper court).

She glanced out the window. Sammy would be coming in for his supper soon. The shadows had turned to dusk. When she was younger, she had wondered if night was darkness conquering the day, or if the day simply got tired and went away. It had been important for her to work out whether light or dark was strongest.

Now ... well, colours changed at dusk; reds that turned to purples, yellows to browns. Her mother had been black once, even though her skin was white. Maybe, thought Zanna, her daughter could be white, even though her skin was black. A bit white, at any rate. The Hendersons might invite Zanna to tennis and a luncheon, but they'd always see her colour. Maybe if her children, when they came, played with the Henderson children, no one would see the colour there at all.

Or maybe they'd still need Sammy's advice. Take it on the chin, he'd tell his children. You won't get tuppence unless you fight. And she'd tell them too. Colour isn't simple, lovey, she'd say. White or black, it's how they see you, not who you are.

She glanced at her easel. It was so easy there. Light and dark; she needed both or she had nothing. Sammy and me, we're white and black combined. And sometimes, Lord, just sometimes, I wish we could live our blackness and forget about the white.

CHAPTER 40

1878–80

ANNIE GROWS UP

The bank drafts arrived from the Sydney solicitors every month. Letters arrived from Papa as well, though not regularly or often, addressed not to Mama or Annie or Zanna, but simply to 'My Dear Family'.

John Roland never wrote, but Papa's letters explained he was at school in Brisbane and doing well, and Annie supposed it comforted Mama at least a little, to know that her son was happy, even if he refused to be her son.

None of this really mattered to Annie at the time. She had more important things to think about. She was growing up.

Zanna was the quietest person Annie had ever known, but Annie missed her far more than she'd missed John Roland. She could visit her in town, of course, but Zanna was no longer only Annie's, and it was never the same.

Most weekends Annie went to the Merryweathers', ostensibly with messages from Mama — can we buy a basket of eggs, a pat of butter, please — but mostly she'd go because there was simply more happening on the farm than at home.

Sometimes Annie wished the Merryweathers had a daughter she could talk to, instead of only Frank, but she realised that part of the reason she was so welcome at the farm was that Mrs Merryweather longed for a daughter, and Annie was the nearest one around.

Mrs Merryweather showed her how to forage for eggs in the hayshed (the dust made her sneeze). She learnt to trim a side of mutton and how to tell tomorrow's weather from a thin, high cloud viewed through the window above the washing-up sink. She learnt how to feel a ram's testicles for lumps (though not in view of any of the men; even Mr Merryweather might have objected if he'd learnt his wife had shown her that), and who'd got the best price per bale of wool at the last sales, and how to make the treacle tart that Frank loved best.

As a child the land around Annie had been adventure. Each year increased the territory she was comfortable with; the bush behind the house, the track up to the Merryweathers', the creek and houses she roamed between at school.

Now with Mrs Merryweather Annie learnt to see the land differently. Land was there to be used, to be assessed. How many sheep could this paddock hold this year; and if it didn't rain by August, how many then? The bush became scrub, to be cleared or ignored. Grass mattered. Trees just got in the way.

Food was fuel for workers, though she never quite lost her mother's view of food as artistry as well. And children, Mrs Merryweather implied with every action that she took, were the reason for it all. Build a world for your children to inherit, as they will do in turn.

Mrs Merryweather baked on Saturdays, because that was when her mother had baked: rock cakes, Banbury cakes, date rolls, Queen cakes, sand cakes, ginger nuts, cream puffs, angel cakes, coronation pudding. Icing thick with walnuts and cakes rich in cherries and lemon peel — different from Mama's and not as perfect. Mrs Merryweather cooked to put a safe layer of fat between her family and the world. Mama made cakes because her cakes were beautiful.

Mrs Merryweather smelt of hot flour. Frank's smell had been the first male smell Annie was ever conscious of, and one day she realised she could remember his scent over all others. (Papa had smelt of cigars and books, but that didn't count — she'd forgotten that smell, though she remembered it years later.)

Frank smelt of grindstone dust when he'd been sharpening the axe in the courtyard. He smelt of horses and stable sweepings and hay dust as he lifted her up to the top larder shelves for a stored pumpkin to take home. There were black marks on his hands from fencing with the wire he brought from town.

It was Frank who bought her sweets when he went to town on Saturday mornings: red ones in a twist of paper. He tossed them to her over the farm table, then handed his mother hers.

'Thank you,' Annie remembered to say, and Frank grinned at her through the ginger whiskers he'd grown this past year and sipped the tea his mother put before him, already sugared, thick with milk.

At school Miss Frances still smelt of damp dishcloths. Miss Emily smelt of mutton and sharp cheese when she burped after lunch. Harold Greggs smelt of liquorice. He gave Annie some. He kissed her behind the boy's dunny, and she kicked his knees, but she met him again the next lunch hour.

— ∼∿◦ —

Frank got a silver watch for his eighteenth birthday. He showed it to Annie over the soup bowls at the Merryweathers' — pea and bacon soup with thick bits of buttered crust to dip in it. The watch clicked into its case and was engraved on the front.

Frank had a silver box for his coins. The sixpences and threepences slipped out like eggs sometimes did when you gutted a chicken. Frank slipped her threepence, the shiniest of them all and winked at her. 'Buy yourself some ribbons,' he whispered.

Annie got the chickenpox and had to stay home from school and, even worse, from the farm. Mama coated the blisters with cool tea leaves, then coated the scabs with calamine. She fried chicken and pancakes in the pan she called a skillet and let Annie eat it all in bed. Frank brought down a whole mass of eels he'd caught, and Jane and Louise, who were fourteen like Annie and in the same row at school, came and gossiped with her through her bedroom window.

Mama had the house painted as Annie lay in bed. Red and cream outside, and blue and cream inside. There were flowers all along the front of the house: zinnias, forget-me-nots that flowered for a week then went to seed and spread along the creek, portulacas like the jewels in Mama's brooch, violas and pansies. The day Annie went back to school Mama bought two rosebushes for two new round gardens on either side of the path to the gate, edged with white painted stones.

The sun crackled the school's tin roof. The words under her nib dried too quickly to bother reaching for the blotting paper. At fourteen Annie was old enough to leave school if she wanted. She was a monitor and mixed the ink on Tuesday mornings in the vat behind the schoolroom. The blue dust got up her nose and made it tickle during prayers.

Mornings were lazy in the heat. Afternoons were more competitive. Miss Serena encouraged competition between the older boys and girls. Whoever answered the most questions in the last hour — male or female — got out of school first.

Whoever got out of school first could grab their bag from the hook on the verandah and run down the track, the dust, thick with dried manure, filling their nose, clinging to their skin like flies' feet and the heat closing your eyes, through the long dry grass of Merryweathers' back paddock to the swimming hole in the creek.

The swimming hole was cold. The water stuck to their body and felt like frozen silk. The casuarinas were a green umbrella between the children and the sun.

There were no swimming costumes here; none for sale at Herring's in town. They swam naked (out of the gaze and knowledge of their elders) or not at all. The swimming hole was for one sex only, so whoever got there first could claim it male or female for the day. There was only one swimming hole within easy run from the school.

Hands flung in the air during the hot afternoons. Ink splattered onto desks already daubed as if they had been run over by a million chicken feet.

'Yes Miss, yes Miss, yes Miss ...' The dates of the Wars of the Roses. The name of Henry the Eighth's fourth wife. All tickets to the water, water clear as a candle flame but colder, trickling under the casuarinas, over the green coolness of the rocks.

'Yes Miss, here Miss, here Miss! Me Miss . . .'

The triumph of getting to the swimming hole first, hearing the boys' bare feet thudding, heard them mutter as they saw a flash of skin, a splash of water.

'Nyahhh! Nyahhh!'

'Shit . . .' They would turn away into the air that smelt of leaves and cattle shush, and move down past three bends, where all they could do was paddle in the shallow water, and throw hot rocks that splintered on the boulders in the creek.

Annie loved swimming. She felt as if she was flying when she lay on her back and watched the clouds. Drying off was almost as good, all sprawled on the hot rocks, feeling the heat seep into their bones and covertly watching each other's bodies; who was getting hair down there or under the arms; whose breasts were biggest and whose hadn't begun to grow; who had the best bottom and who had a skinny one, like a boy's.

Men liked plump legs best, Jane informed them. Her brother had said so. Annie inspected hers and was relieved to see they were still fat, not 'nigger' legs. Her breasts were growing nicely too. But in the afternoons Annie still ate a double helping of apple cake, to keep the skinny legs at bay.

A pair of swallows nested on the newly painted porch at home. At the Merryweathers' that weekend Frank showed Annie the yellow robin's nest in the wattle tree by the back gate. Seven bald heads and wide beaks yelled at the intruders. Frank lifted her up to them. She could see the flecks of dandruff in his hair and the red mark on his forehead from his hat.

'Be quiet, you silly fools, we're not your ma,' said Frank to the shrieking birds.

'Can't we feed them?'

He shook his head. 'Their mother'd smell us on them and kick them out.'

'That's cruel.'

'I suppose it is,' said Frank, putting her down again. (He didn't seem to notice that her breasts had grown.) 'That's just the way it is.'

Frank had new boots from Herrings'. They squeaked when he walked. Then he put oil on them; next weekend they didn't.

－⁂－

Christmas. Mama (who was strangely ignorant of the protocol of birthdays) was good with Christmas. The year Annie turned fifteen, Mama went to town with Mrs Merryweather to buy their presents. The house was decorated with greenery and wreaths and the scent of cooking. There were oranges in a bowl on the sideboard and a big bowl of nuts you could eat at any time. Mama and Annie made sugared nuts on Christmas Eve.

Sammy and Zanna and the baby came over for dinner, and the family sat in the kitchen tossing the hot nuts and shrieking as the toffee splintered onto the floor like diamond daggers.

They opened their presents on Christmas Eve, as Zanna and Sammy would have Christmas Day with his parents in town, while Annie and Mama would go to the Merryweathers'. Annie got a carved box, new shoes and a tin of toffees from Sammy. She had made a fan woven from palm fronds with a silk tassel at the bottom for Mama, who exclaimed over it. She had knitted a hat for the baby (it was more holes than stitches) and had embroidered a handkerchief for Zanna and one for Sammy, with his initials in the corner.

They all went to Church on Christmas morning. The Merryweathers were at Church as well, in the pew in front of Annie and Zanna and little Peter and Sammy, while Mama sat with the choir in the pews at the side.

Mrs Merryweather had a new hat for Christmas, and new gloves, and she wore her good black silk, so she looked as hot and shiny as a chook in summer. Frank had a new hat as well, stiff as a bucket. He looked handsome, sort of red and polished for Christmas Day. He grinned at Annie as they settled in their pew.

Afterwards Mr Merryweather discussed the sky with the Reverend Hornsby: Will it rain before New Year?

And Frank sat on the fence between the Church and the graveyard talking with Mary Bentley in her new pink dress with lace on it and her old frilly hat. Frank and Mary were still talking when Mama finally persuaded Billy Bob to move his carcass and take them home.

Annie and Mama went up to the farm for Christmas dinner. Mama took sugared almonds, crystallised ginger in a squat brown pot and marzipan fruit.

The last was a miracle. Annie was proud of it, and proud of her mother for making it. There were marzipan oranges and apples and even potatoes, all coloured and shaped and wrapped in silver paper. Mama had worked at them for weeks in the cool of the morning before the kitchen began to sweat.

Frank was in the parlour, sitting in one of the faded armchairs sipping Christmas whisky as they all sat down to open their presents.

Mrs Merryweather gave Annie a *Girl's Own Annual* (Mrs Merryweather didn't care for reading but she knew Annie did) and Mr Merryweather gave her a pincushion. Then Frank handed her a present. She had knitted him a face washer with 'Frank', not just his initials, embroidered in the corner. His present in its silver paper looked so much better than hers that it made her blush.

'Well, aren't you going to open it?' someone said.

She opened it carefully so as not to tear the paper.

It was a wickerwork bird, bright with lacquer, red and green and blue, with an open beak and sturdy legs so it stood upright. It had gold eyes and gold feet and glowed as though it was about to conquer the sky.

It was the most beautiful thing she had ever seen.

'Chinese,' nodded Tony McReady, the farm foreman. 'Seen one like it at Lee Pak's last time I were down.'

Annie looked at Frank.

Frank was pretending to be buried in his whisky, but his cheeks were redder than his sideburns.

'Thank you,' she said, and Frank nodded as though his mind was on other matters entirely and turned to Tony McReady to mention that the black-eared cow was barren, they might as well put her down.

Mrs Merryweather smiled as she herded them in to lunch.

~𝕸◎

Columbus discovered America for the umpteenth time since Annie had been at school. Captain Cook discovered Australia and New Zealand again, Napoleon was still the greatest tyrant ever known. The fire spat and hissed in the corner of the schoolroom. Miss Frances taught Annie French knitting that winter, and praised her blanket stitch.

Frank was going to the dance with Mary Bentley. He combed old Rosalind for half the afternoon, till her coat gleamed like the dining table. Annie watched him from the end room where Mrs Merryweather was showing her how to braid a rug with scraps she'd brought from home, all the while explaining how it was good to put spare earnings into fences or better stock or, best of all, more land.

Mary Bentley would have her hair up. Mama had told Annie she couldn't have hers up until she turned sixteen. It had to hang down like a little girl's. Mary Bentley's nose is too long, thought Annie, as she pulled at the darning needle with its length of rag. She'll look like an emu when she's old.

She wondered how much hair Mary Bentley had down there. Annie checked hers every bath night but it was still only a faint down, like wool sweepings from the floor, despite the fact that she was nearly sixteen. The hair under her arms was good and thick. Jane had black hair on her legs, which Annie envied. Jane said some girls never got hairy legs at all.

She hoped Mary Bentley got the stomach ache at supper. She hoped Frank got the stomach ache too.

~᯽◦

The dance came and went. Neither Frank nor Mary seemed to get the stomach ache. Frank still talked to Mary after Church and took her to the next dance as well. Annie's breasts grew bigger. Harold threw stones at their front fence on Saturday until Annie came out.

'Feel on for a walk?'

They walked down the track. Dust seeped into her Saturday stockings. They crossed to the creek and sat by the trickling water. A fly teased her right nostril. They talked about next month's Show. Harold's pa was growing monster spuds, his ma wanted prizes for her jam. Suddenly Harold leant across and kissed her hard on the lips. He sat back to survey his handiwork.

Later they walked home.

Mama took her to town in the Merryweathers' cart. Herrings' was full of the scents of rolls of cloth, the tight sweet smell of lace.

They bought gloves, a new long skirt and Annie's first stays. They pinched and squeezed and she was sure she'd never breathe again; if a cat looked at her she'd crack. But within a week she was used to them.

The stays plumped out her breasts. She admired them in the mirror. Jane's were bigger, but Jane's nipples were pale, like washed out cream, while hers were deeper pink. Annie thought hers were the better ones. Her hips looked bigger in the stays too, but she'd always had good hips, and her legs were still properly plump. It was a pity no one could see her legs, Annie thought, though at least the new silk skirt hinted at their admirable proportions. Annie had the second slimmest ankles in the school. Jane Taylor had used Miss Emily's tape measure to check.

'Going to the dance this Sat'dee?' asked Harold, as he walked her home from school — the long way, because she'd gone to see Jane's new dress first. Annie was in her last year at school. Harold was leaving school too. He planned to go to Sydney to study next year. John Roland did that, said the voice in Annie's head, but she shoved the thought away. It led to memories and a whisper that still said, 'black baby, black baby'.

Harold had pimples, and his voice trilled and trembled when he got out of breath, but he was the tallest boy at school, so all week she'd been hoping he would ask her to the dance.

Wheels rattled on the ruts behind. Frank nodded above them, in the new yellow painted buggy his mother had bought last year. There were boxes on the tray under his feet. He must have been to town.

'Only room for one,' said Frank.

Annie swept her skirt around her legs as she got in. She had to be careful about such things now; no more flashing knees as she climbed into a buggy.

She wondered if her hair was tidy. She wished she were wearing her stays. She glanced down. Her breasts looked like two fried eggs under her dress.

The wheels grunted beneath the buggy. Old Rosalind snorted as they passed McReadys' cows.

'There's a dance at McReadys' shed on Saturday,' said Frank.

Annie nodded. 'I was going to go with Harold but I don't suppose he'll ask me now.'

Harold's indignant face didn't matter here with her head above the dust, feeling the breeze, next to Frank.

Frank clicked his tongue at Rosalind. He looked nervous suddenly. Annie wondered if he'd forgotten something from town.

'Like to come with me then?' he asked.

It was a shock but not a shock. She felt herself glowing like an iron on the hob. She nodded. 'All right.' It was hard to get her tongue around the words.

They'd reached the gate. Annie slid down, nodded and fled into the house.

—⁂—

It was a shop-bought dress, with a high neck. (She wished it were lower. Maybe next year when she was seventeen.) She had new dancing slippers too. Her hair was still down, not up, but she brushed it a hundred times and threaded a blue ribbon through it.

She felt enormous pity for her friends, condemned to boys from school as partners. Jane was going with Harold. She was welcome to him. Louise was going with Bert. Bert!

Frank's cheeks gleamed where he had shaved and his hair was leathery with oil and brushing. He'd cleaned his nails.

This time he helped her into the buggy. After that, they didn't speak. Annie held her hands tight in her lap, and wondered what Mary Bentley spoke to him about.

Horses stamped and kicked and inspected each other in the paddock by McReady's shearing shed. Dogs sniffed tails by the steps. Women cast glances at each other's dresses. Men pulled uncomfortably at their neckcloths.

Then the music started. A preliminary scraping, then the accordion tumbled over itself, someone laughed, old Farrell grabbed his niece and pulled her into the middle, galloping a polka. The floor was smooth with sheep oil and colours flashed. It was a thousand leagues away from the drab of sheep. Billy Randell's whiskers were coated with resin from his bow or maybe it was sweat, his fingers were thick from decades of fencing, but they still flew along the strings. He'd play all night, then fence all day. He had ridden fifty miles to play tonight.

Frank's arms were warm when they danced. Annie didn't stumble once. She didn't talk much either, but it didn't matter while the music played.

They had supper on the verandah with Frank's friends and their girlfriends, talking about fat lamb prices and how the weather was holding for the hay. She knew about these things — she had been listening to Mrs Merryweather for sixteen years. Mrs Merryweather was as good as any man when it came to judging when to sell the steers. Better, probably.

Annie glanced over at Jane and Harold and Louise and Bert. Suddenly they were still children, and she was . . . what?

It was quiet after the dance. Shyness covered her, thick as a blanket. She sat next to Frank in the buggy and didn't speak as they passed O'Hare's and Harrington's, turned the corner by O'Reilly's. Suddenly Frank pulled on the reins. He turned towards her.

The kiss landed on her nose. She had turned to help

him, but the wrong way. The kiss was wetter than she expected, much wetter than Harold's. The second one was better, properly on her lips. By the next she was almost comfortable, close to him now, and she could feel his teeth (and a fleeting thought: it would be revolting to feel Harold's teeth and as for his tongue ...).

'Annie,' said Frank breathlessly, and suddenly they looked at each other and laughed.

After that it was easy. There was the world to talk about, and more.

'See that old stump?' said Frank. 'Remember how old Tebbut tried to blow that with black powder once, but the whole thing fizzled and he was too scared to have a look?

'Listen,' said Frank. 'That's the mopoke.'

'There's one by our back fence.'

'Mopoke, mopoke,' said Frank, his arm around her shoulders, his fingers in her hair. It didn't matter at all that Mama hadn't let her put it up.

'I would've asked you last year,' said Frank, 'but Mum said you was too young.'

They kissed again outside the house. Rosalind stamped and jerked the buggy. They fell back on the seat and laughed.

'Shh,' said Annie, to Frank or to the horse, she didn't know or care.

'You'll come up to the farm tomorrow?' Frank asked.

She nodded.

'I'll come and fetch you then,' he said.

'I can walk.'

'I'll fetch you,' said Frank, and smiled at her.

His lips tasted of the night and of the cheese and onion pasties he'd eaten at supper.

A bat darted black into the blacker shadows. Frank took her to the door. Somewhere inside she could hear the clang of the stove; Mama adding wood, waiting for her to get home.

They kissed. They smiled at each other.

The world seemed very bright. Each second of that night had been an hour. And tomorrow she'd see Frank again, she thought, as she closed the door behind her, then ran to the parlour window to watch the buggy down the road. And Mama would find out about it all, and what would Mrs Merryweather think ...

The only surprising thing about it all, of course, was that no one was surprised.

CHAPTER 41

1 8 8 1

CONFESSIONS

There was something Annie had to do, however. She loved Frank; knew that he loved her. She suspected that Mrs Merryweather loved her, too, and Mr Merryweather would love whoever his wife and son told him was worth loving.

But there was still something she had to do.

She waited till the next Saturday, when she and Mrs Merryweather were in the kitchen, rolling pastry together. (Mama was spending the day with Zanna in town. Zanna had a daughter now, a sister to little Peter. Elizabeth Anne, the most beautiful baby Annie had ever seen, until she saw her own.)

The kettle steam dripped down the windows, leaving clear streaks on the glass. Mrs Merryweather pushed at the pastry with the tips of her fingers. The pastry was for a currant tart. Frank liked currant tart, so it was important to learn to make it well.

'Mrs Merryweather?'

'I reckon you should be calling me Mum pretty soon,' said Mrs Merryweather comfortably, giving the pastry another push.

'I have to tell you something. I mean, I really have to, before I marry Frank.'

Mrs Merryweather looked at her wisely. 'Is this about Zanna then? Her being black and all? About your mama having a touch of the tarbrush too?'

Annie sat down on one of the kitchen chairs with the shock of it. 'You knew?'

'I've eyes in my head, don't I?' said Mrs Merryweather. 'There, I think that'll do it then. Pass the dish over and I'll lay it out.'

'Mama ... Mama was a slave in America. Then Papa married her —'

'And brought her here. Don't you worry, girl, I had that all figured out years ago. I'm not as green as I'm cabbage looking.'

'Does everyone else know?'

'Why should they? Half the old hens round here never look further than their back doorsteps. Besides, your mama has been here longer than most of them now. They'd reckon she'd always been here, if they ever thought about it, in spite of the way she talks sometimes.'

It couldn't be as easy as this. It couldn't. 'Does Frank know? And Mr Merryweather?'

'Phil? No, and what he don't know won't hurt him. But I had a word to Frank a few years back.'

'He doesn't mind?'

'Why should he? You're you and that's the end of it.'

'But what if I have a black baby?' The words were blurted out before she could stop them.

Mrs Merryweather stared. 'A black baby? What put that idea into your head, girl?'

'Sometimes the blackness comes out, years later.'

Mrs Merryweather snorted. 'I've been breeding sheep for long enough to know more'n that. You get out what you put in, sheep or human. The only way you'll have a black baby, girl, is if you cheat on my Frank, and if I thought you'd do that you wouldn't be getting Frank, no mind he fancied the look and ways of you.' She glanced down at the half cut pastry. 'Oh, put that in the larder to keep cool and sit down again. There's something I need to say to you too.'

Annie put the pastry in the stone-floored larder next to the bowl of butter and the egg basket, and came out into the heat of the kitchen. Mrs Merryweather poured water into the teapot, then shoved a cup of tea and the sugar pot and milk jug towards her. For once she seemed to be hunting for words.

Outside, the chooks set up a squawking, arguing over the breakfast bacon rinds. Annie sipped her tea.

'Never told you how I came here, did I?' asked Mrs Merryweather abruptly.

'You came from England,' said Annie.

'That I did, and Frank's pa, too. Six months on the boat, it took us. I asked Frank's grandpa for the money. Thought he'd argue with me, me being six years older than his son and wanting to drag him right across the world, but he didn't. He knew what his son needed. He needed someone to steady him and tell him what to do, and Frank's grandpa knew it.'

Annie was silent. The thought of a wife being six years older than her husband was shocking. Almost as shocking, she thought, as having a nigger mother.

'Well, we bought this place,' said Mrs Merryweather heavily, 'with what we saved working as a married couple for old Higgins and what the bank would lend us. If it had been left to Frank's pa we'd've stayed working for others all our lives.'

Annie didn't know what to say, so she nodded.

'You see why I'm telling you this, girl?' Mrs Merryweather laid her swollen knuckles on Annie's. 'Frank's a good boy. No one could want better than my Frank. But he's like his pa. He needs telling what to do. If a new bull's needed he'll wait a year or ten while he thinks about it, or never notice at all.

'I don't care how much nigger's in you, girl. You'll be good for my Frank, and that's what matters. You know what's what, and how to do it, and what you don't I'll learn you.' She shrugged. 'Besides, nigger's African, ain't it? Not like the blacks or the Chinee. Even the Chinee aren't as bad as they make out either, though don't you say so in front of Frank's pa, he's that down on them.'

'And the black baby?'

'There won't be a black baby,' said Mrs Merryweather, quite confident she could organise that too. 'But even if there was a bit of the tarbrush somewhere there, well, you know, I think it's a bit like lust just how bad I want a baby in the house again.'

CHAPTER 42

1882–84

PATTERNS

Frank and Annie were married the year Annie turned seventeen, at St Stephen's Church, with her mother in grey lace and Mrs Merryweather tearful and joyous in purple, and Zanna and Jane as her attendants and Frank waiting for her up the aisle looking like his happiness would spill over and flood the place.

There had been discussion about whether Sammy or Mr Merryweather would give her away. Mrs Merryweather decided on Sammy, on the grounds that if people were going to talk, let them, though everyone was so used to Sammy and Zanna they hardly noticed the colour of their skin any more.

(It might have been different if they had been Aboriginal, or if there had been more dark skins around. But the district's Aboriginal inhabitants had been moved to a camp on the coast decades before. There was no black community to identify Zanna and Sammy with; they were just themselves, and mostly accepted.)

Annie's father had been gone so long from their lives that she never thought he would return for her wedding. She had hoped, though, that he might write a letter congratulating her — a letter just to her, not to 'My Dear Family', which always sounded hollow. If they were so dear why had he abandoned them?

But his letters had stopped a few months before her marriage. Annie later discovered that her father never even received the one telling him of her engagement.

Her father had managed a station in Queensland for three years. She thought he had been content there. His letters sounded so, though they mostly spoke of the state of the cattle and the brolgas that danced outside his window.

The job must have paid enough for John Roland's school fees, and provided a home for John Roland to come back to in the holidays, although her father's letters never spoke of that. He did mention occasionally if John Roland did well in his exams.

At the end of the three years John Roland left school and became an articled clerk in a solicitor's office. There was a gap in her father's letters then. Five months later a short note arrived from Broome in Western Australia. It didn't mention John Roland, or what her father was doing there, whether he was involved in the pearl fishing or managing a property or just passing through.

There were only three more letters after that, all from an address in far north Queensland, but none of them did much more than enquire after their health and promise another letter when the wet receded and the roads were clear enough for the mail to get through.

Sometimes in those early years he sent his wife and daughter money, but not often, and never very much. They probably had more money than he did, with the regular banker's drafts from the Sydney solicitors. In those years he sent them gifts: a length of Chinese silk that her mother had had made up into dresses for all three of them; a sandalwood box for Zanna and a short letter on her marriage; a stuffed baby crocodile that Annie adored and put on the mantelpiece for everyone to admire. But the gifts stopped. Either there was nowhere to buy them, or he had no money, or his wife and daughters were now so distant in his mind that he had no idea what to buy.

Most of Annie's first year of marriage was taken up with Frank. Frank beside her in their bed, which was even better than she had expected, so it was hard to believe that all married people did this, and never spoke of it. How did those dangly bits on little boys turn into this? All those interesting pale bits that never saw the sun. Frank beside her as they rode down to the creek; discussions with Mrs Merryweather about what Frank would like for tea (it was assumed that Mr Merryweather — Pa, she called him now — would like what Frank liked).

Mrs Merryweather had decided Frank and Annie would live with them until their new house could be built. The house was never built, of course, and by their second anniversary Mrs Merryweather had given up any pretence that it would be. There was no way Mrs Merryweather was going to see her son — or Annie or their children — move even half a mile from her watchfulness. Besides, as she said, how could she listen for the babies in the night with them so far away?

But at times — particularly when her first baby began to quicken — Annie did think of her father. Isolated as her upbringing had been, she did know something of the world from the books she read, the newspapers and magazines her father had bought, then her mother, and that she now got Frank to buy her.

She was aware that her father might have died up north with no one knowing enough about him to let them know. Perhaps they would never know for sure if he were alive or dead; just assume as more and more years passed that they'd never hear from him again.

It was equally possible that he might have remarried, far away from anyone who had known of his first marriage. He might have changed his name, as many men did.

He might have found a woman whose background fitted more closely with his own on one of those northern properties, the daughter of the house perhaps, who would inherit the acres that his first marriage had lost him. Perhaps he had another family now, with no taint of brown skin or memories of slavery and subservience to forget.

Annie never knew what her father thought or did in those years up north. The only clue she had was the draft of a letter she found years later in a book he had left somewhere up north that was finally sent down south to his only known address. The ink in some parts had washed across the page, and there were many crossings out, but it was readable.

It was a letter to his mother. Annie didn't know what year her father wrote it. She didn't know if he ever sent the final copy or not.

In the last part of this letter he referred to 'returning home'. Perhaps this was a reference to his home in the north. Perhaps it meant he intended to come back south to his wife, or that he hoped to visit his childhood home. Annie believed it was probably the last letter her father ever wrote.

CHAPTER 43

1886

UP NORTH

Charles Roland Fitzhenry, now called Charles Forrest, was trying to write two letters. The first was to his mother. He had written several letters to her in the past twenty years, but had posted none of them. The last letter he had sent had been written from another country. It had been a far easier letter to write than this.

He was also trying to write to his wife. Although Charles had written to his family, he had never written to his wife — not a letter to her alone — saying the personal things he had never said to her. He had never realised, for a long time, that there were any that needed to be said.

The trees outside were thin topped and tall. The grass was also tall, and too green from the storms of the past month. The whole world smelt of rot.

This should have been cattle country, but the cattle didn't thrive. Nor did white men. Thin cattle were tended by thin men, their gums pale with scurvy from a diet of rum and damper, their skin shabby with the pus-filled sores of Barcoo rot, their minds weary from the fever and ague that dug their fingers into you throughout the wet season.

Only blacks and sandflies, roos and bustards, seemed to thrive here. The sky was too high, too hot, too blue. The air was thick with damp and heat.

Charles had never consciously decided to leave his wife forever. He had left for his son's sake, and to get the work he was unable to find locally. If, in some crevice of his mind, there had been the thought that, perhaps, without her the life he had lost — the life he had been promised as a child — might return, he had never acknowledged it, had never allowed himself to dream that what might have been could turn again into what might be.

It had been for John Roland's sake that he had changed his name, for the boy's sake that he had come so far. And as time passed it was easier to let more time pass before visiting home.

Home. When he was young it had been a certain place, that house on the hill. All he had to do was survive, and he could come home. He had survived, and that home was taken from him, and now the home he dreamt of was not a house, but a person. The longer he had travelled the more vivid his wife became in his mind.

No, they had not been happy. They had had glimpses of happiness in their children, and at night, but even so the further Charles travelled the more he realised that if he had any chance of happiness at all, it was with her.

She was both closer to him and further from him than anybody in the world. There was no use wishing it were otherwise.

Somehow he had to write to her. But he would write to his mother first.

A curlew yelled beyond the hut. Charles wiped the sweat from his face and watched it drip from his hands onto the paper. He wondered without interest if the sweat came from heat or fever. He dipped his pen into the thick brown sludge in the inkwell.

Dear Mother,
I write from Illawheela Downs, a property of which you won't have heard . . .

It had been too long since he'd written a letter. He had forgotten how. The house on the hill seemed so far away. Everything seemed far away, except when he dreamt.

Time doesn't pass in dreams. Things that happened ten or twenty years ago happen again and again each night. Even here, with the sky so taut you could pierce it with a pin, he still had nightmares of the war of twenty years past.

At one time, Charles thought that if he left Caroline the nightmares would go away. Now he knew that dreams belong to no country. They are a country of their own. There was only one person in the world who could understand his nightmares. Sometimes he dreamt of her.

He'd met a woman, three years ago, on a property where he'd worked as foreman. She was the owner's daughter. Her skin was sallow from the heat, but her eyes were clear and laughing. She'd had white skirts the black girls starched, washing them in the tubs beneath the bauhinia trees where the flowers like flickering moths fell into the tub and rested against the white cloth. It seemed her dresses smelt of them. She had reminded him of Sally, of his youth.

Her name was Eulalie. In the cool bright days of winter she organised a vegetable garden. It withered in the summer heat, but Doo the Chinese cook dried the cabbages and turnips and salted down the pumpkins. The house with its bright Chinese carpets (bought from Afghan traders, like the blue and white china) had a comfort and serenity that reminded him of the house he had grown up in.

She would have married him, as Sally would have, long ago. Half of him considered it, up here in a new world, his name changed, manager of the property. There was nothing now to link him to the other marriage and the shame of his past down south.

Sometimes, watching Eulalie with the darkies, it was impossible not to feel his marriage had been grotesque; some surreal accident where he had gone to sleep imagining he had married the mistress, and woken up finding himself married to the darkie instead.

But it hadn't been like that. He had married the darkie knowingly, and found she was a white woman.

Or was she? thought Charles wearily. Were there secrets behind every dark face? Could each one of them turn white if it weren't for the colour of their skin? And if the only barrier was colour it meant the very fabric of life was wrinkled, the wars in China, Africa, India were meaningless, even his work here a sham, just like the cause he'd fought for. He was manager here because only a white man *could* manage. But if that were not true ...

(The first year up north he had been supervising a mob of blacks building a fence; driving them too hard, he knew that now, trying to prove himself a white man. Finally one of them had laid his crowbar down and begun to walk away.

'You can't do that!' Charles had yelled.

The man looked him in the eye. 'No, boss,' he said, '*you* can't do that.' And he'd walked empty-handed through the scattered limp leafed trees, where no white man could survive unaided.)

Dear Mother,
I haven't written to You before because I was ashamed.

How could Eulalie know the land he had come from? The land of nightmares, the land of war? Only one woman had shared that world.

He had left Eulalie. (Eulalie, Sally, why hadn't he noticed how the two names rhymed?) He'd moved on. Now he was here for another six months, until after the wet when the new manager would come. When the rivers went down he'd ride south, take a steamer down from Rockhampton to Brisbane, and then to Sydney, if his luck held good.

Dear Mother,
I write to ask You a favour for my Wife. I ask that You will meet her. Or if this is not possible (your age or health I know may make this impossible) if You would write to her . . .

My wife . . . the image swam in his mind. Not the slave, or the woman in the night, but her face across the kitchen table . . .

I married my Wife out of loneliness, in illness and confusion, because I'd left my world behind, because the only world I knew was mad, except for her.

Back in the army I dreamt of simple things, clean sheets, the smell of gum leaves. I thought those longings were a symptom of the insanity around me. They weren't. Perhaps you just see things clearly when you're desperate. It has taken me twenty years to realise the life that I want now. A life of simple things, of trees, the sea, and home.

For years I thought that what I felt for my Wife could not be love. Love is what you find in books. Love is an ideal. What I felt for her was too elemental to call love — the pleasures of coupling, of talk at supper when the children were in bed. Now I know that love is made of simple things, just like those dreams.

My Wife is a woman of quietness and gentleness, at least I so believe. So quiet that when I left I only knew from her actions, not her words . . .

Dear Mother,
I left my Wife ten years ago and now I realise, for the first time, that I regret . . .

My Wife is a woman like me, though the world may think we are different in all essentials . . .

I could not talk to Eulalie up at Bobadour. There is a scar on my life that only my Wife can understand.

Dear Mother,
I have a Wife and children and I am going home to them. I pray God that they will have me.

Voices erupted outside, shrill and guttural in the thick hot air. He rose and barked an order out the door.

Charles knew the problem. The local blacks, all from one tribe, objected to the new kitchen boy. Charles had hired him without thinking. He was an escaped Kanaka who had found his way inland from the slave gangs on the sugar fields. A good boy, he'd learnt his cooking on the ships. He'd turn him off, but it would look bad if the blacks thought he had done it just because they demanded it.

A white man stuck by his orders in this country or he was gone. (That's what they'd said twenty years ago, as well, the foolish men he'd fought with. Was it all a lie then? The whole stupid white man game? Though some had not been foolish. Walter and his cows . . .)

Charles blinked, tried to clear his mind, but it was too hot. His mind seemed to swim in the heat.

The voices subsided. Charles stood at the door a moment longer. The air was as stale outside as in, as if the heat had taken all the goodness from it. He had a longing suddenly for sea air, cool air straight off the sea. The moon rose through the trees, brighter than the lamp. A mosquito sipped at his cheek. He slapped it absentmindedly and went back to the table.

The curlew called again.

Dear Mother,

I write from Illawheela Downs, a property of which You won't have heard. I write to ask You a favour for my Wife. I ask that You will meet her; or if this is not possible (your age and health, I know, may make this impossible) if You would write to her. I beg this as your son.

I have no excuse that I can give for my failure in writing to You for so long. It is one failure among so many others. I hope that some day we may meet and I may explain my failures, as I am unable to do now.

I believe that You will like my Wife. Her name is Caroline. She is not black, though as I told my Father she was once a slave. She is a Christian Woman and a fine one. I regret I did not say this to my Father when I told him of my marriage.

My Wife could pass as a white woman and does where she lives. I believe that whatever I have done my Wife deserves some recognition, even if I do not.

Dear Mother,
I have missed You every day since I left to go to war in a strange country. I pray that We may meet again. I will write again when I reach home.
   I Remain, always,
   Your loving Son,
   Charles Fitzhenry

Outside the door the blacks were singing, high as the curlew cry, somewhere under the roof of trees. There was meaning out there somewhere; somewhere a pattern to this strange land, somewhere, perhaps, the love he'd felt for it in childhood. The blacks might know the answer, if only he could stop being white and ask them. But he was too tired now. Perhaps his children might find it . . .

The curlew called again, or was it the blacks' song, out in the black night . . .

He was tired. His hand shook. It was ague, he realised, not the heat. He was sick.

He'd write to Caroline tomorrow, or next week, when the fever left him. There was no hurry. No letters could be sent south now.

Then when the rivers subsided, he'd go home.

CHAPTER 44

1886

JAMES AND EMILY IN THE HOUSE ON THE HILL

When Charles was a baby his skin was like rose petals. Your first child is astonishing. You watch the creases in his hands, the fatness of his feet, the fuzz growing on his bald head. You watch for the first sign that he notices you as you are watching him.

'It's time to dress, Mrs Fitzhenry,' said Blatchett, like a nanny to a two year old. Blatchett irritated her.

'I don't need to dress. I am dressed.'

'Doctor Hatton is coming out today. You'll want to be dressed to see him, won't you?'

Blatchett had wet patches underneath her arms. They were never dry, even in cold weather. She smelt them every time Blatchett lifted her elbows.

'I am dressed. Who did you say was coming?'

'Doctor Hatton. Come on, Mrs Fitzhenry, there's a lamb.'

She stared at Blatchett. She hadn't lost her mind, whatever they said. Her mind was on more important things: Charles' delight when he first toddled into the waves. Blatchett was taking liberties.

'I am dressed,' she repeated.

'You can't wear your nightdress down to breakfast, can you?' insisted Blatchett, wondering if she'd have to call Ellen up to help. It would be easier by far if the mistress had breakfast up here every morning; she could stay in her nightdress all day then. But the master insisted she came down, though God knows why. Feeding her was no problem, she liked to eat, it was just the dressing of her, and the cleaning of her ...

She liked breakfast. At one time, she hardly ate at all. Ladies didn't. For a year or two, as she'd grown fatter, Blatchett had laced her stays looser, but now she didn't bother with stays, and Blatchett didn't bother her with them either. She ate two eggs from the silver warmer and a plate of kidneys and mushrooms, and a slice of ham from the sideboard and toast and bramble jelly.

'I planted these brambles,' she told the man at the other end of the table politely. He was a stranger, but it didn't matter. She'd had fifty years of learning how to be polite to strangers. She knew how to talk to a strange man at her breakfast table. She piled the jelly on the toast. If Blatchett were here she'd make her take less jelly, but Blatchett was having her own breakfast in the kitchen with the other servants. The jelly was hers, anyway. It was made from her brambles.

'I planted these brambles,' she told the man at the other end of the table again, and he nodded his head still reading his letters. Something in the turn of his head reminded her. He was the man who called himself her husband.

She watched him, thinking. They believed she didn't think these days, but she did. The world inside was the only world that made sense. The world outside ebbed and flowed. They kept changing things in the world outside. She tasted the jelly on her tongue and thought: This is a better world. The burp of a baby forty years ago touches me more than the burnt toast at breakfast; more than the man who sits across the flower arrangements (Who does them now? Me? I have forgotten.) who I remember, sometimes, was once my husband.

The man reached for the honey. He had grey sideburns, like an elderly dog. She thought: I could never have married a man with grey sideburns.

There was a miniature on her dressing table of another man. That was a man she could have married. Not this man with spindly knees. A man like this would grunt in the night when he came to you.

James watched her across the table as he ate his

toast. Sometimes she smiled at him, though there was no recognition in it. It was a social smile. She crammed the food into her mouth like a child. She used to eat very little. James wondered what other appetites she had hidden for years.

It was not right, of course, to visit your wife's room when she was like this. Part of him was afraid, too, of finding her too willing, as though her decorous acceptance of his lovemaking had been a sham, like her ladylike approach to food.

It had been three years since he last visited her room.

His penis stirred in the coffin of his under-drawers. (There was too much starch in them now that Emily no longer oversaw the linen room. Yesterday a drop of his urine had mixed with the starch, and the starch dissolved and set again. He'd had to sprinkle water from the wash bowl on to his under-drawers to free himself. The tip of his penis was raw today.)

Three years was too long for any man. He wasn't old.

He could have found a mistress, of course. Old Bartland installed a woman in a cottage at South Down after his wife's death. The woman was supposed to take in sewing, but everyone knew the truth of it. He supposed Bartland paid her well enough for the privilege.

He wouldn't shame the family like that, especially not with his wife still living. He increased his trips to Sydney instead. He went every three months now.

The first place he'd tried in Sydney had been horrible — greasy songs around a piano and upstairs a bed that smelt of musk and powder. Even the coverlet was grubby. Then Bartland gave him an address.

This place was different. From the outside it looked just like a private house. He knocked, and was admitted by a maid in a good black dress and starched cap. She took his hat and coat, and offered him a seat in the hall and then her mistress arrived, in black silk. If it hadn't been for her hair — also black, and a slightly too-defiant shade of black for the wrinkles on her face — he might have taken her for one of Euphemia's friends.

He was shown to a private room. The furniture was good. There was a plush sofa instead of chairs, and a round table set for a meal for two. He sat gingerly on the sofa, his walking stick still in his hands.

The door opened, and he felt a moment's relief as well as embarrassment. She was quite respectable looking, pretty, plump and blonde, in a silk dress with Brussels lace. Her teeth were good, and her small feet wore the polished little boots any lady might wear. (The other had worn a stained dressing gown over her stays, and tattered evening slippers.)

The servant came in again, with a tray — soup, fish, cutlets, a half decent red wine. They sat on the sofa, side by side. His companion ate neatly. They talked (surprisingly) about the Public Education Act. She had been following it in the *Herald*. After that she encouraged him to tell her about his time at Sandringham.

Perhaps she hoped he would start to reminisce about his first visit to a brothel, his first sexual adventure — anything to bring them to the night's main course. If so, she was disappointed. In the middle of his account of troop movements on the northern Indian frontier she bent down.

'Oh, my garter is coming down.'

She put her booted foot on the chair beside him. He could see her white stocking, the swell of her calf, the round knee, a glimpse of flesh above it.

'I must have had too much wine. I can't fasten it.'

It could almost have been unrehearsed.

Part of him was aroused. Another part was angry. It shouldn't be like this, a man of his age, his station in society. He had a wife, he had always done what was right. It shouldn't be like this ...

He bent down and hoped she didn't see his hand trembling. He touched her thigh above the garter. She smiled and began undoing the buttons on his shirt; then she worked on her own fastenings. The dress must have been specially made, as it was soon open to her chemise and stays. Her fingers worked on his trouser buttons. They reached inside.

Her hand was cool. She leant back, taking him with her. (No, she was no novice — she knew his urgency. Or rather, the embarrassment that made him want to finish and get out.) Her fingers caressed him, her skirts were around her waist, so he could see the slit in her drawers and the pink flesh and hair inside. Her hand began to guide him in, and at its touch he shuddered and he discharged a volume of seed over her drawers.

It took less than a minute to dress, to pause at the door and say quietly, 'Thank you, my dear', to pay the servant at the bottom of the stairs (he could have bought a new ram with so much money), to get his hat and coat and be out in the blessed fresh air, away from perfumes and the smell of spending. All he felt was anger at his wife for so deserting him that he was driven to this.

'How was it?' asked Bartland after Church a few weeks later.

He mumbled something. Bartland smiled. 'I told you it was select. Should be at that price too. Try it on a Sunday next time. That's when they have the punishments.'

'Punishments?' For a minute he didn't understand.

'If they've been — naughty.' Bartland licked his lips. 'Twelve strokes of the birch on the bare buttocks, another stroke for every scream. Or the leather strap if you prefer.'

He couldn't help it. 'You mean you watch?'

Bartland laughed. 'Or participate if you'd rather. There's a punishment block in the parlour.' He bent and whispered, 'The girls wear silk drawers sometimes and they wet them first, to make it sting.'

He forced himself to smile, because he owed Bartland that, because he knew he would visit the house in Sydney again, though not on a Sunday. But all the time he was sick with longing for the quiet complacency of his wife and the tickle of her nighttime plait as it rested on his neck.

It wasn't just the marital intimacy. Most of all he simply wanted to talk to her, to tell her about his day, to watch her pull on gloves for evening, to feel her warm fingers straightening his collar. He didn't want to be alone, like this.

All he wanted was his wife.

The man arranged his napkin on the table, and stood up. He kissed her on the cheek as he passed. She remembered him now. There was something she had to ask.

'James.'

He stopped. 'Yes, my dear?'

All at once the question left her. He saw the panic in her eyes and kissed her cheek again. 'I'll see you at lunch,' he said. 'George will be here. I'll be down at the yards till then. Doctor Hatton will be here later.' He paused, then went out.

She took another piece of toast, then peeled an apple. When Charles was young he always took an apple from the table for his horse. He had been seven when they bought him a horse of his own. Not a pony, James insisted. If he rides a pony now he'll always be a pony rider.

The horse was a delicate chestnut. Charles fed it apples in the courtyard and the magpies quarrelled among themselves.

Blatchett came in. She concentrated, to shut her away, to stay in the past with her son.

─∭◎

After breakfast she walked in the rose garden with Blatchett. The sky was hot. Black clouds shimmered on the southern horizon. She tried to think. There was something she was thinking of this morning. Then she remembered. She was thinking about her son.

His hair was peach fluff when he was young; she smelt it every time she held him. He turned his face into her bosom as though he expected succour, but she hadn't any to give him, not by then. Marg Bronsard nursed him, she had a wart on her chin with three hairs sticking out. She was too coarse to be a nanny. James hired that girl in Sydney next trip up. Jane, who married Sam Burnell the fencer. James built the cottage for them down by Honey Creek . . .

She wished Blatchett would be quiet. She wanted to think about her son. And it wasn't a beautiful rose, no matter what Blatchett said. Blatchett knew nothing about roses and that one was scalded by the sun.

When he was three they went to the river for a picnic. She came in later to watch him in his bath. The bath had tigers painted on it and green flowers. The jug steamed on the floor.

'What did you see at the river?'

'I saw the wind on the water,' said her son, smiling up at her, and she smiled back with delight.

Blatchett had her arm again. 'Come on now, Mrs Fitzhenry, he'll be here soon.'

'Already!' She had no idea it was so late. 'My hair,' she insists. 'I want to do my hair.'

Blatchett was pleased. 'That's a good girl.'

She was so excited that she didn't mind the familiarity.

Upstairs she tried to do her hair. It wouldn't curl properly, and there wasn't time to use tongs. She would ask for the hairdresser but they kept him hidden from her these days — so many things they kept hidden, they thought she didn't know. She twisted her hair up into a fresh cap instead. She changed her collar too and dabbed eau de cologne on her wrists.

She refused Blatchett's arm downstairs. Blatchett followed her into the morning room.

There was no one there. No one except a man in a frock coat and a belly too big to ever let him sit on a horse. Gold buttons, quite vulgar. She had no interest in him.

'Where is he?' she demanded of Blatchett.

Blatchett exchanged glances with the stranger. It was rude of her. Blatchett would have to go.

'He's here, Mrs Fitzhenry. She's been ever so good this morning,' she said to the stranger.

'That's not my son,' she cried. 'You told me my son was coming!'

Blatchett soothed her. 'It's Doctor Hatton. You know Doctor Hatton.'

'I want my son!'

'She's that upset. Maybe I should get Mr George,' said Blatchett to the doctor. 'He's in the study. He came up to the big house this morning to do the accounts.' Blatchett put on the sort of smile you'd give a puppy or a wilful child. 'Now don't you worry, Mrs Fitzhenry. I'll go get your son for you.'

She sat down as Blanchett went out to fetch her son. She knew she should entertain the stranger but she was too upset. They'd taken her son from her, they'd hidden him somewhere. They were always hiding things. She wanted her son. She wanted to touch him, smell him again. She wanted to hold him in her arms.

Another man came in, followed by Blatchett. He glanced at the doctor, glanced at her.

'Good morning, Mother, you're looking very well,' he said politely. He tried to kiss her cheek.

He had a red face and complacent eyes. His hair was like a sheep's neck. She stared at him in horror.

'That's not my son.'

'Of course it is,' said Blatchett. 'That's Mr George.'

The curtain lifted suddenly. She put her hand over her face.

'I want my other son,' she whispered. 'I want my son.'

The doctor reassured George. 'It often happens like this. She remembers you when you were a child. Now she sees an adult and thinks there are two of you, that she's got two sons.'

George looked embarrassed. 'Actually,' he said, 'I did have a brother. But that was a long time ago.'

─◉◉○─

She cried all the way through lunch. Finally the man who called himself her husband rang the bell. Andrews came in and led her into the morning room and left her there, to wait for Blatchett.

She opened the French windows. The river gleamed in the sunlight, despite the black clouds on the horizon. She wondered if her son was down at the river. He loved the river. He was probably at the shallows where it met the sea.

She couldn't be bothered with a hat, not at her age, far too old to worry about her complexion. She hurried down the terrace in case Blatchett saw her or those strange men in the breakfast room, eating their lunch at her table as though they lived there. Her heels sank into the white sand, the grains ate at her face as the wind howled up from the south. She called her son.

'Charlie? Charles!'

She was still calling him when the storm broke, when they found her two hours later.

Blatchett dried her, put her to bed with a hot brick at her feet. The pillow was cool under her hot cheek. She could hear the rain outside. She hoped he had found shelter, her little son.

If she were a peasant woman she would be able to wail and rock backwards and forwards. But she couldn't, ladies don't. There was a pain in her chest, so fierce she couldn't swallow. But it was only grief, so she ignored it. She whispered softly to her son, so Blatchett couldn't overhear: 'I can't stand it any more.'

CHAPTER 45

1 8 8 8

AN ENDING OF SORTS

Five years and three grandchildren after Annie's marriage, Caroline heard a knock at the front door.

It was late. The lamps had been lit. Caroline had undressed for bed. The house smelt of lemon polish, and lemon essence from the cake she'd made to take to the Ladies' Guild tomorrow.

For a moment she wondered if there was something wrong at the farm or with Zanna, but if that were the case then Sammy or Frank or one of the farm labourers would have called at the door and just come in. And a swaggie, Caroline hoped a little nervously, would have knocked at the back door, not the front.

Caroline took the lantern from the dressing table, walked down the corridor and peered through the stained glass on either side of the door.

Caroline was forty-one. She had brown hair, so dark it was almost black, with grey beginning at the temples. She had an accent, but everyone had accents: Irish or Lancashire or Scots or barking Prussian. Hers was more acceptably upper-class English than most in the district, including the Fergusons.

Caroline was so comfortably part of the district that if anyone discovered she was one-sixteenth Negro there would be gossip for a week or two, but nothing more. Caroline wasn't the Madam Chairman type; she was unassuming, except in matters involving food, a hard worker. She had a gift for happiness, even though she'd found it late. People liked Caroline, especially since she learnt to laugh.

'Who is it?' When asking questions, her voice still had more of a foreign timbre than in ordinary speech. Caroline still turned a question into a tune.

A voice beyond the door said, 'Caroline', then nothing more.

The silence stretched as though it would crack. Caroline pulled the bolt out from the door and opened it and held her lantern high.

A tall man. For a moment she took him for a tramp, despite the familiar sound of his voice. He had a bundle like a swaggie. Transparent hands, thin feet. The knee of one trouser leg was worn. His eyes were blue. Even in the shadows of the porch she could see his eyes, bright as midday, staring from the thin brown face. The face was so thin it was ghostlike. Only the eyes seemed real.

This was not the gentleman she had waited on so many years before at Miss Elizabeth's. This was not the scared and shivering man she had travelled north with either, nor the man she had lived with, till he left her, all those years before.

This man had something of all those men, but he had changed, as much as she had changed.

'Caroline?' he said.

'Charlie.' Caroline lowered the lantern and stood aside to let him pass. 'Come inside,' she said.

Charlie walked through to the kitchen. Caroline replaced the lantern on the kitchen table, poked kindling into the stove, then poured milk into a saucepan for the coffee that was one of the luxuries she allowed herself. Though the money still came every month from Sydney Caroline now had grandchildren to spend it on, not herself.

Then she sat at the table and looked at him.

Charlie looked around the kitchen. He seemed puzzled, as if he had thought that once he got here he could relax. Now he was here he realised that the journey hadn't ended. Perhaps it never would.

'I hardly recognised the place,' he said at last.

Caroline nodded. There were roses and sweet Alice in the garden, in the flowerbeds out front with white painted edges, and a new white fence and path. The camellias along the side of the house were tall now. Years ago she would have worried that the changes wouldn't please him. It didn't occur to her tonight. She was proud of her garden.

Charles studied her. She had changed, but she was the same as well. His wife ... in the past years he had realised that she *was* his wife. She knew the scars on his soul like no other person, just as he knew the scars on hers.

She moved like a shadow in the deeper shadows of the lamp. Her hair hung thickly on her neck, a hint of grey perhaps, but that was all. Her eyes were still clear as she looked at him, then looked away. The weight of her breasts hung low inside her nightgown. He remembered their warmth suddenly and watched the stove instead.

The milk rose slightly in the saucepan. She lifted it with an old potholder around the handle. It too brought a stab of recognition. Surely it couldn't be the same potholder she had used before he left.

She added coffee essence, then poured the milk into two cups. They were still the cups they had bought together when they first reached Sydney. A skin had settled on the top of the milk. She scraped it off onto the edge of the pan. The edges of the coffee frothed in the cups, rich and milky. She handed his cup to him and watched.

'Are you hungry?'

It was the first thing she had said to him since she opened the door.

He nodded. 'Yes.'

She sat still for a moment. Perhaps she too was remembering. Then she nodded, crossed to the meat safe, drew out bread that the baker had brought yesterday, butter still in the blue butter dish he had bought her their first Christmas together, that she had cradled in teatowels against the jolting of the bullock dray.

She cut the bread smoothly, buttered it, handed him the plate, turned her back to stir the fire again while he ate. She added more twigs from the box by the hearth, pulled the skillet from the wall and put it on to heat, then began to add cold meat, cold potatoes and raw onion to a bowl, and beat in eggs and flour. He remembered the patties that she'd fried in dripping years ago. He could remember the crisp taste of them, had forgotten their name.

She set the table in front of him as the patties cooked, as efficiently and perfectly as she had always done, from those first days at Miss Elizabeth's to the last days before he left her. As always the tablecloth was immaculate, with ironed creases, no crumbs or butter stains or marks from dinner gravy. She must still change the cloth after dinner, every night. He touched it with his finger, saw her looking and lifted his eyes around the room for the first time.

New plates in the dresser, a vase with pink flowers on the windowsill, white curtains, a plaited rag mat on the floor. The smells of the house were different too. There was no yeast bubbling on the windowsill, and there was a scent of lemons . . .

Caroline nodded at his boots.

'They'll be wet. You'd better take them off.'

He hadn't asked if he could stay. Now relief coursed through him like water; even his bones felt liquid. He bent and unlaced his boots.

She took them from his hand. He saw her eyes mark the split in the toe, take in his feet, sockless, ingrained with dirt and calluses. (The last illness had taken nearly all his money. He hadn't looked for work again. He had just come home.) She put his shoes close to the stove and turned the patties in the pan.

'I'll wash in the scullery,' he said awkwardly. She nodded.

The patties were ready when he came back. He ate slowly, tasting each mouthful. She watched him, seated across the table. Outside the wind muttered down the chimney, the windows rattled and were still. He looked up from the plate finally.

'Can I stay?'

She watched him across the table. His hair was grey, not fair (though later she would run her hands through it and find some fairness still remaining). His eyes had sunk, the skin around them like a snake's, cast off the year before (like the skin that Zanna found years ago and hung across the tank stand). A pouch of skin hung from his chin like a doll's reticule. His face was browner by far than hers, and so were his arms and hands.

He was not the man of memory.

Unlike him, Caroline had not been brought up to expect relations with a man to last forever. She had not read novels with love everlasting as their happy ending when she was young and, though she had read novels like that since, she didn't think much of them. Nor was there any financial reason to agree. She knew the bank drafts would keep coming even if she said, 'No'. Charlie had always been an honourable man. She supposed he still was.

This was a stranger in front of her. This should be a stranger. Yet she had no doubt what she'd say.

'Can I stay?'

He wasn't asking for a bed on the sofa for a night or a week. She knew it. He felt her eyes heavy on him, her face as blank as sixteen years ago, the face of a slave who hid her thoughts, hid them best when they were most powerful. Finally, she nodded.

'You can stay.'

He had forgotten how she lengthened words. The sentence hung in the air.

Charles found it easier to speak now he knew what would happen tonight, tomorrow, the day after. 'I had a letter when I was up north. My mother died. I'd just written to her, I hadn't known … anyway, she left me money. An inheritance from her father. I … we … we can move. I'd like to move. Buy our own house. By the sea perhaps, with trees around. I changed my name up north. We can start again. There's no need for the money from Sydney now.'

She nodded. He wasn't sure how much of this she agreed with. Perhaps she was just acknowledging his voice.

'The children — how are they?'

'Zanna has four children now. Annie is married. Did you get the letters? She has three children. The last one, little Jamie, he's just a month old.'

'Married?' It was as though he was adding up the years.

'Five years ago, nearly six now. To Frank from the farm. He's a good man.'

'Married,' he said again. He added, almost as an apology, 'John Roland is well. He's a solicitor up in Brisbane. Engaged to the daughter of one of the partners in the firm.'

'Does she know?'

Charlie didn't have to ask what about. 'No,' he said. 'He changed his name too. It's Forrest. Same as mine.'

Then he said, 'Will you come with me? To a house by the sea, with trees?'

She nodded.

She stood then, checked the stove, moved down the corridor. He could sense, without hearing, all her actions; the door ajar, the chamberpot pulled from beneath the bed, the scrape across the floorboards as the pot went back. Pulling back the sheets, lying between them, waiting for him. Everything the same as it had been when he left. Everything entirely different.

He placed his knife and fork together, carried the plate across to the washing-up bowl, glanced at his shoes drying by the stone. It was time for his final journey now, down the cool corridor to join her.

Chapter 46

1895

SEARCHING FOR CHARLIE

In 1892 James Roland Fitzhenry married his second wife, Henrietta Callaghan, forty-two years his junior. In 1893 she left him, taking with her the sum settled on her at their marriage, most of his first wife's jewellery, the more portable pieces of family silver and James Fitzhenry's reputation as a man of judgement.

He was lonely.

In 1895 he contacted his solicitors, Thomas, Allen and Wiseman, and asked for the address of his older son. He was told that they hadn't acted for Charles Fitzhenry since he took possession of the inheritance from his mother, and had asked that the monthly allowance be stopped. They understood he had changed his residence since then. They did, however, have his previous address.

James Fitzhenry waited for three months, in the house that echoed on the hill. George had married fifteen years before, as carefully as George did everything, to a girl of tidy habits and neater fortune. Her table served sufficient for everyone but no excess, and she made it clear that her father-in-law was welcome at Sunday dinner, after Church, but not more often. There was a coldness in the George Fitzhenrys. It didn't dissipate when Henrietta came and left.

James considered writing to his eldest son. But in a letter he must speak first and, after all, the sin wasn't his. It wasn't for him to say the words that needed to be said. In November of 1895 he instructed Marcus the coachman to drive to Sydney, where he rested for four days, and then proceeded north then west.

He asked for his son by name at the bank, where the bank drafts had been sent. The bank manager was new; he knew of no Fitzhenrys, Charles or otherwise, and they had no account of that name. He suggested that James try at the hotels. Some of the men at the bar were sure to know who was working or living on the properties further out.

James sent Marcus into the first two. When he came out, metaphorically empty-handed, but with a strong smell of beer, James ventured into the third himself.

It was the first pub he had ever been into, and it was bigger than he had expected. The bar stretched twice as long as the morning room at home. The smell of beer was strong. He began to suspect he had wronged Marcus by assuming he'd imbibed.

He tapped on the bar with his walking stick.

'Can I help you?'

'I'm looking for a Charles Fitzhenry. I wondered if you or anyone here know anyone of that name.'

'What you want him for?'

For a moment he was going to damn the barman's impertinence, but he had come so far, and this was the first time someone hadn't immediately claimed ignorance.

'I'm his father.'

The barman called. 'Anyone know a Charles Fitzhenry?'

No one answered, but there was a heaviness in the air around the bar. The drinking and laughter stopped. Finally, one of the men spoke up. 'No one of that name around here.'

He was a big man, heavyset, with dark skin. James' first reaction was that they let blacks drink in this hotel; his second, 'What if that man is my grandson!'. But when he looked at him he realised the man's features were Maori, not Negro, and anyway, he'd said that he didn't recognise the name.

'Well, you'd know, Sammy,' someone muttered.

The big man turned, and the muttering quietened. 'Tell you what though,' he added, with a grin that looked just a little like a challenge. 'You might try out at Burgoon. The Merryweather place, out on the

Burgoon road. Second left straight out of town thataway, then go on for a coupla hours till you get there.'

'Thank you,' said James politely. 'You're very kind. Do you think these Merryweathers,' he tried to think how to phrase it, 'do you think their name was once Fitzhenry?'

The man laughed. 'Jeez no. There's been Merryweathers there since the ark. But I reckon they knew a bloke once, had a name like that. You ask the Merryweathers. They'll set you right, if anyone can.'

Or should, he might have added. There was something in his face James didn't understand. But he thanked him, and the room at large. The laughter and clink of glasses rose behind him as he walked out.

James instructed Marcus to drive on.

It was a weary way to the Merryweathers'. He should have stopped in town for the night before he went on. Houses gave way to horse paddocks; the horses gave way to sheep. James gazed out at them professionally. Some good breeding there. Good fences too.

The Merryweather house was at the end of the road, as the big man had said. There were early roses above the house gateway. The smell of bread floated around him as he walked up the path, above the scent of rose and dog. He knocked on the front door.

No one answered. He wished he had sent Marcus to inquire. His bones hurt. He skirted the old chairs on the verandah and found the kitchen door.

The smell of bread was stronger. There was no need to knock. An old woman with floury hands peered out the door at the sound of his footsteps. He asked his question again.

'My name is Fitzhenry. I'm looking for my son, Charles Fitzhenry. According to my information he used to live in this district.'

The woman paused. Her massive bosom squashed against her apron. Her hair was the colour of the flour on her hands. Her eyes were astonishingly bright in the brown wrinkles round her eyes.

'Mum? Who is it?'

A younger woman stood behind her, a long floral apron wrapped around her waist. She had been cooking too. There was a smudge of jam along her cheek and a dust of flour on one dark brown lock on her neck.

'My daughter-in-law, Annie,' introduced Mrs Merryweather. She opened the door wider. 'Come in, Mr Fitzhenry.' Then, to the girl, 'Mr Fitzhenry is looking for his son. He thinks he used to live hereabouts.'

The younger woman stared at him without expression. Her hands brushed the apron, as though to clean it. James wondered for a moment if she were simple. Then her face came alive again. The older woman gazed at her sharply, then nodded.

'Pour Mr Fitzhenry a cup, love. He must be that parched. We've just had one ourselves,' she told him. 'It's still fresh.'

He sat at the table. It was floury, but well scrubbed underneath. One end was covered with trays of biscuits, still steaming from the oven. A bowl of dough stood among the biscuits, next to a pot of jam.

The girl crossed to the dresser and took down a cup; not the thick china they were drinking from, but thin china, with Chinese scenes on it in blue. She poured the tea, then said, 'Milk? Sugar?'

'Black. One sugar, please.'

The girl added the sugar for him, and handed him the cup, then filled a plate with some of the warm biscuits from the trays at the other end of the table. She passed the plate to James, then stood with her back against the dresser, watching.

James took a sip of tea, and then another, and tasted a biscuit. The jam on top was hot and sticky, but extremely good.

The older woman stood uncertainly for a moment, then crossed to the dough. She kneaded it as if to help her think.

'I don't know that we can help you,' she said finally. 'My husband might. Or Frank. They'll be in later for their dinner, if you'd like to wait.'

The girl spoke for the first time. 'He needn't wait, Mum. I can tell him.'

It was as though she had come to a decision.

'The Fitzhenrys used to live a few miles down the road.'

'When did they leave?'

She calculated. 'Five years ago it must have been.'

'Do you know where they went?'

She glanced at her mother-in-law, as though to gauge her reaction. She shook her head. 'I couldn't tell you.' She paused. 'I did hear tell though that he changed his name when he came back from the north.'

For some reason this shocked him more than anything else. He sipped the tea before he answered, trying not to let the shock show on his face.

'Do you know why?'

She shook her head. And said, 'I can't tell you that. Maybe he just wanted to start again.'

That didn't make sense. 'Can you tell me what their name is now?'

He thought she was about to speak. The two women exchanged a look. The door opened. A child came in. Evidently he'd been asleep.

'Ma? I need to be buttoned.'

The girl buttoned his trousers, gathered him in her arms and came to the table. She sat, still holding the child.

'Matthew,' she said, 'my youngest.'

Matthew peered out between his mother's arms and giggled. His hair was blond and tangled at the back where he had been lying. Fitzhenry had a sudden memory, sharp, of his son doing just that. He could almost feel the soft baby skin beneath his hands.

The girl was looking at her son. He didn't want to ask again. He could feel humiliation turning him to stone.

'I can't tell you for certain,' she said. 'I did hear their name might be Forrest. Something like that.'

'You're sure you don't know where they've gone?'

The older woman spoke this time. 'You might try down Shallow Crossing. That's about a half day down the coast from here. There are Forrests living down that way, though they mightn't be the ones you're looking for. You could ask, anyway.'

He saw himself spending the last years of his life asking in hotels and farmhouse kitchens for his son. His eyes filled with self-pity.

He felt better for the tea. The girl poured him another cup. Something about the way she poured reminded him of Emily, soon after they were married, and his eyes filled with tears again. You cried at the least little thing as you grew old. The child Matthew grabbed a biscuit. He stared at James with bright green eyes — Mrs Merryweather's eyes — then reached out to touch James' glasses with sticky hands.

'Matt, don't,' said his mother. 'Glasses are new to him,' she apologised. 'Neither his pa nor his grandpa wear them.'

He tried to make conversation as he finished his tea.

'You've got other children?'

She smiled. 'Five.'

He hadn't thought she'd be so old.

Her smile widened. 'I started young,' she told him and the frankness was hardly vulgar in their floury kitchen. 'Three boys, two girls, so far at any rate. They're all at school now, except for Matt.'

'Start their schooling young,' said Mrs Merryweather, 'and get them out of your hair.' Her eyes rested proudly on her grandson.

He was starting to feel sleepy. He stood to go. He realised that he would have liked to stay here, in the smell of hot flour and strong tea. But the scent of mutton fat and rosemary was coming from the oven. There would be a roast in there, and they would want to serve dinner to their men. Marcus would want his meal too, and he couldn't ask his coachman to eat here, not with him, even if they invited them to stay.

He had a sudden longing to ask about his son, to ask what he'd been like, how he had spent the last twenty or so years. He didn't.

The women came to the coach with him. The child perched in his mother's arms. They waved. He found he was leaning from the window to watch them wave, in front of the sprawling farmhouse with its tangled roses.

He stopped in town for the night. The Commercial, the best hotel, was full, some dance or other. He had to take the second best. His room smelt of dust. The sheets were damp. They hadn't been ironed. His bones ached even more. It wasn't fair, to ache in summer. He wondered if he were getting a chill.

Shallow Crossing was a hotel and half a dozen houses. He sent Marcus to ask at the hotel while he watched the dogs sniff the coach wheels and raise their legs well back from the horses. There was no other human in the landscape.

Marcus came out. 'They say the Forrests live about five miles out, Sir,' he said. 'One of them's a Charles Forrest.'

James felt a spring of hope. He nodded. 'Drive on.'

The road was little better than a track. This wasn't farmland. Only enough trees and no more had been cut to make the road. James wondered what would happen if a branch fell on the coach. He longed for the smooth green paddocks of his home, two generations away from bush.

The house was on a hill in a square clearing. It was stone, two storeys, and to his eyes quite small. A young orchard stretched out the back, behind the stable and the woodshed and a shed for the cow that grazed beneath the trees. The front was full of flowers, roses just blooming, pinks and whites and deeper red. They looked and smelt the same as those at the Merryweathers'. The sea flashed silver through the trees below the hill. It was the first time he'd seen it since he left Sydney.

He was afraid to leave the coach. Only the thought of Marcus, curious, and the eyes inside the house forced him to move.

The house was quiet. He opened the gate, leaning on it for a moment to gain strength. The front door opened. A man stood there without speaking, the door half shut behind him as if to bar the intruder from the inside of the house.

Was it his son? It could be. He had thought it would be easy to tell. He had thought he'd find the boy of nearly forty years ago. This was an old man, grey-bearded. Sixty? Seventy? Charles would be fifty-five.

'I'm looking for Charles Forrest.'

'I'm Forrest.' No clue in the voice. James realised that he couldn't remember his son's voice. There was no hint of welcome in the man at the door, but no animosity either.

'My name is James Fitzhenry. I'm looking for my son.'

'There's no Fitzhenry here. I'm afraid you've wasted your time.'

It was ridiculous, quite ridiculous, but for some reason he kept on.

'I was told he'd changed his name. To Forrest.'

'You thought I might be him?' The man shook his head. 'It's a common name, Forrest.'

'Is there another near here then? Another Charles Forrest?'

'Not that I know of. Not round here.'

His legs were unsteady. He was old. Couldn't the man see that he was old, ask him to sit down? The man stayed in the doorway.

If he were his son, why didn't he say so? Was he still ashamed? Was he — James felt a shaft of indignation —

angry at being disowned? Or had he — the thought came suddenly from somewhere — somehow outgrown his family, and had no wish to have them back?

No. That was ridiculous.

Could this be his son?

The door opened wider.

The woman was dark, but that might have been the shadow of the doorway. Her hair was black, sprinkled with grey. She moved further into the light. Now he could see that her skin was tanned, but lighter than Mrs Merryweather's. She laid her hand on her husband's arm. 'Who is it?'

'His name's Fitzhenry. He's looking for his son.'

Suddenly he heard laughter. A child ran through the trees further back, a little girl in a pinafore and ruffled skirt, playing with the hens. An older voice called to the child. Another daughter? A servant?

The man and woman stood there, side by side. He swallowed his humiliation. 'Are you my son?'

The man left the doorstep. His voice was gentler. 'It's a strange father that has to ask. I'd have thought you would have known.'

'I thought I would also.' Had he spoken or just thought it?

The man's face was swimming. Was it the light, the too-strong light off the sea, or his own weakness?

'Are you my son?'

'I can't tell you that,' said the man gently. 'Think of me as your son if you like. If it's any comfort to you.'

The woman moved then. She murmured something to her husband, touching his arm. The colours of the garden began to blur. Someone was leading him inside. The room was cool. The too bright light was fading, but the scent of roses stayed. He opened his eyes and they were still there, in a deep vase on a table.

He was sitting by the window in a soft chair. There was a cup in his hand, something hot, not tea. He sipped it. The world cleared further, his fingers grew less cold.

The woman stood before him. Her voice was gentle. 'Are you ill?'

He shook his head. 'Just tired.' He could have said, 'Just old.' Then, belatedly, 'Thank you.'

The man came in the other door. He had been saying something to the child outside, to the person with her.

The man paused. The light was behind him. It was hard to see his face.

'Are you feeling better now?'

'Yes.' He waited, hoping the man would say more, that the woman would ask him to stay longer, but the silence grew. He put his drink down, stood up.

The man helped him. He tried to recognise his son's smell, the feel of his skin, but couldn't. The man's hand was on his arm, leading him to the carriage. Marcus got down to help. His knees trembled. The woman waved from the doorway. The child still laughed under the orange trees among the speckled hens.

'Drive on,' the man said to Marcus.

The carriage moved.

James Roland Fitzhenry wrapped the rug around himself, though the air was hot. He thought of the man he had left behind. Was he his son? Or a kind man unwilling to dash an old man's hopes?

Either way, he was a stranger.

POSTSCRIPT

1915

GALLIPOLI PENINSULA
5 A.M. 25 APRIL

Sitting in a crowded rowing boat, cradling pack and rifle, Charlie Merryweather wondered if today was the day he'd die. A volley of shots floated across the water. It sounded like a mob of rabbiters. It was difficult to believe the targets here were men. Charlie was eighteen, with the mutton fed limbs of a country boy, the hair beneath his helmet faded like old grass on the Burgoon hills.

Already soldiers were leaping from the first group of boats, splashing waist deep towards the cliffs. Charlie squinted into the dawn light. Were those Australians on the shore, or enemy? Charlie had come to fight the Hun, but the enemy here were Turks.

The black sea turned grey silk as the launch towing Charlie's boat drew closer to shore. Yes, those figures on the cliffs were Australians, each digging in with their bayonet to help them climb as the enemy fired from above.

All at once Charlie's world grew small and focused. Confusion vanished, and uncertainty. Charlie knew what he would do, and how he'd do it. Charlie Merryweather was the seed of his grandfather, and even if this cause was not noble he would give it nobility.

The sea was cold, and now the dawn was brightening you could see the blood. Charlie hefted his bayonet and waded towards the enemy.

About the author

About the book

Read on

Ideas,
interviews
& features
included
in a new
section…

Meet the author

JACKIE FRENCH likes to say that her writing career spans 'fourteen years, 46 wombats, 120 books, eighteen languages, eight genres, 3721 bush rats, the odd award (well, actually, they're not that odd), six possibly insane lyrebirds, assorted television segments, radio shows, newspaper and magazine columns, theories of pest and weed ecology and 27 shredded back doormats.' (The doormats are 'the victims of the wombats who require constant appeasement in the form of carrots, rolled oats and wombat nuts', which is one of the reasons for her prolific output: 'it pays the carrot bills.')

She was born in Sydney on 29 November 1953 and grew up on the outskirts of Brisbane. 'I left my mother's house when I was 15, went to uni at 16 and went bush at 18 when I got my degree, with a short break when I worked in the public service for a few years to get enough money to buy this place,' she says, referring to her famous home near Braidwood, which, along with Jackie, has made numerous appearances on TV's *Burke's Backyard*, and lies 'right down deep in a valley, down a narrow dirt road known as The Goat Track, with a house we built ourselves out of stone from the creek, and fruit trees and gardens all around us'.

'My parents separated after many years of unhappiness when I was 12 — it wasn't a happy childhood, which is perhaps one of the reasons I began telling stories… I can't remember ever not making up stories, or playing with words in various combinations. But both my parents encouraged me to read — my mother used to scour the bookshops for me, and take me by tram to libraries far afield. My grandmothers also sent me lots of great Australian books. Books by Australian authors were pretty rare in those days, and I was lucky to be one of the first lot of Australian kids who regularly read words about the land I lived in.'

Jackie wrote her first children's book, *Rainstones*, because 'I was broke. I needed $106.40 to register the car, and sending off a story was the only way I could think to do it — I was living in a shed in the bush with a young kid at the time. The story was accepted, and I went on from there.' The manuscript itself 'was described by the editor who bought it as the messiest, worst spelt one they'd ever received.'

In the same fortnight she was offered a regular column in a newspaper and a farming magazine and discovered that 'writing about flowers and fantasy was a heck of a lot easier than hauling manure in the old green truck to feed the peach trees.' She has been a full time writer and wombat negotiator ever since. Jackie doesn't see 'any real difference between fiction writing and gardening/pest control writing — both involve a close study of the interrelationships of the world, then forming them into patterns that might become stories or theories of weed ecology!' At last count she has had 'about 120' books published, though she adds 'a few more may have snuck out by now.' She is married to Bryan, 'a deeply tolerant man who accepts marsupials in the kitchen and discussions about unicorns or chaos theory at breakfast' and has one son, two stepdaughters and four step grandkids. *A War for Gentlemen* is her first novel for adults. ∎

> ❝ writing about flowers and fantasy was a heck of a lot easier than hauling manure in the old green truck to feed the peach trees ❞

Photo: Paul Gosney/
Australian Women's Weekly

Life at a glance

BORN:

Sydney, 29 November 1953

EDUCATED:

BA, University of Queensland

MARRIED:

To Bryan. Jackie has one son, two
stepdaughters and four step grandkids.

CAREER:

Previous jobs include sugar packer, cook,
echidna milker, chambermaid, gopher for a
private detective, farmer ... now writes (and
wombat wrangles) full-time.

SELECTED PREVIOUS WORKS:

For a complete list of Jackie's books, please
visit her website.

Rainstones (1991)
Back Yard Self Sufficiency (1993)
Jackie French's Guide to Companion Planting
    (1994)
Somewhere Around the Corner (1994)
Plants That Never Say Die (1995)
Mind's Eye: short stories (1996)
Seasons of Content (1997)
Dancing With Ben Hall (1997)
Daughter of the Regiment (1998)
Soldier on the Hill (1998)
Tajore Arkle (1999)
Hitler's Daughter (1999)
Charlie's Gold (1999)
Missing You, Love Sarah (2000)

Dark Wind Blowing (2000)
Lady Dance (2000)
In the Blood (2001)
How the Finnegans Saved the Ship (2001)
The Fascinating History of Your Lunch (2001)
Blood Moon (2002)
The White Ship (2002)
Ride the Wild Wind (2002)
Diary of a Wombat, with Bruce Whatley (2002)
Valley of Gold (2003)
Blood Will Tell (2003)
Flesh and Blood (2004)
To The Moon & Back, with Bryan Sullivan
    (2004)
Tom Appleby, Convict Boy (2004)
Valley of Gold (2004)
Rocket Your Child into Reading (2004)

SELECTED AWARDS AND HONOURS:

Rainstones
1993 Shortlisted in the Primary Age Group of
    the WAYRBAs
1992 Shortlisted, CBCA Book of the Year:
    Younger Readers
1991 Shortlisted, Children's Book Award in
    the NSW Premier's Literary Awards

Somewhere Around the Corner
1995 Honour Book, CBCA Book of the Year:
    Younger Readers
Highly Commended in the NSW Family
    Therapy Association & Victorian
    Association of Family Therapists, The
    Family Award for Children's Books

In the Blood
2002 ACT Book of the Year

Missing You, Love Sara
2002 Shortlisted for the KOALAs
Shortlisted in the Older Readers' category of
    the YABBA
2001 Notable Book: CBCA Book of the Year
Shortlisted for the West Australian Young
    Readers' Book Award (WAYRBA) in the
    Older Readers' category

Ride the Wild Wind
2003 Shortlisted for the Patricia Wrightson
    Award in the NSW Premier's Awards

Diary of a Wombat
Winner, Young Australian Readers' Award
Winner, Kids' Own Australian Literature
    Award (KOALA) for Best Picture Book

Hitler's Daughter
2003 Named a 'Blue Ribbon' book by the
    Bulletin for the Center of Children's
    Books in the USA.
Shortlisted in the Older Readers' category of
    the Children's Choice Book Awards
Shortlisted for the COOL awards
2002 Shortlisted for the KOALAs
Shortlisted in the Older Readers' category of
    the YABBAs
UK National Literacy Association WOW!
    Award
2001 Shortlisted in the Older Readers'
    category of the Bilby (Books I Love Best
    Yearly) Awards
Shortlisted in the Younger Reader's category
    of the WAYRBAs
2000 Shortlisted for the Sanderson Young
    Adult Audio Book of the Year Awards:
    Vision Australia Library
Winner, CBCA Book of the Year: Younger
    Readers

'I am a reading addict. I'll read the phone book if there is nothing else around.

I don't think I'd be able to list all the other authors I admire — there are too many… but I enjoy thrillers and sci fi, and now I write so much fiction I find myself reading it less and less — more biographies and history and natural sciences. I never read gardening books. They are too often wrong (and I get annoyed) or boring.

The Twyborn Affair by Patrick White: For his ability to see the world so clearly — not one phrase or image or insight is a cliché. Don't know any other author who achieves that.

Wyrd Sisters by Terry Pratchett: The most gloriously escapist universe in the multiverse

The Dispossessed and *The Left Hand of Darkness* by Ursula le Guin: The only author who can create true alienness, which still has a punch in the gut for our own reality.

The House at Pooh Corner by AA Milne: The most perfect prose.

Jane Eyre by Charlotte Brontë: I must have worn out four copies of this since I was 8. To hell with the romance — this is a book about integrity.

Lark Rise to Candleford by Flora Thompson: Most perfect evocation of another life.

The Magic Pudding by Norman Lindsay: For its sense of joy.

The Merry Go Round in the Sea by Randolph Stowe

Kind Hearts and Gentle People by Ruth Park ■

Behind the scenes
At home with Jackie French…

An Average Day:

5.30 am: Woken by demented shrike thrush pecking at window.

5.32: Swear at demented shrike thrush. Go back to sleep.

9.00–12.20: Write, with short breaks for aphid or fruit fly counting and mooching around garden.

12.30: Swim in creek if water above freezing or no drought; greet chooks; lunch.

2–5.00: Write; short breaks to pick asparagus, avocados or other stuff for dinner.

5.00– ?: Mooch around bush or garden; say good day to wombat, cook dinner.

After dinner: Answer letters; feed wombat.

10.00ish: Say goodnight to wombat; go to bed.

10.30: Say a very firm goodnight to wombat.

11.30: Rescue chewed doormat and mangled garbage bin from wombat. Speak sternly to wombat. Go to sleep.

Jackie's Garden:

'I am a passionate plant collector. We have about two hectares surrounded by bush; inhabited by two humans, or three when my son's home, two to five wombats, one to three wallabies, 127 species of bird at last count, one echidna, 116 varieties of apple, many of them heritage varieties; also heritage varieties of other fruits — have about 266 different sorts of fruit growing here at the moment, from lilli pillies and emu berries to avocadoes and sapotes, plus a few hundred species of herbs. Don't use pesticides, herbicides et al except to experiment — basically the animals keep the place mown, the birds and other beasties keep pests in check, close planting cuts down weeds, various plant associations cut down disease, and the place does most of its own tucker providing.'

Rethinking Gardening:
'Most Australian gardens follow a pattern — a bit of lawn, some flower beds, maybe a vegie patch out back and a few trees and shrubs.

'Our garden is different. It gets about an hour's work a week. Everything grows together. Pumpkins climb up the avocado trees, strawberries ramble under the kiwifruit and limes, and there are wild parsnips and carrots and parsley coming up in the drive. It's a mess. But it works.

'It's time we started working out Australian ways to grow things. Australian gardens needn't follow the European pattern. Have a lawn if you must — but remember that lawns needn't be grass, needn't be mowed — and can still be rolled on by kids and dogs and host the barbecue on Sunday afternoons.'

Major Influences:
'Wombats. I'm not joking. Wombats are determined, but have a very great sense of the quality of life — which for a wombat means dirt and food. Also the valley where I live, which is part of my life in many senses. And people … but I'd have to list hundreds.'

Advice to Younger Writers:
'No matter how good your writing style, you must have something to write about. Each book should be a small part of your heart and soil, plus about two litres of life's blood. Work out what you love and are passionate about, whether it's hamburgers or history. If you're not passionate about anything you are a deeply boring person and should only write books for snails.' ∎

❝ chokoes wander in the oranges, daisies poke through the lemon branches ❞

The critical eye

'*A War For Gentlemen* is Jackie French's first novel for adults' raved the *Canberra Times*' Dorothy Johnstone, 'and it is an outstanding success. Over the past ten years French has built an international reputation as a writer of children's fiction and an authority on gardening … Genre crossing isn't easy. But French makes the transition with enviable ease … there are many complex emotional and psychological tangles to this book, and French has the ability to go to the heart of them. She writes directly, but doesn't oversimplify … descriptions of tiny schools and country dances, farming methods and small town social hierarchies are offered with a sureness of touch that brings the reader right into the heart of them. A brief but telling epilogue, set in 1915, shows that the attractions, and potential for tragedy inherent in notions of masculine honour, have the power to resurface and take their toll.'

'*A War For Gentlemen* is the tale of one strand in the complex historical origins of Australia' wrote Peter Pierce, professor of Australian literature at James Cook University, in the *Sydney Morning Herald*. 'This is an amiable story — a mild light falls across the half century of Australian history that the novel traverses. If human costs from prejudice and misunderstanding are reckoned, French's perception of the past is benign. That this unusual narrative is purportedly based on a true story is believable … engaging … [one of two recent] earnest, entertaining, thoughtful novels, fit for Christmas and for some reflection thereafter'. The *Australian Women's Weekly* found 'an interesting and entertaining novel about the unbearable pressures placed on an unconventional relationship and the legacy of war'.

Or, as Blair Mahony puts it in his review in *Viewpoint's* Spring 2004 edition, 'Jackie French is a freak. And I mean that in the nicest possible way.' ■

⁶ Genre crossing isn't easy. But French makes the transition with enviable ease. ⁹

The inspiration

THIRTY-THREE YEARS AGO, Jackie French was shown a letter written by an elderly man who was as trying to find a son he had disowned so many years before. 'He found a man who was older than he thought his son should be. He was married to a woman with brown skin, but no browner than any Australian woman who had spent time in the sun. The couple treated him really kindly and asked him in, but when he asked "are you my son", the man wouldn't answer. He never knew whether it was his son, who wouldn't forgive him for disowning him, or someone who wanted to give hope to an old man.'

This was the beginning of the novel *A War for Gentlemen*, although 'for 10 years,' says French, 'I thought I would write this book as a work of non-fiction. But there were too many gaps in the story — and too many places where I wasn't sure if I had found the truth or not. I also came to admire the original Charles and Caroline too much to pretend to know what they had said or thought. They were extraordinary people, with an extraordinary courage to create a world for themselves so far from their own backgrounds. But despite this, of course, much of the book still is fact — the scenes from the American Civil war are based on letters, oral histories, photographs, newspapers of the time. And the skeleton of the story — Charles' decision to go to war, his escape to the north with Caroline, their lives in Australia, are as close as I was able to come to what actually happened. ' She adds that she believes that 'good historical fiction oozes through the cracks in history. Nothing in this book, I hope, conflicts with any history.'

> ❛ good historical fiction oozes through the cracks in history. Nothing in this book, I hope, conflicts with any history ❜

Does the idea of borrowing the lives of real people for fiction cause any guilt? 'Only a slight pang. I think writers are natural vampires, I think every writer does that. I probably feel less guilty about this one than borrowing a conversation with a friend or characteristics that I've used in other books.'

Although the American scenes in the novel give a very strong sense of location, Jackie reveals that she did not actually visit the US sites described in the book: 'The world of a slave, or a civil war soldier, was so very different from the present that I don't think this would have helped. An enormous amount of oral history has been collected in the US from ex-slaves and civil war survivors. I've taken the scenes from those who were there at the time, not the pale reflections in a modern reality. Caroline's world in particular was such a circumscribed world — she was someone who literally was a stranger in her own country; she wouldn't have gone beyond the kitchen yard until she escaped.' ■

Have you read?

Rainstones (HarperCollins,1991, ISBN 0207171246)

The country Helen loves has been dry for nearly half her life. She needs some Rainstones…but the only Aboriginal she knows is the local building inspector, who was brought up in Redfern, not the bush.

Seasons of Content (HarperCollins, 1997, ISBN 0207196451)

A journal of a year in the life of the Araluen Valley in the beautiful Southern Highlands of NSW, a combination of many stories — foxes in the autumn and the first of the asparagus, dashes to the school bus in the mornings and a sleepy lizard nibbling Christmas pudding leftovers on hot rocks, the slow drying of the creek … and recipes too.

Hitler's Daughter (HarperCollins, 1999, ISBN 0207198012)

It began on a rainy morning, as part of a storytelling game played by Mark and his friends. But Anna's story was different this time — about a young girl who lived during World War Two. Her name was Heidi, and she was Hitler's daughter…

'Brilliant' *Queensland Education Review*

The White Ship (HarperCollins, 2002, ISBN 0207197989)

Michel was happy living with his family on a remote island off the coast of France. But one day disaster strikes the island. Michel and the other children are forced to flee from Catherine de Medici's soldiers on the *White Ship* and look for a new land to call home.

'Explores our current debate over refugees and illegal immigrants from a sensitive yet innovative perspective ... Its rich tapestry of personalities, history, fantasy and empathy, together with its contemporary perspective, make this book a rewarding reading experience.' *JAS Review of Books*

Tom Appleby, Convict Boy (HarperCollins, 2004, ISBN 0207199426)

At the tender age of eight, chimney sweep Tom Appleby is convicted of stealing and sentenced to deportation to Botany Bay. As one of the members of the First Fleet, he arrives in a country that seemingly has little to offer — or little that the English are used to, anyway.

'Paints a vivid picture for the reader of life in another time ... combining a great story with historical fact...This is definitely a worthwhile read for any kid wanting early Australian history to be more approachable and interesting.' *Lollipops Magazine*

Rocket Your Child Into Reading: New Ideas, Great Tips & Fun Games (HarperCollins, 2004, ISBN 0207199264)

Written in Jackie French's inimitable style, one of the aims of this book is to help parents and teachers identify children's reading difficulties and then suggest ways to deal with them. Jackie draws on her own experience of being dyslexic to show that there are many fun and rewarding ways to improve your child's reading abilities and stimulate a love of books.

'Strategies and tips for all kinds of readers' *Illawarra Mercury*

Find out more

www.jackiefrench.com
A wonderfully comprehensive site, packed
with resources, and info on Jackie French, her
books, and her passions.

www.arlho.net
Australian Register of Living History: a
website for 'living historians and re-enactors'
which also lists Civil War societies and events
in Australia.

http://valley.vcdh.virginia.edu
The Valley of the Shadow: A digital archive of
original sources that document the lives of
ordinary people living in two communities,
one in the North, one in the South, during
the American Civil War.

JOIN ....

The American Civil War Society of NSW (see
www.arlho.net for contact details)

VISIT ....

Jackie's garden – see her website for info and
details, or send a stamped self-addressed
envelope to PO Box 63 Braidwood 2622

READ ....

*Confederates in the Attic: Dispatches from the
Unfinished Civil War* by Tony Horwitz
*American Scoundrel: Murder, Love and
Politics in Civil War America* by Thomas
Keneally
The poems of Sir Walter Scott, including 'Jock
of Hazeldean' and 'The Field of Waterloo'. ∎